Winner of the

Winner of the European Literature Prize

"*Where You Come From* is a triumph, funny and touching and subtly profound. As it ranges from chronicle to prose poem to folktale, it builds a momentum that dazzles throughout. An exhilarating and powerful read."

—JENNIFER CROFT,
author of *Homesick*

"A *Speak, Memory* for 'The Garden of Forking Paths,' Stanišić's tour of his lost homeland is imbued with wit and affection. He knows stories are all we have, and that some stories can't be bound by a single ending. A marvel and a delight."

—RYAN CHAPMAN,
author of *Riots I Have Known*

WHERE

YOU

COME

FROM

Original title: *Herkunft*, by Saša Stanišić
© 2019 by Luchterhand Literaturverlag, a division of Verlagsgruppe Random
House GmbH, München, Germany
English Translation Copyright © 2021 by Damion Searls

Published by Tin House, Portland, Oregon

Distributed by W. W. Norton & Company

Library of Congress Cataloging-in-Publication Data

Names: Stanišić, Saša, 1978- author. | Searls, Damion, translator.
Title: Where you come from / Saša Stanišić ; translated by Damion Searls.
Other titles: Herkunft. German
Description: Portland, Oregon : Tin House, [2021]
Identifiers: LCCN 2021026141 | ISBN 9781951142759 (paperback) |
    ISBN 9781951142834 (ebook)
Subjects: LCSH: Stanišić, Saša, 1978—Fiction. | GSAFD: Autobiographical
    fiction. | LCGFT: Autobiographical fiction.
Classification: LCC PT2721.T36 H4713 2021 | DDC 833/.92—dc23
LC record available at https://lccn.loc.gov/2021026141

First US Edition 2021
Printed in the USA
Interior design by Jakob Vala

www.tinhouse.com

Cover Art: Natee Jindakum / Alamy Stock Photo, Hilary Morgan / Alamy Stock
Photo, © Eberhard Grossgasteiger / Rawpixel

GOETHE
INSTITUT

The translation of this work was supported by a grant from the Goethe-Institut.

WHERE
YOU
COME
FROM

SAŠA STANIŠIĆ
TRANSLATED BY DAMION SEARLS

 TIN HOUSE / Portland, Oregon

GRANDMOTHER AND THE GIRL

Grandmother saw a girl on the street. Don't be scared, she shouted from the balcony to the girl, I'll come get you. Don't move!

Grandmother goes down the three flights of stairs in her stocking feet, and it takes time, it takes time, her knee, her lungs, her hip, and when she gets to where the girl had been standing the girl is gone. She shouts, she calls for the girl.

Cars slam on the brakes and swerve around my grandmother in her thin black stockings on the street that once bore the name of Josip Broz Tito and today bears the name of the vanished girl as an echo, Kristina! my grandmother shouts, shouting her own name: Kristina!

It is March 7, 2018, in Višegrad, Bosnia-Herzegovina. Grandmother is eighty-seven years old and eleven years old.

TO THE ALIEN REGISTRATION OFFICE

I was born on March 7, 1978, in Višegrad, on the Drina River. It had been raining uninterruptedly for days. March in Višegrad is the most hated month, as drippy as it is dangerous. The snow melts in the mountains, the rivers rise up over the heads of the riverbanks. My Drina is nervous too. Half the city lies underwater.

March of 1978 was no exception. As Mother's contractions started, a mighty storm bellowed over the city. The wind shook the windows of the delivery room and discombobulated feelings; in the middle of one contraction, lightning flashed too, so that everyone thought, Aha, I see, that's how it is, the Devil is being born. Which was fine with me—it's not a bad thing for people to be a little scared of you before it all really gets going.

It's just that this didn't exactly give my mother a positive feeling with respect to the birth process, and since the midwife was likewise dissatisfied with the situation at hand—keyword: "complications"—she sent for the attending physician. As for the doctor, she didn't want to drag out the story unnecessarily any more than I do now. Perhaps it suffices to say that the complications were simplified with the help of a suction cup.

Thirty years later, in March 2008, I was applying for German citizenship and had to submit at the Alien Registration Office a handwritten chronology of my life, among other things. Nightmare! On my first try all I managed to put down on paper was that I was born on March 7, 1978. It seemed like nothing had happened since then, like my biography had simply been washed away by the Drina.

Germans love bulleted lists. So I put in some bullet points along with some names and dates—"· Elementary school in Višegrad"; "· Slavic Studies major in Heidelberg"—even though none of it felt like it had anything to do with me anymore. I knew the information was correct but I couldn't possibly leave it at that. I would never trust that kind of life.

I started over. I wrote my date of birth again and described the rain and how my grandmother Kristina, my father's mother, gave me my name. She took care of me a lot in my early years too, since my parents were studying (Mother) or employed (Father). She was in the Mafia, I wrote to the Alien Registration Office, and if you're in the Mafia you have a lot of time for children. I lived with her and Grandpa, and with my parents on weekends.

I wrote to the Alien Registration Office: My grandfather Pero was a Communist, heart and soul and Party book, and he took me with him on walks with his comrades. When they talked about politics, and actually they were always talking about politics, I dropped right off to sleep, it was great. By age four I could join in.

I erased the part about the Mafia. You never know.

Instead, I wrote: My grandmother owned a rolling pin and constantly threatened to beat me with it. It never came to that, but to this day I have a rather aversive relationship to rolling pins and, indirectly, to pasta.

I wrote: Grandma had a gold tooth.

I wrote: I wanted a gold tooth too, so I colored in one of my incisors with a yellow marker.

I wrote to the Alien Registration Office: Religion: None. And that I'd grown up among, more or less, heathens. That Grandpa Pero called the Church the greatest Original Sin since the Church invented sin.

He was from a village that honored Saint George, George the Dragon Slayer. Or maybe people were really more on the dragon's side, at least that's how it seemed to me at the time. I was visited by dragons from an early age. They dangled from relatives' necks as pendants; embroidery with dragon motifs was a favorite gift; Grandfather had an uncle who carved little wax dragons and sold them in the market as candles. That was nice, when you lit the wick and the little critter looked like it was breathing miniature fire.

When I was almost old enough, Grandfather showed me a picture book. I thought the dragons from the Far East were the best. They looked ferocious, but fun and colorful too. Slavic dragons looked ferocious only. Even the ones that were supposed to be nice, uninterested in laying waste to villages or abducting virgins. Three heads, giant fangs, that sort of thing.

I wrote to the Alien Registration Office: The hospital where I was born doesn't exist anymore. God, the amount of penicillin I had pumped into my ass there! I wrote, but I didn't keep that. One mustn't offend potentially namby-pamby bureaucrats' feelings with such vocabulary, now. So I changed "ass" to "posterior." But that seemed wrong to me, and I deleted the whole fact.

When I turned ten, the birthday present I got from the Rzav River was the destruction of the bridge in our neighborhood, the Mahala. I watched from the shore as this branch of the Drina pestered the bridge with spring in the mountains for so long that finally the bridge said, Fine, take me with you.

I wrote: There's no such thing as a biographical narrative without childhood leisure activities. I wrote in the middle of the page, in capital letters:

SLEDDING

The expert course started up near the highest peak in town, where a tower had watched over the valley in the Middle Ages, and ended after a tight curve right before the ravine. I remember Huso. Huso used to clamber up the hill with an old toboggan, out of breath, laughing, and we too, the children, laughed—laughed at him for being scrawny and having holes in his boots and gaps in his teeth. A crazy man, I thought at the time; today I think he just lived his life without paying attention to the consensus about things like where to sleep, how to dress, how to pronounce words clearly, and the condition your teeth were supposed to find themselves in. He just went about his business differently from most people. Strictly speaking, Huso was nothing but an unemployed drunk who didn't brake before the ravine. Maybe because we hadn't warned him about the last curve. Maybe because he'd drunk his reflexes into oblivion. Huso screamed, we ran over, and then it was a scream of joy: Huso was sitting in his toboggan, which was caught in the underbrush halfway down the slope.

"Keep going, Huso!" we shouted. "Don't stop now!" Fired up by our cries, and especially by the fact that it was easier from where he was to go down than up, Huso heaved himself out of the thicket and hurtled down the rest of the slope. It was unbelievable, we were over the moon, and Huso was shot in 1992, in his shack on the Drina, in his house of planks and cardboard, not far from the watchtower where—as the old epics sing of—either the Serbian hero Prince Marko found refuge from the Ottomans or, depending who you ask, the Bosnian hero Alija Đerzelez leapt across the Drina on his winged Arabian mare. Again Huso survived; he disappeared and didn't come back. No one ever conquered the expert course as expertly as he had.

I wrote out a story beginning: *When anyone asks what "Heimat" means to me—home, homeland, native country—I tell them the story of Dr. Heimat, DDS, the father of my first amalgam filling.*

I wrote to the Alien Registration Office: I'm a Yugoslavian and yet I've never stolen a thing in Germany, except a few books during the Frankfurt Book Fair. And one time in Heidelberg I rowed a canoe into a swimmers-only bathing area. I erased both of those, since they might be criminal offenses and still within the statute of limitations.

I wrote: *Here's a number of things I had.*

SOCCER, ME, AND WAR, 1991

Here's a number of things I had:

Mother, Father.

Grandmother Kristina, my father's mother, who always knew what I needed. When she brought me that little hand-knit jacket, I'd actually been cold. I didn't want to admit it, that's all. What kid wants his grandmother to always be right?

Granny Mejrema, my mother's mother, who told my fortune from kidney beans. She would throw the beans and the beans would throw pictures of a not-yet-lived life onto the carpet. One time, she prophesied that an older woman would fall in love with me. Either that or I'd lose all my teeth, the kidney beans were somewhat ambiguous on that count.

A fear of kidney beans.

I had a well-shaved grandfather, my mother's father, who liked to go fishing and was nice to everybody.

I had Yugoslavia—but not for long. Socialism was tired, nationalism was wide awake. Flags, each their own, in the wind, and the question in people's heads: What are you?

Interesting feelings toward my English teacher.

My English teacher invited me over to her house once. To this day I don't know why. Off I went, as excited as the birth of spring. We ate homemade English-teacher-cake and drank black tea. It was the first black tea of my life. I felt mind-bogglingly grown-up but acted as though I'd been drinking black tea for years, and even came out with the sophisticated comment: "I like it best when it's not totally black."

I had a Commodore 64. My favorite games were the sports ones: *Summer Games, International Karate Plus, International Football*.

A mountain of books. In 1991, I'd discovered a new genre: *Choose Your Own Adventure*. You as the reader decide for yourself how the story continues:

If you shout, "Out of my way, spawn of Hell, or I'll slice your jugular open!" turn to page 313.

And I had my team: Crvena Zvezda, Red Star Belgrade. In the late eighties we won the championship three times in five years. In 1991, we were in the quarterfinals of the European Cup against Dynamo Dresden. A hundred thousand people came together in our Belgrade stadium, Marakana, for important games. At least fifty thousand of them were insane. Something was always set on fire, everyone always sang.

I often wore my red-and-white-striped scarf to school (and in the summer too) and made plans for the future designed to bring me into the vicinity of the team. The path of becoming a soccer player myself and being bought by Red Star for 100,000,000,000,000 dinars (inflation) struck me as unlikely. That meant I wanted to become a physical therapist, or a ball boy, or a soccer ball for all I cared, as long as I could be part of Red Star.

I didn't miss a single game on the radio or the highlights on TV. For my thirteenth birthday, I wanted a season ticket.

Granny asked the beans and said, "You'll get a bicycle."

There was no realistic chance of my wish being granted, if only because Belgrade was a cool one hundred and sixty miles away. The only child in me nevertheless speculated that my parents might decide to move to the capital for my sake.

On March 6, Red Star crushed Dynamo Dresden in the first game, 3–0. Father and I watched the game on TV, our voices already hoarse after the first goal. After the closing whistle, he pulled me aside and said he'd try to get us tickets for the semifinal, if the team qualified. By "us" he meant Mother too, but she just tapped her forehead with her finger.

The second game, in Dresden, was called off due to rioting when the score was 2–1 and ended up counting as a 3–0 victory for us. The semifinal draw was Bayern Munich. Even back then theoretically unbeatable. Again Father and I followed the first game on TV together. During halftime, there were reports of unrest in Slovenia and Croatia. Shots had been fired. Red Star shot too and scored two goals, Bayern one.

Here's how it is: The country where I was born no longer exists. For as long as the country still existed, I thought of myself as Yugoslavian. Like my parents, who were from Serbian-Orthodox (Father) and Bosnian-Muslim (Mother) families. I was the child of a multiethnic state, the fruit and avowal of two people who were drawn to each other and whom the Yugoslavian melting pot had liberated from the constraints of different origins and religions.

It must be added that someone whose father was Polish and mother was Macedonian could declare themselves Yugoslavian too, assuming they cared more about self-determination and blood type than blood and being defined by others.

On April 24, 1991, Father and I went to see the second game in Belgrade. I hung my red-and-white scarf out the window because that's what real fans did on TV. Once we got to the stadium, the scarf was unbelievably filthy. Nobody tells you that'll happen.

On June 27, 1991, the first acts of war took place in Slovenia. The Alpine republic declared itself independent from Yugoslavia. Next came skirmishes in Croatia, atrocities in Croatia, and the Croatian declaration of independence.

On April 24, 1991, the Serbian defender Siniša Mihajlović put Red Star in the lead with a goal off a free kick. It had been awarded for a foul on Dejan Savićević, a technical genius from Montenegro. The roar from eighty thousand throats was deafening, almost monstrous. Today I could say that people were letting off anger, suppressed aggression, deadly fear. But that wouldn't be true. Those feelings were to be discharged later, faced with guns, and from guns. Here there was only one thing: cheering for an important goal.

Torches were lit, red smoke rose up over the stands. I pulled my scarf up over my face. People all around us were cheering, almost all men, young guys. Mullets, cigarettes, fists.

In the midfield, Prosinečki was still causing all sorts of trouble for Bayern, his bright blond shock of hair like a little sun rising over the pitch or—when an opponent didn't know what else to do—setting. A Yugoslavian like me: Serbian mother, Croatian father. Short shorts riding high up his legs. His pale legs.

In the back, Refik Šabanadžović was cutting off Bayern's space: a harrassing Bosnian, stocky but fast. My favorite player—Darko Pančev, known as Cobra—was lumbering around in front of the opponents' penalty area, seemingly half-asleep. The

Macedonian forward, goal scorer in the first game, kept running across the pitch bent forward, shoulders pulled up, as though he weren't feeling well, today of all days. The crookedest legs in the universe. I would have loved to have legs like those.

What a team! There'll never be another one like it in the Balkans, it's not possible. After the collapse of Yugoslavia, new leagues were created in each new country, with weaker teams, and nowadays the best players are traded abroad at a young age.

Bayern tied the match in the middle of the second half on an Augenthaler free kick, the ball rolling right through Stojanović's fingers. Belodedić, the Romanian (Serbian minority) center back, comforted his captain lying on the grass.

My father, this rarely loud man, bellowed and cursed and swore, and I imitated it, imitated Father's anger. I have no idea what my own anger was doing, maybe I didn't have any because everyone around me had so much, or maybe I knew everything would turn out all right. And just when I was about to tell Father that—everything will be fine—Bayern took the lead.

Father crumpled.

Almost exactly one year later he asked me, circumspectly, what objects were important enough to me that I couldn't live without them on a possibly long trip. And by a long trip he meant fleeing our occupied hometown, where drunken soldiers were singing their songs as though cheering for a team. The first object I thought of was my red-and-white scarf. I knew there were more important things. But I took it anyway.

Father said: "Don't worry. Everything will be fine."

If it had stayed 2–1, there would have been extra time since we'd won the first game. Maybe Bayern would have had the stronger legs and better ideas, enough to make it into the finals. And maybe then absolutely everything would have turned out differently—war wouldn't have come to Bosnia, nor I to this book.

I didn't see it become 2–2. At that moment, in the nintieth minute, everyone was standing, the whole stadium was on its feet—in fact maybe the whole country was standing as one, standing behind something together, for the last time. I could see the winning attack up until the moment the ball, deflected by Augenthaler, started its journey toward the goal, but then the men in front of us, next to us, moved, the whole stands moved, to the right, upward, I was pushed, and for a second I lost my balance and sight of the ball . . .

How many times have I watched a replay of that goal? Definitely a hundred. It is burned into my memory down to the smallest detail, like only those moments linked to great love or great misfortune. Augenthaler was trying to defend the flank, his foot hit the ball at an unlucky angle, and it looped up and into his own goal.

Here's a number of things I had:

A childhood in a small town on the Drina.

A collection of reflectors unscrewed from cars' license plates. The only time my parents ever hit me was because of that.

A grandmother who had mastered the language of kidney beans and advised me to work with words, for the rest of my life, and if I did, then admittedly not everything would work out but some things would turn out better. Or else work with precious metals. The beans hadn't made a final determination between these two options.

I had two parakeets, Krele (light blue) and Fifica (don't remember).

A hamster named Indiana Jones, to whom, in the final days of its much too short life, I gave an Andol headache pill ground into a little spoonful of powder (that's what I took for headaches myself) and read Ivo Andrić's short stories aloud.

Frequent headaches.

An improbable trip with my father to an improbable game played by an improbable team, who after making it through the semifinal in Belgrade would go on to win the tournament and thereafter become completely unthinkable.

An unthinkable war.

An English teacher I never said goodbye to, and will never see again.

A red-and-white scarf that I refused to wash after the match in Belgrade, but then it ended up in the washing machine anyway. Today, Red Star Belgrade is a team with a lot of aggressive far-right fans. Back then, I took the scarf with me to Germany, and I don't know where it is today.

OSKORUŠA, 2009

To the east, not far from Višegrad, there is a village in the mountains, hard to reach at the best of times and absolutely impossible to reach in inhospitable weather, where only thirteen people still live. I don't think those thirteen people have ever felt out of place there. They didn't come from anywhere else and they've spent most of their lives in that village.

Equally certain is that these thirteen will never leave. They will be the last. Up in that village (or in a hospital in the valley) they will end their days and with them their farmsteads—their children won't take them over—their happiness, and their creaking hip joints. Their schnapps, which blinds the sighted and makes the blind see again, will be all drunk up, or maybe not; soon no more will be distilled here (a wooden cross in the bottle). The fences will no longer separate anything that has meaning, the fields will lie fallow. The pigs will be sold or slaughtered. I don't know what'll happen to the horses. It'll be an end to the leek plants and the corn and the blackberries. Though the blackberries might make a go of it alone.

I was here for the first time in 2009. I remember that when I saw the power lines I stupidly wondered out loud whether the electricity would be turned off after the last person here died. How long would the current still hum between the poles?

Gavrilo, one of the oldest men in the village, spit a juicy glob into the juicy grass and shouted, "What's wrong with you?! Almost the second you get here you're talking about dying. Let me tell you something. We've survived *life* here, death's not the problem. As long as you tend to our graves, maybe put some flowers on 'em and talk to us every now and then, things will continue here. With or without electricity. But no one needs to put any flowers on me, what'm I supposed to do dead with some flowers? So. Off we go, open your eyes, I'm going to show you a few things, you clearly have no idea about anything."

Oskoruša, the village was called. The old man had come to get us on the side of the road, with hands that looked as if baked from clay. I say "us" because I wasn't alone. The trip was my grandmother Kristina's idea.

Stevo was there too—he'd driven us. A somber man with incredibly blue eyes, two daughters, and money troubles.

Grandmother was wearing black, unimpressed by the day-time sun. She talked a lot, remembered much. In retrospect, it seems like she had an inkling that her past would soon be slipping away from her. She was showing Oskoruša to herself once more, and to me for the first time.

Grandmother had her last good year in 2009. She hadn't started forgetting yet, and her body did what she wanted it to. In Oskoruša she walked up and down the roads she'd walked half a century before as a young woman with her husband. My grandfather Pero had been born here and spent his childhood in these mountains. He died in 1986, in Višegrad, in front of the TV, while I was in the next bedroom shooting at plastic cowboys with plastic Indians.

Earlier, when I was ten or five or seven, Grandmother had said that I would never lie and deceive, only exaggerate and make things up constantly. I probably didn't know the difference back then (and even today I don't always), but I liked that she seemed to trust me.

The morning before our trip to Oskoruša, she repeated that she'd always known: "Exaggerating and making things up—that's what you make your living from now."

I had just arrived in Višegrad and wanted to relax after a long reading tour for my first novel. I had a copy of it with me, as a gift, but it was in German, which made no sense.

Is the book about us, Grandmother asked.

And I was off: Fiction, as I see it, I said, creates its own world, it doesn't portray ours, and the one in here, I said, slapping the book's cover, is a world where rivers speak and great-grandparents live forever. Fiction, in my view, I said, is an open system of invention, perception, and memory that rubs up against real events . . .

"Rubs?" Grandma interrupted, coughing, and she heaved a giant pot of stuffed peppers onto the stove. "Sit down, you're hungry." She draped the book on a vase like a museum piece on a pedestal.

And then came the line about how I made my living.

The stuffed peppers smelled like a snowy day in the winter of 1984. The Winter Olympics were happening in Sarajevo and on my sled I was pretending to be an athlete like our Slovenian heroes racing down the mountain in their splendidly tight-fitting, crazily colored suits. I won every race (by going down only when there was no one behind me who might catch up).

Now, waiting for the peppers, I see on the slope the Kupuses' house, which was shot up during the war and has stood empty since. At the time, when I'd sledded back to Grandmother's house, she served peppers. My fingers itched terribly, she held my hands and warmed them up, and on TV Jure Franko was winning the silver medal in the giant slalom. Not even peppers come without footnotes of memory in Višegrad.

Grandmother poured me some water. It's very important, she'd said in 1984 and said in 2009 with just as much conviction, to drink a lot of fluids. The glass was the same, too. I recognized it from the little crack in the rim.

"Grandma, you need to throw this one out."

"You have eyes, don't you? Drink from the other side."

I did, and she watched. Watched me eat. Watched me question her. How are you doing, Grandma? What do you do all day? Do people come see you? Questions I'd asked over the phone too.

She was curt, not wanting to talk about herself. Only when I asked about other people, about neighbors, did she give longer answers: "No one's died or gone crazy since the last time you were here. Rada's still around, Zorica's still around. And Nada up on the fifth floor. They're only a little crazy. It happens as you get older. But it's okay. It's good they're here. Even crazy I like them."

Just then the doorbell rang.

"And here's my Andrej!" Grandmother cried, hurrying to the door. I heard a man's voice and Grandmother tittering like a girl. Heard bags rustle and Grandmother say thank you. She came back and immediately cleared my plate. I wasn't done, actually, but I was more or less full.

"Who was that?"

"My policeman!" Grandmother cried, as though that explained everything.

I wanted to wash the dishes but Grandmother sent me out of the kitchen, saying that was no job for a man. She'd said it before too. About vacuuming, making beds, cleaning. Grandmother came from a family and a time in which men sheared sheep and women knit sweater vests. Customs were still oriented toward practicality, dreams remained unspoken, language was crude and precise. Then came Socialism, with its discussions about the role of women, and the woman herself would leave the discussion and go back home to hang up the laundry.

My grandmother's older sister, my great-aunt Zagorka, didn't want to wait for the new era any longer. She wanted to go to school, wanted to go into the sky, into space. To become a cosmonaut. She had the stubbornness, then had the reading and math, thanks to the rachitic twins, Todor and Tudor, who themselves wanted to share the curious secrets of numbers and letters with her. At fifteen, not long after the Great War, she turned her back on the cliffs of her childhood, taking with her only the goat who had been her most pleasant companion on the mountainside, and set off for the Soviet Union. Along the way, she learned how to fly a plane from a Hungarian pilot in Banat and fell in love, one warm night on a runway in the Pannonian lowlands, not with him. In Vienna she spent three long years cleaning toilets in military barracks, learning Russian on the banks of the Danube from Aleksandr Nikolayevitch, a pale Soviet sergeant in the veterinarian service. Aleksandr sang and played guitar, badly but with enthusiasm. This Russian from Gorky on the Volga sang songs on the Danube for my great-aunt Zagorka

from Staniševac on the Rzav—songs of beautiful rivers and cities and eyes, brown eyes, sometimes blue, it didn't really matter
what color the eyes were, and my great-aunt wanted something
different from the singing Russian than he did from her. She
left Vienna with her trusty goat and some money, as well as a
Russian sergeant's papers and a short haircut. She got to Mos-
cow on her nineteenth birthday. She finished military pilot
training with honors and was accepted into the outer echelons
of the First Cosmonaut Group of the Soviet Union in 1959. It
was too late for her high-altitude dreams—the Americans were
soon whizzing around the moon and the Russians didn't want
to be second anywhere. One warm Monday in February 1962,
she walked into Vasily Pavlovitch Mischin's office and said she
had an idea and a goat, old but still healthy, and a mere six
months later my great-aunt Zagorka's goat, from the village of
Staniševac in eastern Bosnia, was blasted into orbit around the
moon. The goat remained nameless and may have died upon
reentry into the earth's atmosphere.

Zagorka died in 2006. At the end she wasn't especially
tired, nor especially sad. She was hard of hearing and had no
teeth left. My grandmother looked after her little sister, as she
called Zagorka, until her last breath, and I was just about to sit
back down at the table when Grandmother said: "What are
you doing? Come here this minute and do the dishes! What's
wrong with you?"

There was a dishtowel hanging under the sink, roughly as
old as I was. Red and white checks, soft and threadbare from
thousands upon thousands of spins in the washing machine. I
dried off a plate, a fork, a knife, the glass with the little crack.

SAŠA STANIŠIĆ

Grandmother stood behind me, having changed clothes. Black blouse, black pants, only her rubber boots were yellow. I couldn't help but think of Supergirl, who could get into costume in seconds flat, except my grandmother's hair wasn't long and blond, it was in a perm and purple, and her cape was one of mourning.

"Where do you want to go?"

"We're going to Oskoruša."

"But I just got here."

"Getting here can wait. Oskoruša's waited long enough." A horn honked. "The driver's here too." She tied her black scarf under her chin, examined herself in the mirror, took it back off.

"Listen," she said. "You should be ashamed that you've never been up there." And when I still didn't move: "Saying no has never told a good story."

I have no idea where she got that from, but it sounded good.

"How long will we stay there?"

"Once you're up there you'll want to stay forever."

Shopping bags of groceries were standing in the hall. "Her policeman" must have brought them. Now it was my turn to carry them. Grandmother smiled at me. "Welcome home," she said. "My little donkey."

If there'd ever been a Mafia in Višegrad, Grandmother would have been the Godmother. As a child I knew about three petty criminals, famous around town, who were afraid of her and did errands for her. When she was having her hair dyed purple in the salon, one of them would usually be standing out front, as if by chance, cracking pumpkin seeds. Grandmother, freshly permed, stepped out into the street and whispered

20

something to him, at which point he disappeared at top speed down the alley on whatever assignment it may have been.

Grandmother never went to school. Boys had to go to school, even though they'd have preferred to run around outside, she said; the girls would have rather gone to school but they had to stay home. Her mother taught her sewing, mending, housework.

The illusion that my grandmother could be and do anything, my faith that she would easily deal with life and with getting old, vanished as she got sicker. It started in spring 2016. She misplaced things and couldn't understand why they'd disappeared. She went hunting for the right word and once she'd caught it forgot what she was trying to say with it. She could no longer figure out the remote control and broke it. She went to the hair salon only when someone took her there. She let a salesman talk her into spending two hundred euros for a pillow, while before she would've threatened to box his ears and sold him an old pillow of her own.

In 2009 she was doing well. In spring 2009 my grandmother went down the three flights of stairs to the courtyard easily. The engine was running in the blue Yugo; the driver in jeans and a T-shirt hurried to help her into the car. He introduced himself as Stevo and added, with a nod at Grandmother: "The chauffeur."

The hard and bumpy dirt road to Oskoruša wasn't great for the car. The little Yugo tried hard to get out of the potholes without breaking an axle, but soon Stevo had had enough, or at least had mercy.

We set off on foot until we reached a forest; someone called my grandmother's name from somewhere, and the mountains, friendly but firm, chiseled the echo into air humming with spring.

Grandmother smiled.

At first we couldn't see who'd called her name, then a young man stepped out of the woods and leapt down the slope, precise and capricious as a mountain goat. A young man who grew older and older the closer he came. Pine needles were stuck in his beard.

He took off his hat and called Grandmother's name a second time, when he was only a few steps away from us. They looked at each other long enough to tempt one to write "tenderly."

A handshake for Stevo, then turning to me with an expansive gesture and belting out my name too—all of it was slightly too much: the turning around was too loud, the eyes too brown, and under his fingernails, dirt.

"The grandson. I'm Gavrilo. We're related—I could tell you how but I'd rather show you."

The showing started at the cemetery: Grandmother wanted to visit her parents-in-law's grave. Gavrilo briskly brought us to a slanting field bordered by slanting trees. The view looked out to the west, where a mountain towered up over gentle hills scattered with houses and farms. The mountain had thick green forests almost all the way to the top, then bare rock, a cliff reddish in the sun. The dead have a nice view in Oskoruša.

I tried to keep up with Gavrilo as we marched between the graves through the midday heat and high grass and I peered at the mountaintop. Then the old man stopped and slapped a hand onto my chest. "Watch your daydreaming!"

A snake was crossing our path.

"*Poskok*," Gavrilo hissed.

I took a step backward and it was like I was stepping back in time, too, to a similarly hot day in Višegrad many years before.

Poskok meant: *A child—me?—and a snake in the chicken coop.*

Poskok meant: *Rays of sunlight slicing between the boards through the dusty air.*

Poskok: A rock that Father's raising high over his head to crush the snake.

There's *skok*, "jump," hidden in *poskok*, and the child pictured the snake as: *jumping at your neck, spraying poison into your eyes.*

Father said the word and I was more afraid of the word than of the creature in the chicken coop.

Poskok contained everything a child needs for a good scare—*poison* and *Father wanting to kill*. It's almost like Father was a partner in what the word unleashed in the child, me. The word is the animal and more than the animal. I was scared of *the word* and *the animal* and *the father* at once. I was standing behind Father, off to one side, with a good view of the snake. A premonition whispered to me: Father'll miss. Father'll miss and the word will start its *skok* with *its jaws open wide*. I was frantic with fear and curiosity. What would happen if Father didn't ___ the snake, what if the snake ___ Father? I can feel the fangs in his neck, *poskok*.

Father slammed down the stone.

The translated word, "horned viper," does nothing to me.

The horned viper in the Oskoruša cemetery turns around, green, relaxed, in the crown of a fruit tree, to get a better angle of view on the intruders. It arranges itself amid the branches, in the sun, turning itself into its own nest above my great-grandparents' grave.

At the grave were waiting food and drink and a very tall woman cutting smoked meat into thin slices with a giant knife, unmoved even when the reptile wound its way up the crooked tree trunk just a few yards away.

Gavrilo took his hand off my chest and kept walking, over to the woman. Grandmother and Stevo caught up to me and said hello to her. She set the table with the meals she'd brought, the drinks in plastic bottles. The gravestone was the table. Meat and bread and flies and knives. The snake paid no further attention to anyone. It could have been just imagination, just language. Grandmother lit candles.

I turned away. I walked from gravestone to gravestone, reading them. I read *Stanišić*. Read *Stanišić*. Read *Stanišić*. On almost every gravestone and wooden grave marker was my own last name, and from the little photographs, eyes looked at me, proud or embarrassed. It seemed like that's all there was: pride and embarrassment.

Moss had grown over a few names, time had faded some. "We haven't forgotten any of them," Gavrilo assured me later, at the grave of my great-grandparents. He pointed at the illegible ones and said: "He's another one, and this is one too. Stanišić. Stanišić." And, after a short pause: "This one nobody knows for sure anymore."

The tall woman held out her hand to me in greeting, then a schnapps. "I'm Marija," she said. "Gavrilo's my husband. Did you bring the fruit?"

There's Marija: tall as a tree under the trees. A stiff brown dress like a blacksmith's apron. She's from a village a few valleys away, I've forgotten its name. On the day Josip Broz Tito died, a girl with red hair came into the world in that village, an occurrence both unusual and beautiful. At two years old, apparently, the girl started speaking Latin, an occurrence which was also unusual but more impractical and pointless than anything else. People taught her herbal medicine; before long the girl could predict the future, with relative precision, every Tuesday. Some of the predictions came true, others didn't. In 1994, looking for bloodwort—someone from the village had been complaining of a nosebleed for days—she stepped on a landmine.

I gave Marija the bag with the oranges and pineapple. She placed the fruit on the grave.

"They liked fruit?" I asked.

"Dunno," Marija said, beheading the pineapple with her giant knife. "But I do. D'you want some?"

Marija was so tall that when she stood next to me I could see the tiny blood vessels under her chin. She was also agile and quick. The way she sliced the pineapple. The way she jumped down from the grave to get something, and climbed back up again. I couldn't help thinking of fencers.

Overhead, in the crown of the sorb-apple tree, lurked the *poskok*, the horned viper. Today it is September 25, 2017. I am sitting in a streetcar in Hamburg, with two people in their midforties next to me chatting about Pokémon and Angela Merkel. Words lurk over my head, they unnerve me, delight me, I need to find the right ones among them for this story.

The story started with the disappearance of memory and with a village that was soon to disappear. It started in the presence of the dead: at my great-grandparents' grave I drank schnapps and ate pineapple. The air smelled of earthworms, of dandelion milk, of cow shit, depending how romantic you wanted to be. The houses were made from limestone and beechwood hacked out of the local mountain and forest, respectively. Beautiful, maybe. I asked Gavrilo about the beauty, too—Gavrilo the pig butcher, Gavrilo the hunter, I asked him if he'd ever thought Oskoruša was beautiful.

Beauty, aside from his wife's, had never meant anything to him, he said, and he kissed Marija's shoulder. I was sure he'd add something businesslike, a proverb about the eternal drudgery, the soil, the harvest, but Gavrilo just poured himself some schnapps from a soda bottle and sat down on the grave.

Oskoruša is a beautiful name. Actually that's not true. Oskoruša sounds harsh and grumpy. No syllable you can cling to, zero rhythm, a bizarre sequence of sounds. From the very beginning: *Osko*—what's that supposed to be? who talks like that?—and then the plummet to the hissed end, *-rusha*. Hard and Slavic, the way things end in the Balkans.

I could leave that in, people would probably accept it from me, seeing as I'm from the Balkans myself. *Hard Slavic endings?* Right, of course, those Yugos with their wars and their ways, you know.

Actually, though, the image makes no sense. What are we supposed to picture as these "hard Slavic endings"? Slavicness is not a gentleman's hat, something you can be sure about as long as you know what gentlemen and hats are.

But maybe someone's reading this here who takes no pleasure in the ironic multiplication of clichés and prejudices, and who, on the other hand, knows what Oskoruša means, what an *Oskoruša* is. It's a kind of fruit. A widely valued kind, to be precise: a respected variety of beam tree with high, as they say in English, "agricultural credibility." So say those whose respect is at issue: agriculturalists. The *Oskoruša* is the Serbo-Croatian name for the *Sorbus domestica*, the sorb or sorb-apple tree.

The sorb is a tricky fruit. At full ripeness, the side facing the sun glows red, the rest is yellow. The sunny side tastes sweet, the shady side bitter. Parasites avoid it, so it requires no special protection and doesn't need to be sprayed. The trunk and leaves of the tree, in contrast, are at high risk of parasite damage.

In the Bosnian mountains, in the farthest eastern regions of this perpetually tragic land, there is a village that soon will no longer exist. Oskoruša. In the eighties, hundreds of people lived there. One played the gusla. One hosted dominoes nights. And there was one who carved wax dragons. They got through the winters in furs and heated arguments over dominoes. In the summers they slathered up nicely with oil. One time, a backpacker from Iceland ended up there; he smiled a lot and came in a respectable fourth place in one of the dominoes tournaments.

Oskoruša's isolation was presumably a lifesaver during the wars. The village remained unscathed, except for the men who voluntarily joined this or that side and were lost. Those who stayed died for better reasons.

In the Oskoruša cemetery, I shared with the dead my name and my bread. We ate smoked meat on my ancestors. Then Gavrilo started talking.

"Here," he said, pouring a schnapps on the ground, "lies your great-grandfather. Your great-grandmother drank only in secret." On her side, too, he placed a tumbler and then turned away—we all turned away—so that she could continue to drink in secret. We clinked glasses.

No task was too much hard work for my grandmother at her parents-in-law's grave. She scraped birdshit off the black slabs, pulled up weeds, trimmed bushes. She dragged two boulders up, for reasons I couldn't decipher; I helped, she said she wanted them there and there.

Today this fussing about these graves is one of her most reliably returning memories. Grandmother had laid out the gravesite herself. "No one wanted to take care of it," she kept repeating, "not even the ones who wouldn't exist if the ones resting there hadn't existed."

The graveyard heat tasted salty and sounded like cicadas. Gavrilo tried to catch my eye. I nodded to him and immediately felt that it had been inappropriate to nod in a graveyard.

"D'you see that?" He pointed into the landscape. "There's where the house stood," he said.

"My great-grandparents'?"

"Of course your grand-grandparents'. Pay attention!"

"There?"

"No, there."

"Where you can see the fence?"

"No, there, where you can't see anything."

I laughed. Gavrilo didn't seem to think it was funny, and that was the moment when he asked me where I came from.

There it was—where do you come from—same as always, I thought, and I let rip: Not a simple question! First it depends on what your *where* is aiming at. The geographical location of the hill where the hospital was? The national borders of the state at the time of the final contractions? Parents' provenance? Genes, ancestors, dialect? However you look at it, your place of origin is just

28

a construct! A kind of costume you have to wear forever once it's been put on you. And so a curse! Or, if you're lucky, a possession, owed to no talent but granting you privileges and advantages.

I talked and talked like that, and Gavrilo let me finish. He brought the bread over and handed me the heel of the loaf. Then he said: "From here. You come from here."

I bit into the bread. Waited for him to explain. From here? What did he mean, from here? Because of my great-grand-parents?

Gavrilo rubbed a cucumber clean on his sleeve, and while he ate it he talked about how genetically modified vegetables were gaining ground. When I'd almost lost the thread, he grabbed my arm, as if wanting to see how big my muscles were, and cried: "From here. You come from here. You'll see. Are you coming?"

"Do I have any choice?" At least I wanted to be funny.

"No," Gavrilo said. And Grandmother, whispering: "Don't be ungrateful."

I looked up at the snake and was almost sure that it was about to say something too. It was a native, after all; it under-stood the language of these mountains, understood what was going on here possibly better than I did. Maybe even under-stood what I was supposed to be grateful for.

We packed up. Stevo and Marija carried the bags away while I followed Grandmother and Gavrilo. They led me to a well, in fact to the prototype of all wells—stone lining, pitched wooden roof, crank, rope, bucket—and Gavrilo said: "Your great-grandfather discovered this spring and he dug this well and his last wish be-fore he died was for his wife, your great-grandmother, to get him another sip of water from it. Her answer was: Get it yourself."

I was supposed to drink from the well. I wasn't thirsty, and I was afraid of germs, but I didn't want to disappoint anybody, not my great-grandfather and not Gavrilo and Grandmother, so I drank, and it was the best water I'd ever tasted in my life, and as soon as I filled my water bottle with it Grandmother said: "Your grandfather was born in Oskoruša. He drank from this well, he went mushroom-hunting in these woods, and he brought down his first bear before he was eight years old."

"Where do you come from, boy?" Gavrilo asked again, and I caught myself thinking: All "belonging" is just kitsch! I knew that wasn't true, but I also knew that I wouldn't let my guard down over a little water.

Grandmother took over again: "Your great-grandfather was born in Oskoruša. All this was his land. It's your land too. Up there is where he built his house."

"Come on," Gavrilo said, and they both set off. "It's the best view down into the valley and up to Vijarac."

But there were only a couple of rough-hewn stones, the remains of a house wall or something. Grayish, covered in spiderwebs. I tried to figure out a floor plan, clambered through burning nettles up to the remains of furniture in the ruins. A shelf, broken, no longer a holder of anything. A squirrel crouched fearlessly on the skeletal iron bed. And through an opening in the wall that had once been a window, branches reached in, grasping at my grandfather's childhood dreams. But what, please, what was all this supposed to mean for me?

I have drunk water from my great-grandfather's well and I'm writing about it in German and you're reading it in English. The water tasted of the burden of these mountains, a

burden I have never had to bear, and of the wearisome light-
ness of claiming that something you've never touched belongs
to you. No: the water was cold and tasted like water. I'm the
one who decides, I am!

"Where do you come from, boy?"

So now from here too? Oskoruša.

LOST IN THE STRANGE,
DIMLY LIT CAVE OF TIME

I live in Hamburg. I have a German passport. My place of birth lies past distant, unfamiliar mountains. Twice a week, I go running along the Elbe River I know so well, and an app counts the miles I've put behind me. I can barely imagine how someone could get lost here.

I am a fan of Hamburger SV. I own an expensive racing bike that I practically never ride because I'm afraid someone will steal it. I recently took a visit to the botanical garden, surrounded by stuff in bloom. I asked a guy wearing all green and a name tag if there was a sorb-apple tree in the garden. No, he said, but there are plenty of interesting cactuses.

People occasionally ask me if I feel at home in Germany. I alternate between saying yes and saying no. They rarely mean it to be exclusionary. They justify the question, saying: "Please don't take it the wrong way, my cousin married a Czech."

Dear Alien Registration Office, I was born in Yugoslavia on March 7, 1978, a rainy night. Since August 24, 1992, a rainy day, I have lived in Germany. I'm a polite person. I don't want anyone to feel uncomfortable just because I'm not Czech. I say: "Isn't Bratislava beautiful?" Then I say: "Hey, is that Axl Rose from Guns N' Roses?" and when the person I'm talking to looks, I turn into a German butterfly and flutter away.

My three-year-old son is playing in a front yard near our apartment. The neighbors say that the owner doesn't like seeing children in his yard. A cherry tree is growing there. The cherries are ripe. We pick them together. My son was born in Hamburg. He knows that a cherry has a pit, a *Kirsche* has a *Kern*, and that a *Kern* is also a *košpica* and a *Kirsche* is also a *trešnja*.

I was shown cherry trees in Oskoruša. One man showed me his bear fur, another his smokehouse. One woman talked on the phone to her grandson in Austria and then tried to sell me a cellphone. Gavrilo showed me his scar, which looked like giant teeth had made it. There were some things I wanted to see and hear, others not so much.

When I asked Gavrilo how he'd gotten his giant scar, he handed me a few blackberries and tried to give me a piglet as a present, and far up above, in the mountains, a story hissed and spit and it started like this:

Far up above, in the mountains . . .

The story begins with a farmer named Gavrilo, no, with a rainy night in Višegrad, no, with my grandmother who has dementia, no. The story begins with the world being set alight by the addition of stories.

Another one! Another one!

I'll take more stabs at it and find a lot more endings. I know how I work. My stories just wouldn't be mine without digressions. Digression is my mode of writing. *My Own Adventure*.

You find yourself in the strange, dimly lit cave of time. One passageway curves downward, the other leads upward. It occurs to you that the one leading down may go to the past and the one leading up may go to the future. Which one do you decide to take?

I have a hard time concentrating. I am reading about dementia and snakebite poisoning in the Eppendorf University Clinic library. A medical student is sitting across from me holding index cards with illustrations of organs. She spends a lot of time on the liver.

Gavrilo handed me another schnapps.

I offer the medical student a hazelnut wafer but she doesn't want a hazelnut wafer. A tiny impulse, the idea of an idea, is enough to make me lose what is happening in the main event— now a memory, here a myth, there a single remembered word.

Poskok.

The non-main event gains weight and soon seems indispensable; the snake looks down at me from its tree and into me from my childhood; the remembered word, the semantic panic, I choose the passageway leading down and just like that I am thirty years younger, a boy in Višegrad. It's summer, a summer in the restlessly dreaming eighties before the war, and Mother and Father are dancing.

A PARTY!

A party for Father and Mother in the garden under the cherry tree. Music is playing on the porch as Mother twirls under Father's arm. The radio is playing for them. I'm there, but the party is not for me and means nothing to me. I hear the music and don't understand what my parents understand. I sweep the porch. I sweep the porch with a child's broom that doesn't sweep very well. It's missing the most important thing, it's missing what makes a broom a broom: the plastic "bristles" are too far apart from one another. Anything smaller than a cherry slips through them. I scrape along the porch in time to music not meant for me.

The dog barks at my parents, jumping around their legs. It's not our dog. Our only pets are birds prone to melancholy and hamsters quick to die. The dog was here yesterday too. My parents act like they don't notice him, or at least don't take him seriously. He gives up and turns his attention to something hopping along in the grass.

My parents are moving in a way that makes me not want to hang around them. I let the broom drop with a deliberate crash. They keep dancing.

I follow the wandering dog to the field where the Roma have set up their stands and bumper cars and merry-go-round. The dog sniffs at some bushes. It's boring.

My parents showed affection to each other less often than they did toward me.

A few hours before my parents started dancing, Father had wanted to explain to me how canalization worked. He dropped a little red wooden ball into the drainage canal and we ran to the spot in the river where he thought the ball would have to come out again—an opening in the dike. We ran fast, Father and I. It was great, running somewhere together at top speed so that we wouldn't miss what was going to happen.

Someone was fishing from the dike. Hook and bobber on his hat. Father slowed down, stopped, and, still out of breath, started chatting with the fisherman. I still remember thinking: No, it can't be! He can't just be abandoning what we came here for. If nothing else, his own heavy breathing must remind him!

I said something. I pointed to the world. I said: "Father . . . The ball!" Father raised his arm.

I squatted. The men got louder. The fisherman's name was Kosta. Kosta and Father argued and laughed. Maybe that's what Father wanted to teach me: that you can have friendly joking and bitter cursing on a Saturday by the river. But I knew that already. It would have been something new if Father's belligerence had grown to the point of pushing the other man into the river.

Push him, Father! I thought. I had half a mind to do it myself. The stupid little bell on the line tinkled, the man went to work and caught something.

We wouldn't find the red ball. I wanted to throw another one in. Father stroked my hair.

Back home he did push-ups (thirty-three) in the yard, fell asleep, woke up, took off his shirt, mowed the lawn, sent me for the newspaper, read. Father read and sweated, his neck hairs sticking to his skin.

He called me over to read me something. He was already furious again. Maybe he wanted to share his anger, same as with the fisherman. Some people from some academy in Serbia had written something or other. I didn't understand everything Father said. For example, I didn't understand the word "memorandum." I understood "serious crisis," but not what the crisis was. I knew the word "genocide" from school, but here it wasn't being applied to Jasenovac, it was about Kosovo. "Protest" and "demonstrations" I sort of understood, and I could also picture what "prohibition of assembly" meant. I just didn't know why the demonstrating and assembling were prohibited, and whether Father thought that was good or bad. I understood "riots."

I had questions. Father, a calm man, was crumpling the newspaper and screaming, "Unbelievable!" I didn't ask any of my questions.

He clambered up the cherry tree and back down it. He dug a hole and shoveled the dirt back into it. He turned on the radio and found music. The screen door rattled and Mother slipped out of the house as if called into existence by the tune. My parents hugged each other. Mother fell into Father's arms so naturally that it was like they'd agreed to it beforehand. They danced and Father wasn't mad anymore—it didn't go together, everything else goes with anger but not hugging and dancing.

At the fairground: I call the dog's name. I pet the dog. I ask the dog: Whose dog are you? His quick tongue is orange. The dog finds a piece of fabric in the bushes, blue and white and red, like the flag. Unbelievable, I whisper. The dog smells like freshly mown grass. I bore the dog.

A boy whistles through his teeth. The dog breaks free and runs to answer the summons. The boy is my age, and right away I know that he can do lots of things I can't. He waves me over. He performs for me. He walks on his hands. I turn away, I've seen enough. Everything else he has to show me I can just as well imagine, I console myself in my cowardice.

I slink home. Father and Mother are not in the yard anymore. On the radio, two men are speaking seriously to each other, then they both laugh, like Father and the man by the river. It's like everything can be everything at once, serious and funny, furious and dancing.

What are the chickens doing? The chickens are hanging around in the summer. I peek between the boards into the henhouse. Rays of sunlight slice through the air. I go in, thinking I'll look for eggs. Sitting on the platform is the snake.

What do you say to a snake?

"Prohibition of assembly," I whisper. The snake raises its head. It smells in the henhouse the way it always does. The radio is talking about the weather. High of ninety-five. The snake slithers down from the platform.

"Protest!" I shout. Or: "*Poskok!*"

Father yanks me out of the henhouse. I struggle, as if he were trying to hurt me. Father's blue faded jeans. Mother puts her hands on my shoulders and turns me to face her, trying to make me look at her. So now she's dancing with me. What I actually want to look at, though, is: Father versus the snake.

Don't be scared, Mother says.

I'm not scared of any snake!

Father brings the rock from the garden. Father, on the threshold of the henhouse, raises the rock above his head. He walks in, trying to get closer to the snake, and the snake is trying to do something too, probably get out. It had it good before we showed up. It flows toward the door, toward Father, is it about to jump? Father takes a step back and the radio plays more dance music.

Father shows me the dead snake.

I ask if I can hold it.

I hold the snake, and think: This isn't a snake anymore. Father is Father, covered with dust. It would have been so great to find the red wooden ball.

The snake is heavier and warmer than I'd imagined. Holding it like this is like not knowing what to say.

"Were you scared?" Father asks.

Why is everyone always talking about being scared?

"Were you?" I ask back.

"It wasn't too bad," Father says. He wipes his brow with the back of his hand and then wipes his mouth. Dust and sweat. I can't help but think: Disgusting.

Father says, "*Poskok*. It jumps at your throat and sprays poison in your eyes." He pinches my cheek, and then takes Mother's hand.

That was my parents' last dance before the war. Or the last I witnessed. I never saw them dance in Germany either.

Father washed himself off with the garden hose. I dug a grave for the snake. It's still there: *poskok*. Unbelievable.

THE CREAKING OF THE FLOORS
IN VILLAGE LIVING ROOMS

The grilled meat and the walk to the ruins of my great-grand-parents' house had made Gavrilo and Grandmother thirsty and talkative. On the way back, they drank water from the old well and began their sentences with *Do you remember?* The snake in the crown of the sorb-apple tree was sunning itself.

"Do you remember the first time you came here?" Gavrilo asked. "Your dress, your hair, everything was brown except your cheeks were so red!"

Grandmother nodded. Of course she remembered. Her nod wasn't an answer to the question, it was recognition that, yes, she was not alone with the past. It must have been in the fifties, Gavrilo was still young then.

"I'd come with Pero. Father-in-law came back from the fields late that day."

"Bogosav wasn't your father-in-law yet."

"But I knew what I wanted! I knew what would happen with Pero and me." Grandmother laughed. "Pero was in the bedroom, reading. I helped Mother-in-law with dinner. Father-in-law called her but I ran out instead. I introduced myself and he said he knew who I was. Good. I tried to pull off his boots, as is the custom, but no. 'As long as I can do it myself, no one has to do it for me,' he said. I insisted. So he let me. He was wearing thick wool socks.

"I wanted to go back to the kitchen, but he said: 'Stay a minute. Talk to me. Who are your people?'

"'Pero must have told you all about me?' And in walked Pero like he'd been summoned. He hugged and kissed his father and took my hand. But Father-in-law wanted to keep talking to me alone.

"'I want to hear it from you,' he said. And that Pero only told him what he wanted to hear. 'What did you learn from your people?'

"I knew he was really talking mostly to Pero. Pero had lived in Višegrad, gone to high school, read books. He hadn't wanted anything to do with the farm and the countryside. As an oldest son!

"So I told Father-in-law who my parents were. Farmers like him. Wheat, corn. Lots of sheep, four cows, two horses. I said there wasn't much Mother could do with her hands and with wool that I couldn't. And that I'd learned to read and write. Late, but I learned. 'And my mother's also taught me how to make a good polenta.' Then I went into the kitchen and made polenta. I think he liked my leaving him alone for a minute.

"I never had any trouble with him.

"Of course there's no way he could have known that you have to be a real idiot to mess up polenta."

Gavrilo was smiling already. Probably because he knew the polenta would come back at the end. He knew the story, it couldn't have changed any, after all. Down to today, no matter how treacherous my grandmother's memory may be, the polenta punch line is still there.

If Gavrilo knew it all already, who was she telling? Me? Father-in-law himself? Speak well of the dead, but never lie to them?

Now it was the living's turn. Grandmother asked Gavrilo about his daughter (going to college), his mother (immortal because she can't stop cursing), his brother. When it came to his brother, Gavrilo grew serious and pointed at the mountains: "Sretoje's feeding the dragons . . ."

Grandmother nodded. "Heard anything about Radenko?"

"He'll have to stay in the valley." Whatever that meant, it made both of them look down at the ground.

Marija, Stevo, and coffee were waiting in Gavrilo's yard. On the porch was a washing machine, running; on the machine was a cat, dozing. Under a lean-to and covered with cardboard was an old yellow Lada.

"Does it still go?"

"Doesn't need to." Gavrilo pinched the back of my neck. "What are you doing standing around, tired already? Here, have some coffee."

The coffee tasted wonderfully burnt, and the inventory continued. This person came to Oskoruša only in the summer; that one didn't come at all anymore. Someone named Radoje had sold all his cattle after calculating that the money would last him until he died, but now he's lived much longer than he expected and is barely getting by. Plus he misses his cows.

Someone named Ratko broke his leg up on Vijarac, on the fire cliffs. The fracture wouldn't heal. Only after an herbalist woman started working on him did it get better. Ratko refused to say what she'd asked for in return, but the fact is that every time he says *ee* or *i* his face twists in pain. He's gotten real inventive and now sounds like a fine gentleman, saying *mutton* instead of *sheep* and *supper* instead of *dinner*. He doesn't *shit in the shithouse* anymore either, he *passes stool over at the outhouse.*

Lots about bodies. Who's sick, what's broken and how bad. Bones, boils, skin, blood. Same with the earth. How the soil's doing, the harvest, what's the rain up to? "Blackberries," Gavrilo screams. "Everyone's planting blackberries! All because one guy from the valley made a mint with blackberries years back!"

The Dragulovićs were trying it too. The newest folks here; their daughter was the only child in the village. They couldn't find work in the city and now were trying blackberries in Oskoruša.

Once Grandmother and Gavrilo had taken care of the past and the present, it was time for pastries. Marija offered us a blackberry tart. We took, chewed, praised.

Gavrilo leaned back in the sun. Grandmother looked him over. So, you're still alive, her look said. Still here, still healthy. The old woman and the old man were linked by earlier encounters in these mountains and by looks they kept giving each other when the other one wasn't looking: bashful sympathy.

Today Grandmother sometimes remembers Gavrilo, sometimes the name means nothing to her. A veil of The Past has covered her Now. Fictions are woven into it. I can work with that. My grandmother is a little old woman who will never die.

"I've always had a good welcome here," she said to Gavrilo.

"You were always honest, it was easy."

"Not always. I wanted my Pero. I did stretch things a bit here and there."

Now Gavrilo, admiring Grandmother, seemed much younger to me than she did. Earlier it was like they'd rehearsed their dialogue. Now Grandmother was improvising, breaking through the ritual of their common, identical memories.

"What did you trick us about, Kristina?" he said, bending forward.

"You mustn't ask a lady that." Grandmother pretended to be outraged. Grandmother was no lady.

Gavrilo nodded, seeming satisfied with her nonanswer.

"You never made trouble for me. Not the village, not Pero's parents," Grandmother said. I liked that. Not making trouble for people: that's exactly what everyone should always do. "And if I was ten years younger, this one here"—me—"would've had to build me a house."

"It's not too late," Gavrilo said.

"Not for him."

"For me it'd be too far away," I said.

"Too far from where?" Gavrilo asked.

"From Germany."

I didn't want to say that I couldn't imagine living in Oskoruša. But Gavrilo would probably have rather heard the truth. Or maybe I was just projecting again, asking myself a question that no one else was asking me.

I took refuge in the schnapps, drinking so as not to have to explain myself further. And when Marija started clearing the table, I was happy to follow her, carrying the dishes into the house. The others stayed sitting outside.

The creaking of the floors in village living rooms.

Paneled walls. The only decoration: Two wooden figures. A knight on horseback pointing his lance at a dragon. He with curly hair under a hooded cape and halo-gold, his steed with such a fiery gaze that I seriously thought there were candles in the eye sockets. And the dragon, reptile-green, blood-red, twisting and turning, trying to avoid the lance, twists and turns. The horse's tail is spattered with blood.

The images sparkled. The light was so full of adjectives, I had to squint. The knight and the dragon were moving back and forth like they were really fighting. I was drunk. I turned away.

The massive table, with oilcloth on it. Marija brought out plates of meat, cheese, and bread from the kitchen. When we'd just eaten cookies! Six place settings. I asked if they were expecting someone else.

"You never know how many people'll turn up," she said.

A small TV in the cabinet. A little curtain hanging down over the screen. Crocheted doilies on the box and two framed photos on the doilies: of the war criminals Radovan Karadžić and, in uniform, Ratko Mladić.

I had to sit down.

"More?" Marija asked. She couldn't seriously mean did I want more food? The gray meat was piled up in front of me; I hadn't managed to get a single bite down. Or did she mean more pictures of death-soaked life in this country and overladen dishes of food at the same time? More "Where I Come From" kitsch to put into a book?

Maybe she meant the porcelain dalmatians in the cabinet next to the war criminals. Would I like a little more shaking of the cabinet?

Maybe she meant Gavrilo, her husband. Would I like him to show me around any more?

Or did she mean herself? More biography: a woman who went to school in a country called Yugoslavia, eight grades, Young Pioneer salute, a field trip by train to the Ethnology Museum in Sarajevo—the farthest she ever traveled in her life.

Did she mean the knight and the dragon? And that I could see more in it than what was visible on the surface, if I wanted? I did want that! Along with the adjectives. The dim light, the stuffy room, Vijarac's rough peak.

The dragon had been hit, and blood was running from its neck. I swear, there hadn't been that much blood there before. The saint with the lance had the same brown eyes as everyone here. The brown of my eyes.

He's the monster, I thought. *He* is.

Marija, right in my ear: "The dragon slayer." Her breath smelled of roast lamb. She spit on the floor of her own house three times, took my hand, and said, "I have bigger hands than my husband does."

Her hands, this house, Oskoruša. This bittersweet day with the living and the dead, a real live snake or a symbolic beast. The picnic at my great-grandparents' grave. It's all a kind of primal scenery for my Self-Portrait With Ancestors. Which is also a portrait of my not being able to meet the demands of a self-portrait.

The others came back in, washed their hands, and sat down. Each of them tired in their own way. Gavrilo asked if I liked traveling. Finally, I thought, something I can excel at. I rattled off country after country, told stories of this branch of the Goethe-Institut, that university or publisher, this or that grant to go abroad footloose and fancy-free. I had been to the US,

Mexico, Colombia, India, and Australia. Every place I listed—
each one farther from Oskoruša than the last—seemed more
and more absurd. I heard myself say that I'd drunk the best
tequila of my life in Guadalajara. I assumed Gavrilo would take
drinking good liquor as an accomplishment, and I was trying
to please him. Gavrilo showed no reaction. The war criminals
in the glass case didn't either.

Gavrilo started telling us about *his* travels. One day, he said,
some linguists turned up in the village. They stuck a micro-
phone in front of his nose and said: Speak into this, please, we
want to hear how you sound.

He was tempted to chase them off, because you're not supposed to stare at someone's mouth, only at what the person says
with it. But he restrained himself and asked the linguists what
they had to say.

Yes, then they talked about his dialect. That it's special because it contains certain expressions that otherwise appear only
someplace in Montenegro, hundreds of kilometers away.

Now Gavrilo liked that. That someone so far away would
speak just like him. He wrote down the name of the place, and
then he chased off the linguists. That same day he loaded up
his horse and headed out. Day after day, just the horse and him,
or in other words one horse and one old donkey, Gavrilo said.
And he said that he'd found what he'd hoped to find. He took a
leather-bound notebook out of the cabinet, opened it, and said:
"The story of how it all started."

The notebook was manufactured to look old. Artificially dis-
tressed paper. A photograph glued onto the first page showed,
not too clearly, a piece of parchment with writing on it. Two

semesters of Slavic studies sufficed for me to recognize the language as Church Slavonic, but not for me to decipher what it said.

"How it all started!" Gavrilo cried again: "There were once three brothers from Montenegro who rebelled against the Ottoman governor by stealing either his horse, his jewels, or his wife—the story isn't totally clear about which," he said, "but it doesn't really matter. They fled the city. A price was put on their heads, and not a small price either. Two left on foot but the third"—and here at the latest the whole story became very strange, but who am I to judge something for being strange?—"the third flew off as a dragon, to scour the countryside for dangers and find a suitable place for a new beginning."

"As a dragon?" I said.

"Horses don't fly too well," Grandmother said.

"One Stanišić, another Stanišić, and a third Stanišić," Gavrilo exulted. He was breathing fast; he stood up to have more room. The air was heavy with forebodings and forefathers. "And they found a suitable place," he cried. "Right here! Oskoruša! This is where they settled down! Stanišić, Stanišić, Stanišić. And now—here you are!"

Was he telling me this so I could write about it? Ancestors and descendants, graves and tablecloths and revenants. Survivors. And now probably dragons, too.

I asked what happened next with the dragon, and Gavrilo gave me a little knock on the forehead, saying I shouldn't take everything so literally. Maybe that brother was just the fastest of the three.

Stevo took us back to Višegrad that night. At home, Grandmother insisted on making my bed for me. I couldn't fall asleep, so

I turned on the light and did some research on the internet. There was no mention of the Stanišić dragon-brothers. I felt relieved.

Grandmother knocked on the door and came in. She'd seen that the light was still on and wanted to check if everything was all right. She tucked me in. Stood for a while next to my bed, as though I were still the boy whose hands she would warm in hers when he came back in from the snow.

I didn't know if she was waiting for me to say something, and maybe she didn't know if I was waiting for her to say something either, and so neither of us said anything.

During the next few days I took a lot of walks alone through the city. One time, I came back from a stroll and found Grandmother in the company of a young man. Hair slicked back, good-looking guy. A jeans and white T-shirt type. He was sitting next to her on the sofa.

Grandmother proudly introduced him as "my Andrej." Grandmother's Andrej shook my hand, not letting it go for two seconds longer than I would have liked, during which he said: "So, you're the writer."

I looked at the vase. My book was no longer on it.

"And you're the cop," I said.

Sticking out of the vase was a sunflower.

GRANDMOTHER AND THE SOLDIER

Grandmother goes to the butcher shop, but where Grandmother is rattling the door the butcher hasn't had a shop for ten years. Grandmother is cooking bean stew, because her husband is about to come home from work. Bean stew is his favorite food. She eats alone.

Ever since she's been less steady on her feet, Andrej has been doing most of the shopping for her. He is not corrupt like the other policemen, she says; one time he stopped Emir Kusturica and when Kusturica said, "Don't you know who I am?" he'd replied, "License and registration, please. It'll say on there."

She never asks the retired officer on the fifth floor for a favor, even though he keeps offering. Grandmother doesn't like bearded ex-military men. Besides, her policeman always brings a little something with him and is nice enough to stay for a coffee.

Sometimes my grandmother wonders where all the German soldiers suddenly disappeared to. She lived through the wars at home. World War II in Staniševac, her childhood village, and the Bosnian War in Višegrad.

My grandmother took the one big trip of her life in early 2000, to visit her son and daughter-in-law—my parents—in the US, where they'd emigrated to when they were no longer allowed to stay in Germany.

Grandmother's plane was due to land at 8:00 PM but she managed to get onto another that arrived at five. "What was I supposed to do for all that time?" she said to my amazed parents after showing up at their door unannounced. A pale Slovakian was carrying her suitcases. They could understand each other thanks to the Slavic roots of their respective languages. Grandmother wanted the Slovakian to come in for a coffee, but the Slovakian said he unfortunately didn't have time, and left in a hurry.

In 1944, German soldiers came to Staniševac. In 1944, Grandmother was twelve years old.

"Do you remember them marching in, Grandma?"

"More like crawling in. They were cowering, ducking at things from all directions."

"Were you scared?"

"Everyone was scared. The Germans were scared, that's why they were scurrying around like that. And we were scared because they were scurrying around. We knew the stories. Everyone was scared of each other, and that's what scared me.

"We came out of our houses, hands over our heads, and the Germans went in, hands on their guns. But since no one in the houses was about to shoot, or even capable of shooting anything, they lowered their weapons for the time being. Then, since it was hot and they were sweating like pigs in their uniforms, we offered them water, but they wanted to drink from their own canteens."

Aside from the offer of water, the first time the two sides spoke to each other was a little before nightfall. The soldiers had to sleep somewhere too, that was obvious, and the moment something was obvious everyone's fear got a little smaller. The animals could probably be moved from one stable to the next, but not the stench.

No one slept well that first night. Or the second. Every time the villagers could wash their faces in the morning without seeing someone hanging from a nearby tree or hearing that someone had been stabbed in the night, it got easier for them to fall asleep, and eventually the soldiers' steel helmets came off too.

Zagorka knew which house the soldiers would be in, crouching by the stove with their chests naked, delousing one another. Grandmother went there with her sister. Zagorka asked if any of them was a pilot. She had already decided to go away with a pilot when the Germans left. There were no pilots. Zagorka was disappointed, and a little mad, and the soldiers were disappointed too, somehow, probably because they all would have loved to be pilots.

Grandmother told the story that an officer stayed at her family's place. He had delicate hands and sensitive skin like a child's. And teeny tiny glasses. He washed himself in the morning and at night, and before he went to bed he would ask politely if there was any milk, offering something as a trade, unfortunately nothing that anyone could use. Although Grandmother would've been happy to take the chalk, but her father didn't let her.

After he got his bowl of milk, the officer shut himself up in the bedroom. When he came out, the bowl was empty. He said thank you, and then good night, in German for a few days but then someone taught him *laku noć* and also *mlijeko, mo-lim*: "Milk, please." And then at some point, at some point, my twelve-year-old grandmother wanted to see what it looked like when a German soldier drank milk.

She hid in the wardrobe and peered through the crack of the door. The officer came in—Georg was his name—and put the bowl of milk on the floor, setting his little glasses down next to it. Then he kneeled, hands clasped, and began to whisper something. It was very, very quiet.

Afterward he crossed himself and brought the bowl to his mouth with both hands, to drink the milk.

Today he visits Grandmother every so often too. Like the girl on the street. My grandmother's German officer kneels on the old railroad embankment. Grandmother can see him from the window. Tiny glasses and everything.

He doesn't need help, the way the girl does. Grandmother doesn't leave the apartment for him. She thinks he wouldn't like to be disturbed.

MIROSLAV STANIŠIĆ SHOWS HIS SHEEP HOW IT'LL BE

One mustn't speak ill of the dead in their presence. The only thing worse would be not to speak of them at all. The earth is hardly a mute companion. But it lacks the warmth of the human voice and our tendency to digress. The earth is taciturn, the earth is businesslike. Dead people like exaggeration.

Oskoruša's most recent dead person, as of spring 2009, was named Miroslav Stanišić. Gavrilo showed us his grave.

"May the earth sit easy upon him," Grandmother sighed.

"Miki predicted his own death," Gavrilo said. "May the Triple-Horned Winged One forgive his presumption."

"Predicted it how?" I asked, even though I was actually more curious about the Triple-Horned Winged One.

"'You'll see,' he always said. 'On this day, at this time,' he said. And it happened. On that exact day."

"How could he do that?" I asked.

"He was a punctual man, that's how."

"Holds the dominoes record," Marija said.

"You're related to him," Gavrilo said, as if trying to give more weight to what was to follow. "In the months before his death, Miki trained his sheep. The drills were, well, unusual. We didn't understand at first what he was up to.

"'Miki, what the heck are you doing?'

"'I'm showing them how it'll be,' Miki answered.

"'How what'll be, Miki? May the lightning strike you softly.'

"'How it'll be without me.' He kneeled in front of his sheep and talked to them. Demonstrated something or another. They did exercises, bleating on the meadow."

"He'd lost his mind?" I said without thinking, at which point everyone, even Stevo, looked at me as if I were the one bleating and belly-crawling on the grass.

"Saša, Saša, my little donkey," Grandmother said pityingly.

"It would've been crazy only if the sheep didn't learn anything," Gavrilo explained. "But they did learn. Soon they could do everything he wanted them to do, everything he'd tried to teach them."

"One could open doors," Marija said.

"One was like a guard dog, warning of danger," Gavrilo said.

"Three of them learned how to scoop water out of the well."

"One time, one sheep ran into Cigo, that's my brother Sretoje's dog, feisty little fella, and the sheep soothed Cigo's anger by licking its barking maw. Never seen anything like it."

"Never." Marija nodded.

"They're still around. Well, some aren't, old age. The herd is though! There's still the herd. Our Miki taught the herd how to survive! On the morning of the day when his heart would beat its last, he set the sheep free, and they went up into the forests on Vijarac in a column, like soldiers or ants or something, what do I know." Gavrilo took off his cap. "And Miki lay down and left us."

"May his coffin stay sealed," Grandmother said.

"May erosion spare the cemetery," Marija said.

"The sheep," Gavrilo cried, "wander free across the land! They're multiplying. They're thriving, Saša. The sheep are thriving!

Miki's herd will outlive us. That's how well organized they are. The whole countryside would do better under those sheep than under the band of criminals! I'm not joking. And all because someone spoke their language. Miki."

"May the earth sit easy upon him," I sighed.

"Four months, undefeated," Marija sighed, making the sign of the cross in Vijarac's direction.

I looked up at the peak. The sunlight blazed blinding white on the cliffs—a lighthouse in the ocean of hills.

"And I'm related to Miki," I said. As if trying to give more weight to what was to follow.

LITTLE CHECK MARKS ON OUR NAMES

We have little check marks on our names. Someone who liked me called mine "tiaras" once. In Germany, I've usually felt them to be a hindrance more than anything. They put bureaucrats and landlords in a skeptical mood; passport control at the border takes longer for you than it does for Petra in front of you or Ingo behind you.

Plus, during the twelve semesters I was at university, it said in my passport that I was authorized to stay in Germany solely for academic study. So the most assiduous border guards would ask me what I was studying. The fields were listed in my passport too, but they asked anyway, as a test: if you hesitated or stammered like you didn't know your own major, the visa was possibly fake.

At the Frankfurt airport on my way to the US to take a job as a teaching assistant in German, a border-control officer indulged in so much time over my passport that the line behind me was reconnoitering the emergency exits. At some point the officer, as if he'd only just noticed the visa, shouted: "So! You! Are a student. What! Are you studying?" He was screaming. Somehow, he managed to scream every word as if it was the most important.

"Slavic!" I replied at the same volume.

The answer released a nod of recognition from him. "Must need a lot of math," he cried. He turned more pages and had another question: "What were you! Doing! In Tunisia!"

"All! Inclusive! Package! Tour! And I! Especially! Liked! The buffet!"

I tried not to care too much about this exotic quality of my name; anyway, I had trouble grasping some German names too. One time, in a conversation about a couple I didn't know, I asked which one of them was the woman, Hauke or Sigrid. They both were! Assumptions busted.

In any case, once you've gone to twenty apartment open houses and never made the short list, *Saša* is going to turn into the German *Sascha*. After that I didn't get an apartment either, at first, but at least it was because of my job. ("Only doctors, lawyers, and architects live in our building. And one classical philologist, we can't get rid of him.") Then I won a literary prize, and for six months it looked on paper like I was making good money. All of a sudden neither my name nor my job was a problem.

Before I saw the cemetery in Oskoruša, I had never thought much about where I came from in the sense of family roots. My grandparents were just there. One grandfather was still alive, the other wasn't. One was a friendly fisherman, the other had been a fanciful Communist.

I didn't know much about my grandmothers' pasts—I just took them for granted as part of my present. Nice to me, full of life. A little weird about beans sometimes. I always thought there'd be plenty of time for us to get to know each other better.

Places, too, weren't overburdened with feelings of belonging. Višegrad was Mother's story about being in the hospital in a rainstorm. It was running through the streets as cops and robbers, it was the softness of fir needles between my fingers, the stairs to Grandmother's apartment with its countless smells, the sledding, the school, the war, the childhood interrupted.

Heidelberg was fleeing and a new beginning, precarity and puberty, first time being stopped by the cops and first love, salvaged furniture and university. Eventually it was the defiant self-confidence of shouting: Because I can!

But then I read my last name on every other gravestone in the Oskoruša cemetery. And all at once, my origins—both the unknown relatives and the well-known places—meant more to me. I had been to Oskoruša only as a tourist in shorts. Someone who drank a shot of schnapps under his ancestors' fruit tree. Who thought the landscape was unbelievably beautiful and the ruins unbelievable. Who had never asked himself: What kind of people were they, my people? Including the ones who were still alive. Grandmother, standing next to me with her curled hair dyed purple, eyes closed, saying: "I see nothing but the spring in Oskoruša."

Why did she say that? I would understand only much later: it was always in the spring that Grandmother had been in these mountains with Grandfather. Our trip, too, was full of April.

In fact, after the cemetery visit I started thinking crazy and irrelevant nonsense about how I was the last male Stanišić. That I might be a dead end, if I didn't have children. I began thinking about my origins, revisiting and documenting my biography in diaries and notes and fictions, trying to find what aspects of where I came from might have turned me into the man I am today, then questioning the whole thing. It seemed old-fashioned, regressive, even destructive to talk about *my* origins or *our* origins in an age when where you were born and where you came from were once again being misused as distinguishing features, when borders were hardening and so-called national interests rising up from the drained swamp of small-country particularism. In a time when exclusion and refusal of entry were on the ballot again.

Most of what I wrote after Oskoruša was in some way explicitly about people and places, and what it means for these people to have been born in these particular places. Also about what it means not to be allowed to live there anymore, or not to want to. What does a particular genealogy, being the product of a particular origin, give you? And in the same way, what does it make impossible? I wrote about Brandenburg, about Bosnia, the geographical location didn't make much difference at all, struggles with identity don't care about the latitude. I wrote about racism, violence, fleeing. Hardly any of my characters stay in place. Few get where they originally wanted to go. All are afraid. Being sedentary rarely turns out well for them. They are refugees from something more or less existential. Their lives in transit are sometimes a burden, sometimes a gift.

They rarely talk about homelands, or home. And when they do, they don't mean any concrete place. Home, says Mo the globetrotter in *Trappers*, is where you have to pretend the least.

Home, I say, is what I'm writing about now. Home was both the past in a Višegrad I knew the way a child can know things, and the later past I'd been given by a Heidelberg that had started out foreign and turned complex like this sentence. Home is this sentence.

Grandmothers are home. When Grandmother Kristina started losing her memory, I started collecting memories.

My other grandmother, Mejrema, I called *Nena*: Granny. What will remain of Granny? That she was a passionate movie-goer, my mother told me. In the seventies and eighties, she saw every single movie in the Cultural Center. Even ones like *Rambo II*. She took me to my first horror movie, some version of *Dracula*: I was much too young, it was pretty much a disaster and we had to leave the theater before the end. I forgot the images over the years, luckily. All that stays with me is a kind of timid sympathy for bats.

That Granny was a heavy smoker is something I experienced myself. Pass me the ashtray, would you mind? That she liked to sit cross-legged. That she sewed a lot, to smoke less. That she waited by the window when she knew someone was coming over to visit, or coming home from somewhere. The beans had told her more or less when they'd arrive. That she gently swayed her upper body back and forth when she was excited or worried, and also when she was tired and calm.

What's left of her father, my great-grandfather?

He was a raftsman on the Drina. The first thing I heard about him: he was one of the best.

The second: that he couldn't swim.

FRAGMENTS

My cousin had her second child last year, a girl named Ada. They live in France, in Montpellier. My cousin's husband is a doctor with a mustache. His parents are Tunisian immigrants; he is French. He gives his mother my books as presents. "Because they're about being made to feel foreign." After all their years in France, that's his mother's favorite subject.

My family lives scattered around the world. We shattered along with Yugoslavia and have not yet been able to put ourselves back together again. What I want to say about where I come from has to do with this scatteredness, too—it has meant, over the years, that where I am is practically never where my family is.

Where I Come From is Grandmother. And the girl on the street invisible to everyone but Grandmother—that's Where I Come From too: memory and imagination.

Where I Come From is Gavrilo, who insists when we say goodbye that I take one of his piglets with me to Germany.

Where I Come From is the boy with my last name in Hamburg. He is playing with a toy airplane. I ask: "Where are you flying to?"—"To Split, to Grandma." He is riding a balance bike. I ask: "Where are you going?"—"To Africa, to the dinosaurs."

Where I Come From is his Grandma, my mother. Living in Croatia for the past few years, after Germany and America, in an apartment building where she can see the Adriatic from the balcony.

Where I Come From are the sweet-bitter accidents that brought us to all these different places. It's a belonging to which you contribute nothing. The unknown family in the acidic soil of Oskoruša; the unknown child off in Montpellier.

Where I Come From is war. Here's what war was for us: Mother and I fled through Serbia, Hungary, and Croatia to Germany. On August 24, 1992, we arrived in Heidelberg. Father had brought us over the Serbian border and then turned back to Višegrad to stay with his mother. He joined us six months later, bringing with him a brown suitcase, insomnia, and a scar on his thigh. To this day I haven't asked him where the scar came from.

If you're from the Balkans, a refugee, and don't speak the language, those are your only qualifications and references. Mother, the political scientist, landed in an industrial laundry. For five and a half years she handled hot towels. Father, the sales manager, toiled away in construction.

Were they happy in Germany? Yes, sometimes. And yes, not often enough.

In 1998 they had to leave the country again. To avoid having to go back to ethnically cleansed Višegrad, they emigrated to Florida. There they found jobs they could never have dreamed of in Germany. They played poker with their American friends and grilled meat with the Bosnians. They put aside a little money and one time they found an alligator in their garden pond.

And so, today, a life as American retirees in Croatia, though they can only ever stay for a maximum of one year before they have to spend three months in a non-Schengen country. In

2017, about forty-seven thousand people emigrated from Croatia. Croatia is yet another European country completely blind when it comes to questions of migration.

Our first place in Germany was in an industrial park between the cities of Wiesloch and Walldorf, right off the highway. The only good thing about it was that the train station was nearby and you could leave easily. Our house was the only residential building for miles. We were surrounded by smokestacks, manufacturing plants, car dealerships. "Heidelberg Printing Presses." "PENNY Distribution Center." "Self-Service Auto Center: Car Wash, Vacuums." I don't know if all those places existed back then—I'm reading them off Google Maps today.

Six other refugee families lived in the building. Everyone was frustrated with everything: the authorities, the prices, the fact that only two burners on the stove would get hot, themselves. We were all waiting for good news and a better life—better would be fine, it didn't have to be good. Still being alive was good.

We children were allowed to watch TV as much as we wanted. We watched wrestling and softcore porn, and wrestled on old mattresses in the yard. The matresses didn't smell too good. They still bore their previous owners' dreams and dandruff. Body slam. Pile driver. Neck breaker.

The star attraction for most of us was the bulk trash. People just putting their stuff out on the street! I thought it was disgusting. But we had no furniture and no money and so no choice. For a long time I slept on the floor anyway, in protest. I was too proud. My favorite wrestler was Undertaker (he still is).

Mother and I spent hours in the phone booth at the train station. When someone else wanted to make a phone call, we left and Mother had a cigarette. We tried to reach someone, anyone—husband, father, brother, grandmother—but usually couldn't. For weeks at a time we didn't get through; for weeks at a time we didn't know if the person we wanted to talk to would have a voice to talk with.

Mother still remembers the tattered phone book, the stink of sweat, and the graffiti on the window: a black heart. We weren't able to decipher the two letters in the heart.

With the move to Heidelberg, some things got easier. We lived in a bungalow with my aunt Lula's family. She (my mother's sister) and her husband had come to Germany as so-called guest workers just before the war broke out. When the people at the Munich airport detained Mother and me and wanted to send us back, my aunt and her husband wrote a guarantee letter testifying that in case of emergency they would support us. Only then were we allowed to enter. Some people had no one to guarantee for them.

We spent four years under one roof.

After the war, my aunt's family was able to return to Zavidovići. The town was in the Bosniak-Croat part of the newly created federation; their apartment was still their property and almost undamaged. They repainted the walls and replanted the garden. They bred chickens (aunt) and carrier pigeons (uncle). By that time, strangers from who knows where were living in our house in Višegrad. Grandmother fought long and hard to get them to pay rent.

I don't know what my aunt does for a living nowadays—I think probably nothing. For some reason I don't want to ask. I know what makes her happy: folk dancing and, in the summer, spending a couple of days on the Adriatic. Also chickens, probably. Every phone call brings another story about the chickens; she posts pictures of chickens on Instagram. Her account also reveals that the local branch of the Social Democratic Party, the party she almost got onto the city council to represent, enjoys day trips out into nature (comrades sitting on a strange boulder in a forest, looking earnestly at the camera). My aunt makes a very good pita and has a cooing laugh like a pigeon's, which makes me happy. My aunt was never mean to me.

Her sons, my cousins, are both in their early thirties. The elder one is a sports agent in Germany; he has very broad shoulders and a little, fast son. He knew that Hamburger SV would be demoted to second division long before they were, and he knows they'll make it back into the Bundesliga. In Wiesloch his favorite wrestler was "Macho Man" Randy Savage.

The younger brother studied German language and literature, to work in Bosnia at a German call center. Eventually he opened his own call center. Now he's developing a fitness app in which pro athletes show you their training methods. If the app ever goes live I will recommend it to anyone who wants to do push-ups like Mario Götze, as a way of promoting my cousin. In Wiesloch, his favorite was Undertaker, same as me.

My uncle, my mother's brother, was dragged into a hotel bathroom in August 1992 by the Serbian paramilitary, who tried to force him to get undressed so they could see if he was circumcised. He told stories and did this and that and joked around. His act was good, but he knew that he had to be at his best for this scene with his bearded compatriots—it was a matter of life and death. The soldiers laughed. The soldiers asked if he was crazy. The soldiers went silent. There was no applause. It wasn't his best performance, in fact, but he'd won some time. Another uniform entered the bathroom and this soldier recognized my uncle immediately. "Let this one go," he said. "He's just an actor."

From then on my uncle was supposed to report to the police daily. Those who obeyed and reported soon disappeared. In Višegrad, they say: "Darkness swallowed them up." My uncle didn't report; he and his family escaped the city, the darkness. They were on the road for months before finding a new home in Salzburg.

Uncle tried to think of something he could do as a thirty-four-year-old actor in a foreign country where he didn't speak the language. The theater didn't want him, agents didn't give him a chance. So he played newspaper deliveryman for a year, until he thought of a part that didn't need the language. Yugos don't hire clowns but kindergartens and Austrian real-estate offices love them. He found a partner and blundered around birthday parties in a red nose, rode unicycles at office parties. Eventually he even went on a little US tour with a show that consisted of a one-hour attempt to climb over a tiny wall.

After an argument with his partner, he hung up his clown shoes, built a poker table, and started a regular poker game with his two daughters, in their room. First they played with the neighbors; soon people were coming from the whole city.

On weekends, Uncle went fishing in the Salzach; lately he's been fishing in the Drina again. He built a little house near Višegrad. For life as a retiree. Six months a year in France with his daughters and grandkids, six months on the Drina waiting for the catfish to bite—that's how he pictures his last act.

So, his daughters, my cousins, live in France. As children in Višegrad, we used to play together a lot. We played grocery store. I handled the money. We played dolls. I beat the dolls, the girls cried a little, then we played something else.

There is a photo of my cousins and me taken two years before the war started. We are sitting on some stairs. I've put my arm around the younger cousin while the older one leans her head on my shoulder. We're wearing sweat suits. Squinting into the sun, smiling for the camera. I have never in my life felt more like I had siblings than I did then.

When we visit each other nowadays, we talk almost exclusively about our current lives. Talking about the past would take calm and time and above all the courage to ask questions. We have never once spoken about Višegrad since we fled. I don't know how they reached Salzburg—or rather, I do know parts of the journey, I know the route, but I don't know their feelings, what they saw along the way. Despite being close family, I feel like asking to share this kind of existential experience would be too intrusive. So I don't ask and we don't tell. They will read these lines one day. For now, we talk almost exclusively about our current lives.

When we were kids, of course, the present was enough for us too. The sun. Relaxing before the next game. Now we have kids ourselves, so we talk about them. What they're playing. Their tantrums. How we handle gravy (directly on the noodles, randomly around the plate, or in a little side bowl). We say it would be great if our children saw one another more often. All three of us still have copies of the photograph of the three of us on the stairs in the sun.

DO RAFTSMEN NEED TO
KNOW HOW TO SWIM?

My younger cousin's husband has the same name as my mother's father: Muhamed. The blue railroad uniform belonged to my mother's father, and in winter he had a coat to wear over the uniform. It was incredibly thick and heavy so that Grandfather wouldn't freeze on the train. My grandfather Muhamed was a brakeman. He sweated in the brake cabin all summer, froze all winter. He'd loved trains since he was a little boy. He'd rather have been an engine driver, but okay.

In 1978, trains stopped running between Sarajevo and Višegrad and Grandfather Muhamed was put into early retirement. On his first day as a retiree, he folded his heavy coat, tied it up with a cord, put the rest of the uniform and the cap on top, and headed out to the railroad office.

The lady who worked there smoked and read. She gave him a wave of the hand, telling him to wait. There were no windows in the hallway and no chair outside the office. My grandfather was in no hurry. The ceiling above his head was moldy; he stood somewhere else. The building was very quiet, the only sound being the turning of pages in the little office.

Then the lady waved him in. A narrow room, messy and smelling of smoke. Papers everywhere, including on the visitor's chair. Grandfather stayed standing up. He said hello again and stated his name, number of years of service, and service number. The lady lit another cigarette.

He didn't know her. She was not young and not old; she was pale. She asked why he was there. He said he wanted to hand in his uniform and coat and say thank you. He smiled; she coughed. He didn't know what to do with the clothes. He put them down on the floor. Kept smiling, possibly because he wasn't exactly sure anymore what he wanted to thank the railroad for. Or maybe because he remembered how that coat had saved his life in the winter of 1975. Possibly he even briefly considered the thought that he should say thank you to the coat.

The lady kept smoking. In the magazine she'd been reading there were lots of photos. Grandfather smiled. Then he said, All right, and picked up the coat again and left the office.

The sun was shining. Back home, he hung up the coat, took off his shirt and good shoes, and put on overalls and rubber boots. He packed his fishing gear and swung the stool over his shoulder. My grandfather was fifty-seven years old. He walked to the Drina, and he was still smiling, I imagine, when he cast his line.

Grandfather Muhamed was the nicest man. Everyone thought so, everyone noticed. His wife, my Granny Mejrema, said it too now and then—What a nice man—as if talking about a friendly, helpful stranger. She just couldn't help blurting it out sometimes; she sounded honestly disbelieving, as if she couldn't stop marveling at her husband's gentle nature.

He dropped by almost every day to ask if we needed help with anything. He brought us freshly caught fish, went shopping for us, sharpened my pencils. If something was broken he tried his best to fix it, and only rarely broke it worse.

For a long time I'd been scared of, maybe disgusted by, earthworms. Grandfather Muhamed dug three up out of the ground and held them in his hand to show me. The earthworms crawled across the lifeline of his palm. If I wanted to, he said, I could put my hand next to his and the earthworms would come over. I put my hand out and the worms stayed on Grandfather's. Even they must have felt his kindness (he later impaled them on his fishhooks). I overcame my fear of earthworms some other time.

My mother says that he smelled like coal throughout her childhood. No soap could get rid of it. On the day we went fishing with the earthworms, he smelled like shaving cologne and soil.

Maybe the best description of his nature comes from the war. Grandfather left Višegrad with an aid convoy, which was stopped outside the city. Armed men stormed the buses and ordered everybody to get out. Among the soldiers, there were two men from Višegrad whom grandfather knew. He smiled, shook their hands, and asked how they were doing. Everyone survived the incident.

In 1995, we managed to bring him and Granny to Heidelberg. They both mostly stayed home. Grandfather occasionally ventured out on a walk through the vineyards or a shopping trip to the Edeka supermarket a few blocks away. Every couple of days he filled up his canteen with water from a forest spring because he didn't trust German tap water. He learned no German, helped around the house a bit, and liked to watch Formula 1 racing on TV.

One time he came into the living room while *The X-Files* was on. He watched the two agents at work for a while, and at some point asked if he could bother me with a question: "What was that thing on TV just now?"

"A creature from another planet," I said.

Grandfather chuckled and said, "Like me!" He gently ran his rough hands through my hair. In Germany he was still the nicest, most friendly man, theoretically. He didn't get many chances to show it.

Before she met my grandfather, my grandmother had been married once already. Hardly anyone in the family knows that. Failed marriages weren't talked about in Yugoslavia in the fifties and sixties; it was practically an offensive subject. People stuck it out with each other, shared their lives even with partners they didn't want to live with. If they separated, they did so in secret and in shame.

I don't know anything for certain about Granny's first husband. He was probably a Macedonian, because the family had "given her away" to Skopje. Six months later she came back to Višegrad. She was thinner than before, had started smoking, and laughed a lot. It's hard to say what all that was a sign of. If she ever did talk about her short marriage, the people she told never said a word about it.

At the time, Grandfather Muhamed was living in a barracks on the outskirts of the city, looking for work. He had time on his hands, and since he didn't join the Party, he used it too. Whenever he could he liked to spend it along the river under the weeping willow near Mejrema's parents' house. It was a good place to fish and to watch the trains from. Young Muhamed liked doing both, and probably also liked the chance to maybe see Mejrema. From the weeping willow you could see the house in whose garden she would sit under a mulberry tree, sewing

72

and—when her parents weren't there—smoking. And someone up there could, in turn, see you under the weeping willow too.

At some point, Mejrema came down to talk to him. He jumped up at once and waited with cap in hand to say hello.

She didn't say hello to him. She asked what he was doing there all the time.

That threw my grandfather for a bit of a loop. So he didn't say hello either—probably the first time he'd failed to do so in his adult life—and instead asked back if she liked fishing.

She replied with another question: Did she look like someone who liked fishing?

And what do you say to that? Everyone could like fishing, even pretty young women such as Mejrema! Looks don't matter when it comes to fishing. Best to change the subject. But again Muhamed could only think of fishing, so he asked her if she wanted to learn a knot from him.

She was sure she knew more knots than he did, she said back. Invisible ones, too, from knitting.

He wanted to drive trains, he said then.

Why?

Fishing and knots won't get you that far, he said.

And then she smiled and asked if he wanted to go to a movie with her.

He was six years older than her and had always greeted her nicely, his whole life long, I imagine.

My granny Mejrema's father was named Suljo—that was the raftsman. A tempestuous craft on the Drina, lots of calluses and cuts, and my great-grandfather Suljo at the rudder with cap and cigarette stub.

This image: my mother as a little girl on his raft, sitting astraddle on a loose log. A little Drina boat captain. Her grandfather called her Kitty. Her voice ringing out in the canyon when the river makes the raft shake: "*Dedo!* Grandpa!"

Her grandfather has told her that she has to stay quiet, she's not actually allowed to travel with him. But how is she supposed to stay quiet in all this great swaying and tossing?

Suljo masterfully steered the raft around a rocky outcropping that reached far into the river. He was too proud not to show off his granddaughter to the other raftsmen and let them hear her voice.

Below the mouth of the Žepa, the Drina rushes down two foaming stretches of rapids; Kitty has to get out before the current speeds up, it's too dangerous. She follows her grandfather, running along the shore, so as not to miss it when he flies over the rapids. Before the second, still narrower, still stronger rapids, lots of raftsmen jump ship, swim to the shore, and abandon their vessel to its fate.

Her grandfather can't or doesn't need to swim. He stays on his raft with his partner at the rear rudder. The raft dips, water laps over the railing, someone shouts something—maybe the river—and then they're past it, and my mother claps wildly.

After 1963, when they built three weirs, no one needed any more raftsmen. Dams had tamed the Drina.

I wasn't yet born when Suljo left this world. He didn't die on the river, he died of kidney failure. Could he swim or not? There's a story about that. I can't say what's true in the story and what's not.

My great-grandmother Rumša went to do the laundry in the Drina. An illiterate woman who sang old songs. According to the story, Suljo heard her voice for the first time when he was on his raft and thought it was a vila, one of the creatures who, as everyone knows, have haunted the Drina ever since the bridge in Višegrad had been built against their will. Suljo apparently jumped in the water, either to save himself on shore or drown, anything to avoid being cursed to serve the vila for eternity.

As he was going under he saw where the song was really coming from, and he wanted to head there. So he swam to the point on the shore where Rumša was crouching with her washtub, singing.

"Huh, what an ugly fish I've caught" were supposedly the first words my great-grandmother said to my great-grandfather.

Suljo liked to say when he told the story that in retrospect he wasn't sure which would have been worse: the vila's curse or his future wife's sharp tongue.

When she told the story, Rumša described a raftsman in a white shirt and cap—or sometimes, even better, shirtless—drifting down the Drina several times a week. She said that with his cap and the swing of his arms he was the only one she could recognize from afar. And since she didn't want to have to look at him only from afar, she started singing.

"I sung my Suljo to me, and he didn't even know he was mine yet! I'll sing you the song from back then for a few pennies. Or any other song."

Great-grandmother Rumša came from a big family that had been decimated during World War II. Maybe it was the losses that left her, the survivor, crafty, funny, and full of song.

People used to say about Rumša that she had a voice as clear as truth, but that she wouldn't utter this truth for just anybody. In 1944, she was supposed to sing for the Germans, who'd turned a former stable into a stage for their amusement. They ordered her to sing, so she did, but no one said she had to sing well . . .

Suljo and Rumša built themselves a house on the Drina. The façade was white, the shutters were aspen wood, and moss soon crowned the roof. Five children came into the world. On the porch you could sip your coffee over the river and hear Rumša singing. In the shadow of two black mulberry trees, the children played in the yard, a table stood, the pumpkins flourished.

Rumša braided my mother's hair and taught her how to braid it herself, in many variations. She sang for her and for the river. Her grandfather took Kitty with him on the Drina in his boat many more times. Both great-grandparents were drawn to water their whole lives.

And the water came to them. In March 1975, it rained for fourteen days straight, the snow melted in the mountains, and when the flood receded my great-grandparents' house was uninhabitable.

The family gathered in the flooded living room, ankle-deep in mud. The children cleaned, the granddaughters—my mother and Aunt Lula—cried. The previous day, they'd all cleaned the house together. Rumša couldn't bend over so well by that point, or stand back up so well either. Before long she would be a walking upside-down L.

Amid the tears and the devastation, she spoke up: "You did a bad job cleaning," she said, "so I asked the Drina to help."

In a 1951 documentary about the Drina rafstmen, there's one in a cap and shirt.

When Rumša died I was two months old. They'd heard her laugh out loud once in the night, and curse once, and the next morning she was dead. In the one photograph of the two of us together, I'm lying in her lap. She is looking at me, her mouth slightly open. Today it's August 24, 2018. I put my ear to the faded colors and listen.

GRANDMOTHER AND
THE CIRCLE DANCE

Grandmother Kristina is a pragmatic woman. On that particular day in Oskoruša she told Gavrilo, "I get your TV set if you go before me."

The TV was on at Gavrilo's that afternoon, but everyone was taking a full-bellied nap in front of the Mexican telenovela. The flies drank from our hair. An hour later, we were awake again. Grandmother linked arms with Gavrilo and they left the house. They didn't have to say anything—I followed them.

They walked up ahead, talking quietly to each other. I imagined that the topic alternated between memories and money laundering. At one point, Grandmother laughed in disbelief like a girl, her voice rising into a squeak.

A herd of sheep came out of the forest and trotted toward us, their bells jingling and bonging in a minor key. Grandmother and Gavrilo stopped at a fence. Weather-beaten, obviously. Three wooden boards, post, three boards, post. Grandmother and Gavrilo looked around, discussed something with each other, then she asked if she could take a picture of me. I was surprised, and suggested one of the three of us.

No, just of you. "Sit there on the fence."

I handed her my phone. Did she know how to use it?

"Don't be a donkey, of course I don't."

I showed her.

"Climb up on the fence."

"Here?"

"No, farther left. A little farther. Stop. Okay, don't move."

I didn't move.

A meadow in front of me, the herd of sheep and Vijarac's peak behind me. And then here's what happened: Nothing.

"Grandma? What now?"

"Stay there."

"Take the picture!"

"Stop fidgeting."

"Just tap the red X, Grandma."

"Calm down."

It was totally ridiculous. After three minutes or so I'd had enough and I climbed down, but Grandmother and Gavrilo both shouted, "Stop! Get back up there!" They were serious.

I climbed back onto the fence, almost apologizing.

"A little to the left," Grandmother said.

The sheep tottered past us. One opened the gate to the next meadow. The others slipped through it. Nothing surprised me anymore. The last sheep lay down in the grass behind me. Gavrilo lay down too. A bird screeched. Grandmother cried: "There! There!" I turned around to look. There was nothing there anymore except the mountain and the sheep and the bright blue sky. I looked forward again and Grandmother pressed the red X, taking a picture of me in Oskoruša.

The picture is nothing remarkable. A young man in the hills, sweaty hair plastered to his forehead. A sheep lying in the grass. The mountain looming up over his shoulder. Large birds circling the peak. The sky a harsh blue.

Today is February 7, 2018. Almost nine years have gone by since that picture was taken. Does anyone still live up there? Why not? Maybe a painter from Leipzig passed through Oskoruša and painted twelve pictures of fruit trees with snakes lolling in them. A middle manager in a large bank, in charge of arts spending, happens to like snakes in trees and buys the series for her bank's lobby for three hundred thousand euros; her wife, a yoga instructor, falls in love with the region depicted in the paintings, drives there, and the real view is even more beautiful. She buys an empty farmhouse, has it renovated, and holds summer yoga workshops for yoga lovers from the greater Leipzig area. A burned-out business consultant moves there. His girlfriend, a solo bassist, creates a nice atmosphere in the silence of night. The painter returns and paints portraits of Gavrilo, Marija, Sretoje, and Miroslav's sheep. Two alternative-medicine healers press cider in a barn. It's now a commune. The new residents fight and fall in love with one another in various constellations. Tourists interested in communes come by to see it. Hippies with practical talents repair Gavrilo's washing machine and teach him how to meditate. Meanwhile more houses are fixed up. Social media accounts are deleted, fruit is boiled. Artisans open workshops. A dermatologist from Halle fills a market gap in the sustainable-vacation sector with her *sustainable vacations in the Bosnian mountains*. The burned-out business consultant finds a scale from a large reptile on Vijarac and is able to get a good night's sleep again if he has the scale under his pillow. Everyone buys milk from Marija and, one time, five piglets from Gavrilo to roast for a party. A year later, the cries of the first commune babies ring out in the mountains. A Russian woman decides, after a yoga class, to buy up everything that doesn't belong to anyone. There's some stress with the commune until they get to know the Russian and realize she's actually quite *khorosho*. Her husband buys Višegrad in the bargain. Stevo gets a new job, because the Russians in Višegrad are boosting industry. The war criminals in Gavrilo's glass cabinet turn out to be a negative example he wanted to keep in mind. The former Yugoslavian republics are all systematically acknowledging and thoroughly processing the past.

I phone up Grandmother and ask how she's doing.

"I'm not doing well," says my grandmother, who never says that she's not doing well. She hums a tune. I imagine her eyes are closed. A cough interrupts the melody.

I ask if there's anything she needs. Which is an idiotic question, so I quickly add, "Does anything hurt?"

"Yes," Grandmother says, and she hums. "Did I ever tell you how I met your grandpa?"

Yes, she has. Two or three times just this week. "No, you haven't, Grandma."

"At a circle dance. In Oskoruša. He took my arm and stepped on my foot before the music even started. And again once it did. I tried to stay at a safe distance during the next dance. Pero followed me and stepped on my foot again. I wanted to be in the circle next to someone who wouldn't step on my foot, and sat out the third round. So of course he did too."

I picture Grandmother smiling as she talks. She coughs. In the next dance, Grandfather danced on her toes again, and this time Grandmother just stopped. The circle of dancers strained and shuddered like a necklace about to break, opened and closed again, and circled on, without my grandparents.

She suggested they sit down—which he took as a sign of her friendliness and she intended as the consequence of his boot-stomping. Grandmother hums. I know the tune: it's a Serbian dance, quick and simple.

"What happened next?" I ask. The answer is more humming, then her breathing, slow and heavy. "Grandma?"

She says, "You have Pero's long legs."

When I was a child I liked that comparison, I think, because I liked Grandfather. Over the phone it sounds like it's not only about our physiognomy, but as if I need to answer my question about what happened next myself.

The day after our call, Grandmother was admitted to the hospital with pneumonia. Rather than take her illness as an occasion to visit her, I stayed in Hamburg and wrote about her. My parents went to Višegrad. Today is March 7, 2018; they've been there for a month. They tell me that Grandmother is doing better, physically, but that her dementia is worse than before. She talks to people only she can see, and asks after people who aren't alive anymore.

Today I phone her so she can wish me happy birthday. I want her to remember my birthday. The conversation burbles along. Grandmother speaks so softly that I don't have to ask how she's doing. I say: "I want to go back to Oskoruša soon." She says nothing. I say: "Do you want to come with me?" She says nothing. I hum the circle dance. I'm about to stop when something comes to life inside her and dances again. This time she is in the circle "with a man." She doesn't say "Pero," or "Grandpa." *A man* steps on her foot.

I ask when exactly that was.

"On a Saint George Day. Not so long ago. We danced right here in the clover field," she says, as though she were there, as though tables and benches were set up under the trees, as though she could hear the meat grilling, the musicians. And it's strange. I don't want my grandmother to be dancing with some random man. I want it to be Grandfather stepping on her feet. I want her to be remembering dancing her first dance and exchanging her first words with her future husband.

"Was that with Grandpa?"

"What?"

"You were at a circle dance with Grandpa, right? In Oskoruša? With your Pero?" I hum the tune again, but suddenly feel like an animal trainer and break off.

"With Pero?" Grandmother says, hesitantly.

That's enough for me.

"Over there, under the sorb tree," she says, "we talked. It was easier to talk with Pero than to dance with him, that's for sure. The girls from the region are all big and rugged, you know. Like oak trees. I have small bones, my Pero liked that."

Grandmother clears her throat.

"Grandpa spends a lot of time with you," she says, her voice different now. Firmer, full of conviction. "I like watching the two of you together. You roam around the city. Talking the whole time." And she says that every other seven-year-old can beat me up, but that I can trick any of them into giving me what I want from them. "You got that from Pero too," Grandmother says. "You're both troublemakers with words."

Grandfather rarely answered my countless child's questions directly, instead wrapping the answer in a little story. I don't know who told me that but I liked it, and I've used it as a good explanation for why I like making things up.

I ask Grandmother over the phone if it's true, about Grandfather explaining the world to me in stories.

Grandmother says, "He always wore a sports jacket, despite the heat. Such a show-off. A handsome show-off."

She hangs up.

Many years after my grandfather's death, his name is still on the doorbell of my grandmother's apartment. Petar Stanišić died in 1986. For thirty years, people have been ringing the bell of someone who isn't there anymore. Grandmother wouldn't let anyone take her husband off the doorbell. She knew that if his name wasn't on the bell it wouldn't be anywhere except on a gravestone where you light a candle every now and then.

My pushing for the circle-dance story is strange because I know that the whole thing can't really be true. My grandparents didn't meet at a dance, and not in Oskoruša either. Grandfather was going door to door as a tax collector one time, in a village named Staniševac, doing what he needed to do. He stayed longer in the biggest house. He drank and ate with the men of the house while a young woman brought the dishes to the table. She exchanged not a word, not a glance, with the stranger.

A year later, Grandmother fell off a horse and broke her arm. She went to the hospital in Višegrad, where by that point Grandfather was working as a bookkeeper. They ran into each other under the fluorescent lights in the corridor. He still remembered the young woman who'd brought the polenta out of the kitchen, and she the young man with his sports jacket draped over the chair. Sometimes, that's enough for a start: common memory of a moment that at the time seemed insignificant.

My name is on a doorbell in Hamburg.

I've danced the circle dance a few times as a child. I don't remember the steps anymore.

My son has my long legs.

HONEST, LOYAL, TIRELESS

I was born in a country that doesn't exist anymore. November 29 is the Day of the Socialist Federal Republic of Yugoslavia. On that day, Yugoslavians, who don't exist anymore, meet in symbolic, Yugoslavically laden places. And if they come together on November 29, the Day of the Socialist Federal Republic of Yugoslavia which doesn't exist anymore, then it does exist. Self-determination, right? On November 29, I have seen old men and old women with tears in their eyes singing:

> *Širom sveta put me vodio*
> *Za sudbom sam svojom hodio,*
> *U srcu sam tebe nosio,*
> *Uvek si mi draga bila*
> *Domovino moja mila,*
> *Jugoslavijo, Jugoslavijo!*

> *My path led me out into the wide world,*
> *I followed my fate,*
> *Carrying you in my heart.*
> *You were always dear to me,*
> *My beloved homeland,*
> *Yugoslavia, Yugoslavia!*

One time, the get-together was by the Neretva River. Another time, lamb was grilled up on the Igman. Ljubljana, Belgrade, and Jajce had their turns. In Jajce, the Germans had come within a whisker of killing Tito. The people gathering there take selfies in the cave where Tito and his staff hid. The light is bad in there, so the pictures are too, but what can you do.

For the evening's entertainment, the Yugoslavs hire a choir. The choir sings folk songs and songs of the epic heroes. The most important thing is that they don't charge too much. They stand in the background, the choir, when speeches are being given. There is always someone whose speech is about anti-Fascism, including discussions of the current European situation. Once an anti-Fascist, an anti-Fascist to your dying day.

Everyone there, except the choir (who are mostly young), was born and grew up in Yugoslavia when it was still Yugoslavia. They fell in love there, married there, or not, but most did. They had their appendix out in Yugoslavia, bought a Yugoslavian car, got into debt and paid it off, lived through crises and joys, and some even still have their appendix. The only thing that none of them will ever be able to do in Yugoslavia is die. The earth is the same, but not for them.

They have trouble accepting this end to the story. Well, they accept it—they're realists. Yugoslavia's over. But they're not. For a day and a night, they bring Yugoslavia back to life, with full room and board, speeches, slideshows (sometimes PowerPoint too), photographs from the fifties and sixties and the more reckless people even show some from the eighties. No one can show photos from the nineties.

Hej, Slaveni, jošte živi
riječ naših djedova,
dok za narod srce bije
njihovih sinova.

Hey, you Slavs, the words
of our forefathers live on,
as long as the hearts of their sons
still beat for the People.

Everyone sings along, standing under the flag with the star. Hand on heart (not the choir), children of Socialism, brothers and sisters of the Peoples of the World. They are dealers in relics, well-read retirees, farmers, grandmothers. They are members of the Tito League in the Society for the Truth of the People's Liberation Struggle. They debate, their chairs in a circle. Only the person with the relay baton is allowed to speak. The years under Tito were their best years. They believe that the same is true for everyone else. The present is the Hell that followed Paradise. Except for the ones who profit from this Hell: the political hard-liners, the conscienceless businessmen, the exploitative foreign investors.

One time, at a hotel in Mostar, there was a gynecologist convention at the same time, with much better catering. Late at night, one of the Yugoslavians squeezed his old Pioneer's cap onto his head and brought his fist to his temple in salute, to which everyone responded by saluting too. He recited the Young Pioneer Pledge and the others chimed in. The earth cracked open, Tito came back into the world up a golden escalator, and said that he was giving everyone there a medal, but it turned out it wasn't Tito, just a confused gynecologist staring into the Pioneers' eyes. He apologized, backed away, and fled, sorry to have disturbed anybody.

I'm a little like them. I believe in the old ideals. I, too, know the Young Pioneer Pledge by heart, even now:

Today, as I become a Pioneer, I give my Pioneer's word of honor:

    That I shall study and work diligently, respect parents and my seniors, and be a loyal and honest comrade and friend.

    That I shall love our homeland, the self-managed Socialist Federal Republic of Yugoslavia.

    That I shall stand up for the ideas of brotherhood and unity and the principles for which Comrade Tito fought.

    That I shall value all the people of the world who are working for freedom and peace.

Isn't that beautiful? Value all the people of the world! It sounds so simple.

After breakfast, a hungover walk along the Neretva. Someone tries to piss into the river and falls in. Several comrades leap after him—an eruption of solidarity and insanity. The Internationale resounds from the water; downstream, a fisherman shouts, "Shut up, you morons!"

And: "A job for anyone who wants to work."

And: "Yes, there was a bit of censorship, and a handful of political prisoners. Much less than in the Soviet bloc countries though."

And: "Social security, equal education, freedom to travel."

And: "Yes, but you've got to earn your cult of personality."

And: "If Tito were still alive, there wouldn't have been a war."

And: "If Tito were still alive, Yugoslavia today would be like Switzerland, just less uptight."

And: "If Tito were still alive, Yugoslavia would've won the World Cup. Just imagine, a soccer team with players from all the Yugoslavian republics together!"

And: "Comrades, ladies and gentlemen, quiet please. Our next speaker is Milovan Radivojević. Milo needs no introduction. His talk is titled 'Josep Broz Tito and the Truth about His "Lower-Back Pain" During the Fortieth Anniversary Celebrations of the Great Socialist October Revolution.'"

And: "We're Yugoslavian. That is where we come from. Our origins, and our future."

At night, the choir dissolves, the men's neckties loosen, and almost everyone—very few have turned in—push the tables against the wall. There is dancing and, even though it's not allowed, smoking. A clear sky over Mostar. Some of the stars have long since burned out, but their light is still visible. A member of the hotel staff asks if anyone needs anything; he's about to call it a night.

No one needs anything.

Yugoslavia dances in the light of the dawn. Someone from Split is dreaming in a chair. Someone from Ljubljana goes up to his room. A man from Tuzla says good night and goes upstairs with a woman from Titograd. Someone from Novi Sad has fallen asleep on the toilet. Someone from Skopje sets his alarm clock for 1:00 (PM).

Good night, comrades, good night.

HALF BLOOD

In 1986, the world record holder for number of push-ups in twenty-four hours (29,449) was Miodrag Stojanović Gidra. A Yugoslavian.

The Yugoslavians won the men's European Basketball Championship twice in a row, in 1989 and 1991.

Also in 1991, the Red Stars competed for the Intercontinental Cup against a Chilean club with an Indian in their logo. I was allowed to stay up deep into the night and watch the match. We played a whole half a man down and won anyway, 3–0.

Yugoslavia manufactured products that maybe weren't exactly good, but were good enough. Or maybe not even good enough, but cheap.

Yugoslavia provided the backdrops for spaghetti westerns, the greatest movie genre in the world if you loved Karl May and pistol duels as much as I did as a child, or as much as Granny Mejrema loved Clint Eastwood's penetrating eyes in a face almost totally covered in dirt.

Yugoslavians were good. Good at sports, good at war, good at peace, good between war and peace, and outside the two blocs. In the story of Yugoslavia, everyone is pulling at the same rope, with equal rights, irrespective of age, sex, job, or ethnic identity.

All problems came with a promise that they could be solved if everyone worked together. Maybe that wasn't entirely honest, but it was optimistic. Some were solved, some weren't.

The problem of astronomical debt remained unsolved for decades and led to inflation.

The problem of critics of the government was solved by locking them up on an island, and that definitely didn't feel exactly great, of course. I didn't hear anything about that as a child. Yugoslavia was also very good at that: keeping quiet about whatever was less good.

Yugoslavia encouraged and supported young people, because the youth were the future. Meaning me too. It was quite a bit of pressure, to be honest: having to stand up for something and worry about something that hadn't happened yet. Actually, it was totally crazy to entrust the future to someone who wanted to see what would happen to a ficus tree if you put it in the washing machine, complete with pot and soil, but okay.

My Pioneer friends and I swept the banks of the Drina; I was whistling "Wind of Change" by the Scorpions, my favorite song at the time. I learned poems by heart and even wrote some, with rhyming partisans as my lyric personae.

Not long before the war I rounded up donors for a blood drive.

One Saturday in January or February, we all swarmed out, went door to door, and asked people, "When was the last time you donated blood, Comrade?" The neighborhood I was assigned to was around Grandmother Kristina's house. I knew the people in the neighborhood, they knew me. "What do you think, don't you want to donate blood again?"

No country donated as much blood as Yugoslavia, definitely, I thought at the time. The remarkable blood of the Serbians, the Croatians, the Bosnians, the Macedonians, the Slovenians, and the other minorities who weren't necessarily listed by name when reciting the formula of the different peoples but their blood was super-great too. Definitely.

I was a half blood. I was reading Karl May's Winnetou novels.

In 1990, a riot started at a match between Dynamo Zagreb and Red Star Belgrade. Spectators went at each other—Croatians against Serbians, Serbians against Croatians, the players in the middle. Hundreds of people were hurt.

In 1992, the Yugoslavian national team was dissolved.

In August 1992, the Bosnian Serb Army massacred a whole village not far from Višegrad. Barimo. That's what the village was called, Barimo. Twenty-six people were killed.

In 2001, the push-up world record holder Miodrag Stojanović Gidra was shot and killed in his car. One bullet in the neck, five in the chest.

DEATH TO FASCISM,
FREEDOM TO THE PEOPLE

By the time of Tito's death in the eighties, if not sooner, holes had started to appear in Yugoslavia's multiperspective story about itself—cracks in the federation's foundation. Above all, the economic chasms could no longer be bridged with slogans about unity and brotherhood. The richer republics were no longer willing to put up with sharing goods and capital, and ethnic resentments reinforced the efforts to separate—giving rise to more ethnic resentments. Politics didn't lessen the fear and anxieties, if anything it fueled the animosities.

The glue of the multiethnic idea could no longer withstand the corrosive potential of the various nationalisms. Tito proved irreplaceable as the central voice telling the story of Yugoslavian unity; the folksy accents of the new narrators were vulgar and brutal. Their manifestos read like incitements to ethnic hatred. Intellectuals supported them; the media popularized them and repeated them so often that by the mideighties they were inescapable. Father had been reading some before he danced with Mother and the snake.

The new narrators were named Milošević, Izetbegović, Tudjman. They went on long reading tours, visiting *their* people, telling them a new story.

Genre: Rant with overtones of call-to-arms.

Context: The erratic political milieu of the eighties—economic crisis, inflation.

Subject: Their own people as victims. Loss of honor. Injustices suffered, battles lost. The Other as enemy.

Main characters: The underpaid and unemployed of today; the fallen warriors of centuries past.

Time covered by the story: Eight hundred years (apx.).

Style: Imperative. Symbol after symbol. Violent images. Dark forebodings.

Point of view: Omniscient. First-person plural as the narrator's pronoun of choice, with "we" used in such a way as to exclude the "them" who don't belong. "We will no longer let ourselves be whatevered by them," etc.

Message: Rise up to perform new acts of heroism! History can be made right! Our blood is strong! Nikola Tesla is a Serbian / Dražen Petrović is a Croatian!

Line of argument: Claim that there is a people whose national and cultural integrity are threatened and which therefore must be defended. Claim of (pick one or more): racial / religious / moral superiority to legitimate territorial aspirations. Folklore of origin as proof of individuality. Everything the other side says is a lie.

Audience: Men with jackknives and deodorant in their hip pockets.

Here of all places! In the Balkans! At the crossroads of East and West! Everyone in the Balkans had been deployed from somewhere else at some point, everyone! They took hold, they were defeated (or not), they retreated. And they all left something behind. Rome, Venice, the Ottoman Empire, Austria-Hungary. And all the Slavs. Jews came from the Iberian Peninsula and stayed. Enclaves of Roma are everywhere in the region. Germans slept in my ancestors' beds. They were all here, where you can sing the same song in different keys, *depending*. Here, where you drink Turkish coffee, use German and Arabic loanwords without thinking twice, dance in the woods with primeval Slavic vilas and at weddings to Croatian and Serbian pop songs, both equally terrible. Didn't we cheer the Red Star goals together?

Today is August 29, 2018. In the past few days, thousands of people in Chemnitz, Germany, have demonstrated against open borders. Immigrants are being demonized and the Hitler salute hangs over the present.

In the Yugoslavian coat of arms, six flames, ringed by ears of wheat, burned for the six peoples. Roasting atop the flames was the five-pointed star. The child I was thought the coat of arms was awesome, although he did wonder why the wheat or the star didn't go up in flames.

In 1991, affiliations and identities turned explosive. Everyone was drinking the same gasoline. Anywhere you came from could turn out to be the wrong place. People were fanning the flames.

In 1991, after the fire started blazing in Croatia, I campaigned in Višegrad for peace. I belonged to a group of eight- to fourteen-year-olds who'd put together a show in the name of togetherness and sanity. Grandmother Kristina helped us find a good stage. She knew the owner of a restaurant near the center of town, who apparently owed her a favor. We were allowed to perform in the beer garden for free, and even got drinks for free too.

We put red stars on the tables and hung little flags and wreaths on the walls. The wreaths were supposed to look like peace wreaths, but actually they made it look more like Santa Claus was on his way.

We recited poems of praise: To Yugoslavia. To the People's Liberation Struggle. To community, to childhood, to the rain, to Red Star Belgrade (that was me).

We sang partisan hymns and American pop songs. We hosted a talk show on various topics. I remember the dinosaur episode and the anti-Fascism episode. Grandmother organized a raffle, and won the prize herself, of course. My English teacher gave a speech about something, I don't remember what, I was staring at her lips the whole time. Our mothers made sandwiches for the buffet. By the end, they were so expensive, due to the inflation, that we gave them away for free.

Along with peace I was also pursuing a girl at the time. After the show there was music, and she danced with me, and everything felt unbelievably *good* and *right*. Then the girl danced with another Saša, which felt unbelievably *bad* and *wrong*. They even danced to—how painful, how mocking—"Wind of Change."

Almost exactly a year later, a Serbian soldier would be searching for my mother in Grandmother Kristina's apartment. He would open all the doors and even check that she wasn't hanging off the side of the balcony. He would pour himself a glass of milk and ask my grandmother how she could allow her son to marry "a Turk." As he was leaving, he would give Grandmother one more piece of advice:

"Take Tito's picture off the wall!"

SAŠA STANIŠIĆ

"Racists are fundamentally impolite people," Grandfather Pero apparently said once. In Yugoslavia things were pretty good for a long time when it came to fighting racism and Fascism. Which made it all the more shocking how confident the racists were, how obviously right they thought their cause was, when they went on the march in the nineties in Belgrade, in Zagreb, in Vukovar, and also in Višegrad.

Worlds die away if you don't quickly and decisively oppose the people who want them to. Today is September 21, 2018. If there were a national parliamentary election in Germany this Sunday, the far-right AfD Party would get 18 percent of the votes.

Tito's portrait is still hanging in my grandmother's apartment. The children of Višegrad once sang for peace:

My path led me out into the wide world,
I followed my fate,
Carrying you in my heart.
You were always dear to me,
My beloved homeland,
Yugoslavia, Yugoslavia!

GRANDMOTHER AND TITO

"Tito's dead!" Grandmother whispered. She emptied her coffee cup into the sink, wiped her mouth with the dishtowel, opened the apartment's front door, and shouted into the stairwell: "Tito's dead!" I grabbed her arm, and she proclaimed it again, even louder. Was she happy or mad? "Tito's dead!"

Grandmother had never been political. Politics was my grandfather's domain; he was the one who'd hung Tito's portrait on the wall, and the only reason she hadn't taken it down was because Tito belonged to her husband. She herself divided people into good people and bad people, depending on whether they ate well or badly and whether they cared about their families well or badly. Caring about included life after death, too: tending the graves and the memories. Anyone whose family came first to them came first to her.

Tito looked well fed in his photographs, and he cared about the Yugoslavian family. That would have been enough for Grandmother. Still, her outburst seemed excessive to me. She knocked my hand away: "Tito's dead!" She wanted to go downstairs, out onto the street.

"Today, as I become a Pioneer, I give my Pioneer's word of honor." I hadn't said it loud, but Grandmother stopped. I whispered: "Tito's underground. In his cave in Jajce." I slid the zipper of my lips shut with my thumb and index finger.

Grandmother nodded. Her eyes were shining. She hesitated, turned around. She got the Tito biography off the shelf and opened it and looked at the pictures. She had me read her the section about Tito hiding in the cave in Jajce. Asked me to close the windows and door, and then said, quietly: "Tell me the truth. Does he need our help?"

"The Revolution needs everyone who faithfully wants to serve the proletariat's struggle," I said, raising my fist to my temple.

"I'm saying I want a gun, you donkey," she whispered.

I said I'd see what I could do. "Maybe I'll ask Andrej."

"What Andrej?"

"Your neighbor. The policeman?"

"There's no policeman here," Grandmother said, waving my comment aside.

I understood: "Here" wasn't today. Grandmother was back in the year of Tito's death, 1980.

I kept reading in the biography. She seemed elsewhere. My mentioning Andrej had made her unsure of herself. She stared straight ahead. At some point she lay her head on the giant book and fell asleep, with Tito's likeness beneath her cheek.

IN SHOEBOXES, IN DRAWERS,
IN THE COGNAC

Grandmother took a lot that belonged to her husband out of the apartment. She kept: papers and photographs that attested to his life; Grandfather's little library (books she never read and never would); his lapel pin; his three sports jackets (one fits me like it was tailored, the other two are hideous). While she slept on Tito's biography, I walked through the apartment in search of traces of him. Her nap came at a good time—I didn't want her to know what I was doing. I have no idea why not.

Grandfather was a gap in my memory, papered over with other people's anecdotes about him and ones I invented myself. Now I wanted to have something like an encounter with him based on facts. On ID cards, on electricity bills in his name. I started with a glass of his cognac. The bottle was older than I was. I didn't have the courage for more than a tiny sip. It tasted too sweet, it tasted like futility.

Petar "Pero" Stanišić is sitting in shoeboxes, in drawers, wrapped in plastic. Ever since Grandmother has been sick, incessantly traversing bygone times, brooding like a poet, she's started talking a lot about him again. Usually it's impossible to tell if she's really remembering something or making up stories. What's certain is that she wants him with her, one way or another. I have no memory of them being in the same place.

SAŠA STANIŠIĆ

But here they are in a photograph of a party—a festive meal right in this apartment—sitting next to each other. Grandmother and Grandfather among their guests. It's hot in the room; you can taste the laughter above the dishes. The bottle of cognac is on the table. Draped over the back of Grandfather's chair is his sports jacket—the one that looks good on me.

I put the jacket on.

Grandfather is facing Grandmother. She's standing at his side with a hand on his shoulder, the other hand gesturing. Grandmother seems to be telling a suspenseful story; the gesture is of a clutching hand, her eyes ready to attack. No one will ever know what the story was. She presumably doesn't remember. And the guests at the party are all dead.

Grandmother definitely didn't intend to put up a memorial to her husband. She just didn't throw away a few things she thought were important. I also found a shopping list though (bread, milk, apples, flour, salami), and flipped through a greasy little notebook of children's songs. It was her private archive. No one else needed to understand it.

GRANDFATHER IS ARMED
AND NONCHALANT

Today is July 18, 2018. I can't think of any way to present what I've found out about my grandfather except by listing the findings, like ingredients in a recipe for a biography. The great storyteller-grandfather is now a dusty list.

TRANSCRIPT, RUDO PUBLIC ELEMENTARY SCHOOL
Stanišić, Petar, *son of* Bogosav, *d.o.b.* 10/14/1923, *place of birth*: Oskoruša, *religion*: Serbian-Orthodox, *finished* fourth *grade in 1934–35 with the following record*:

All 4s (the second-best grade). Including in *Singing, Handwriting,* and *Crafts Using Folklore Motifs*. One 5 (best grade), in *Religion and Morality*.

Conduct: 5
Absences, excused: 3
Unexcused: 0

PHOTOGRAPH: Grandfather as a sixteen-year-old, black and white
A knife in his belt. Cap askew, expression defiant, hand on hip. Grandfather is armed and nonchalant, and I think: Maybe that's really you.

YUGOSLAVIAN ARMY (YA) MILITARY ID

Comrade: Stanišić, Petar.

Place of residence upon entering the YA: Oskoruša

Civilian profession: Agriculture

Height: 5' 9"

Weight: 159

Period of service in YA: 2/12/45–1/18/46

Category: Infantry

Skills learned in military service that might be of use in civilian life: Fighting

CERTIFICATE OF RECOGNITION

Comrade: Stanišić, Petar. This Certificate of Recognition acknowledges your part in the reconstruction of our homeland.

Death to Fascism – Freedom to the People!

Višegrad, 12/5/1948

PARTY ID #B-H 01 456416

Stanišić, Petar *is a member of the Yugoslavian Communist League, since* 9/8/1949.

ENVELOPE (containing a watch from the hospital)

10/1/1967 – For 20 years of faithful service.

PHOTOGRAPH: Family party, black and white

A richly laid table. Mother, laughing. Grandfather has his arm around her. Both grandmothers with perms, without eyeteeth. Grandfather Muhamed is smiling shyly. He has all his teeth. Would no doubt rather be fishing than staring into a camera. The bottle of cognac looks confident. Raise your glass! Granny's arm stays in her lap, she doesn't drink. Are they celebrating my birth?

TEST RESULTS from the clinic for cardiovascular and rheumatic illnesses in Banja Vrućica, No. 3605, for Stanišić, Petar
DIAGNOSIS:
Calculosis renis 1. sin.
Varices cruris bill.
Hypertensio arterialis osc.
Myocardiopathia hypertensiva comp.

I googled it all right away: kidney stones, varicose veins, illness of the heart muscle due to high blood pressure. Due to greater resistance in the arteries, the heart pumps harder, the left chamber of the heart increases in volume, and over time it loses strength.

I noticed my own beating heart. Researched preventative measures (exercise, diet). My father got a new prescription for blood-pressure medicine a couple of months ago.

The patient stopped his bicycle ergometric test after 11 min./ 150 W (=heavy physical effort) due to fatigue and shortness of breath.

I called my doctor and made an appointment for a stress test ECG.

PHOTOGRAPH: Grandmother, Grandfather, and me at the table, in color
Birthday cake, eight candles. Grandmother is wearing a red dress and looking at me. Grandfather is wearing his sports jacket and looking into the camera. The child is wearing a sweater vest and looking at the cake. It is our last photo together. Months later, I show it to my son. "Who's that?" I say, pointing to the boy in the sweater vest. "That's me," my son says.

DEATH NOTICE from the local paper, 7/24/1986
Petar Pero Stanišić, bookkeeper in the hospital, fighter for the people's liberation, Communist, excellent socio-political worker, died unexpectedly . . . The tragic news deeply saddens his family, in Višegrad, in his birthplace of Oskoruša . . .

Accompanying the notice is a photograph of the giant line of mourners. The coffin at the front is way on this side of the bridge while the end of the column is still on the other side. I am not in the line. I wasn't allowed to come to the funeral—my parents were afraid it would be too much for me. I stayed at a neighbor's and we played dominoes. Today I'm jealous of the people who carried him to his grave. That too—my not being there in the funeral procession—brought me here today, to these shoeboxes.

Here is my only honest memory of the farmer's child, the partisan fighter, the Party functionary: an old man and a boy bent together over a crossword puzzle. The old man gives hints disguised as simple questions, until the boy, seemingly on his own, arrives at the word they're looking for. The boy writes the letters in the little boxes with a thick, four-color ballpoint pen.

Oh, all right, one more sip. In the sideboard bar behind the cognac bottle, one last find—hidden in such a way that *you're meant to find it*: a photograph of Grandfather sitting on a wooden fence (three boards, post, three boards, post), with a backrest of mountains behind him. They are the forests and fields of Oskoruša, and the peak of Vijarac.

Grandfather looks relaxed. His angular face—is that what you call it? High cheekbones. A severe expression that seems playacted: you get the sense that he's about to smile as soon as the shutter is clicked.

Who took this picture, Grandmother?

She walks in as if summoned. "Pero, what are you doing there?"

"It's me, Grandma."

Grandmother needed a moment to get oriented, in space and in time, it seemed to me. She picked up one of the photos, looked at it, and stroked the paper like she was caressing someone's skin. "You can't just dig through other people's lives, even dead people's, without asking permission. —What are you looking for?" She came closer.

"I don't know . . ."

"Then think about it first!"

"I'm sorry."

She stood in front of me. "You should get a haircut."

"Why do you say that?"

"Pero wouldn't have liked it like that."

I asked if she liked it like that.

"It's okay." Grandma leaned heavily on my shoulder. "Show me more," she said. She wanted to see more photographs. I showed her Grandfather in uniform. If it was him. With his cap, and a beard, it was hard to say. I asked, "That's Grandpa, isn't it?" And I added that he'd apparently been wounded. It said so in his military ID booklet. Where? I asked. What happened?

Grandmother looked at the photo for a long time, then put it aside and said, "He wasn't in the war. My Pero despised the war."

My memories are coefficients of longing. Grandmother's memories are coefficients of illness.

She tapped the photo of Grandfather on the fence. With Vijarac's peak under her finger. "There," she said. "That's where he went. Up to the fire cliffs. But why is he staying so long?" She took her finger away again. There was a ghostly silhouette above the peak. Like a worm. Lint on the camera lens? Like a dragon, with wings outspread. Wings? Lint on the camera lens.

Grandfather is sitting in the exact same spot on the fence where I was on the day Grandmother took me to Oskoruša.

Wings? Lint. A blur. A mountaintop.

"Where are you now, Grandma?" I asked.

"Where are you?" Kristina asked . . . me?

GRANDMOTHER AND
THE WEDDING RING

Grandmother can't find her wedding ring. She looks everywhere. It's gone. She sees a man on the hill. He looks familiar. A tall man in a sports jacket. That profile, it's him—she's almost certain. Grandmother hurries downstairs, crosses the courtyard, gets to the hill, and calls his name: "Pero!" Grandmother cries. "Pero!"

The man isn't there anymore.

A woman walking by asks if everything's all right.

Nothing's all right, Grandmother replies. But that isn't the woman's problem.

Today is April 17, 2018. My grandmother is waiting by the garages in thin black socks. She is waiting below Vijarac, and it is a spring day in Oskoruša, ca. 1960. She has an umbrella with her; the sky is clear and yet it's raining.

Her husband is off in the mountains. She doesn't quite know what he does there. Sometimes he looks for mushrooms; sometimes he hikes up to the top, to reflect. This time a rainstorm is coming.

Grandmother twists her wedding ring on her finger and thinks about what she should do. Was the ring on her finger the whole time? Doesn't matter. The important thing is that it's back.

Grandmother turns around. She doesn't climb up after her husband to look for him in this dark forest. Not yet.

CLOSER TO THE NORTH POLE

Zoki walks into the classroom, puts a piece of paper down on the teacher's desk, and shouts: "Everyone write your name."

There are three columns: *Muslim / Serb / Croat.*

We all gather round, we all hesitate.

"Come on, guys." Zoki writes his name under *Serb.*

Kenan takes the pen from Zoki and writes his name under *Muslim.*

Both Gorans put their names under *Serb.*

Edin puts his name under *Muslim.*

Alen puts his name under *Muslim.*

Marica puts her name under *Serb.*

Goca puts her name under *Serb.*

Kule asks what this is all about.

Zoki says: "So we know."

Kule says: "Fuck you."

Zoki says: "Anyway, you're Muslim."

"What I am is *Fuck you,*" Kule says.

Elvira makes a new column, writes *Don't know* at the top, and puts her name there. Alen takes the pen back and crosses his name out and writes it again under *Don't know.* Goca too.

Marko puts his name under *Serb.*

Ana puts her name under *Don't know,* thinks for a second, crosses it out, adds *Yugoslav* as a fifth heading, and puts her name there.

Zoki writes *Kule* under *Muslim*.

Kule says: "Zoki, you dumb horse, I'll fuck your mother."

The Gorans plant themselves in front of Kule and the one with the long incisors says: "What's wrong, Kule? Shoes too tight?"

Kule grabs the pen out of Zoki's hand and tries to scribble something on Goran's forehead. Goran shoves him, Kule shoves back, and we move between them.

Everyone's shouting all at once until Kule raises his arm—the gesture says, *Everything's cool, I'm cool*. He goes up to the desk and makes a sixth column. On top it says, *Fuck all of you*. Kule writes *Kule* in that column, stomps on the pen, which breaks, and leaves the classroom.

No one follows Kule. The list disappears.

A couple months later, Muslims in several cities are ordered to wear white armbands.

An Eskimo family lived in Višegrad at the time, above the supermarket on Tito Street. Actually they had no connection with the Inuit—it was just a joke answer on the 1991 census, which was included in the actual statistics and then recognized by the state. The father repeated it during the Serbian occupation, but no one laughed. So he left the city, with his wife and baby daughter. Today they live closer to the North Pole and speak decent Swedish.

THE CRUCIAL QUESTION

I never took any religion classes. No one I was close to ever practiced any faith openly; there wasn't even anyone who would have said, "I don't believe in the God of the Church, but a Higher Being certainly might exist." I am very happy about that. As a child, I seriously thought that you were a Muslim *because* you didn't eat pork—a Muslim for me was someone with a special diet.

Granny Mejrema believed in kidney beans and Clint Eastwood's acting talent. I never saw her pray. If she had any relation to Islam at all, then it was very discreet. Allah came up in a couple of turns of phrase. That we all used.

Grandfather Pero was probably the only believer in the family. He believed in the Victory of Socialism, and since he didn't live to see its defeat, he was never disappointed in the quasi-religion department.

Grandfather Muhamed was too kind to people to believe in a God. How could you be religious when you were as good as a saint yourself? Friendliness, fishing, and family—that's what mattered to Muhamed, the most selfless person I have ever, to this day, had the privilege of knowing.

That and a good razor blade. Grandfather Muhamed owned the same razor his whole life—a little chrome-plated straightedge with a comb on the end, a German model made by

Rotbart. Embossed on the handle: *Mond Extra.* He got it from his father, who got it from a German soldier in exchange for something or another. Grandfather kept the razor in a red tin can with the color flaking off. The razor, too, had lost its shine in a couple of places. Grandfather protected it like a treasure. He would shave every two or three days, and always ended up with a very clean shave.

In April 1992, an unshaved man in a camouflage uniform climbed up onto the roof of his house in Sarajevo and shot a whole magazine at the sun, because it was too hot for him that day. He crossed himself, or kneeled and faced Mecca, and said: "Peace be with you." Then he clambered down from the roof, grabbed his rucksack, and headed into the mountains, and that was the war.

In April 1992, someone shouted my mother's name on Tito Street in Višegrad. Mother flinched. A man was sitting on the little wall in front of City Hall, waving at her. Policeman's shirt, gun belt, sweatpants. Mother thought his face looked familiar, but she doesn't remember anymore what his name was.

When she was standing in front of him, he repeated her name softly, pretending to be concerned. He asked Mother if she knew how late it was. Mother knew he didn't mean the time of day but that's what she told him anyway.

MY MOTHER LIKES A CIGARETTE
WITH HER COFFEE

Mother learned to tell time early—the fate of a railroad worker's daughter. She knew all the arrival and departure times and knew what time her father was due home. She would wait for him on the platform, in all weather. Dirty, tired, and heavy as smoke, he got off the train, picked her up, and carried her home, where a warm dinner was waiting.

To this day, what travel means for my mother is the pleasure that someone she loves has arrived at wherever. What she wants from me, from all of her friends and relatives, is that we let her know when we've reached our destination. I have never once heard her excited about a trip of her own, whether short or long. Her childhood on the railroad line was just that: a childhood on the railroad line. Trains didn't carry any wanderlust. The family couldn't afford any holiday trips.

My mother moved through the confident Yugoslavian sixties with the modest drive of a young woman achieving what mattered to her. She got good grades, had good friends. In high school she read Marx and Kant; she could cook everything her mother could cook. My mother was beautiful as a young woman. She wore her hair long and loose. We never discussed being in love. Neither her loves nor mine.

Mother went to university in Sarajevo to study political science, emphasis on Marxism. Not because she was ambitious but because she was interested. Now she often took the train between Višegrad and Sarajevo on her own, and on one of her first trips, two older women were singing a partisan song. Mother didn't sing along, she thought it was too sappy. One time she traveled in a train that her father was the brakeman for; they arrived late.

The railroad line ran through the Drina River valley. Mother read. Studied. Didn't waste time. Outside, Yugoslavia passed vaguely by. *Violence is the midwife of every old society pregnant with a new one.*

The heat in her dorm constantly went out during the winter. Mother slept in full gear, as if climbing snowcapped dreams. Sarajevo bloomed and stank and danced and fought. Mother got pregnant. I studied for exams with her, but no longer remember most of it.

It seemed harder to get excellent grades if you were a woman, my mother says, and so she just studied more than the men. *People make their own history, under conditions already present, given, handed down from the past.*

Mother took out a small student loan and could afford only one hot meal a month outside the student cafeteria. Grandfather brought food from Višegrad with him when one of his trains stopped in Sarajevo. Mother waited on the platform. He got off, grimy and smiling. Smelled of the coal that had kept her pita warm in the engine.

In 1980, she moved back to Višegrad with just barely the best final grades in her year. She became a Marxism teacher at the high school and stood in lines for overpriced goods of questionable quality. She got worked up over incompetent leadership and social inequality. Feared rising nationalism and also didn't really take it too seriously. For Mother, like for most people, the crisis was something to stick out and get through, until it became life-threatening. Until, in a police uniform and sweatpants, it threateningly gave her a friendly warning.

Mother suffers from the past, unromantically. She had overcome the obstacles of her social origins—her parents weren't rich, they had to borrow money. As a woman from a nonacademic environment, she was the only one of three children to go to university. In 1990, when it was still unusual to do so, she opened her own business.

Her ethnic origins, though, hung around her neck like a stubborn rumor due to her Arabic name. It was a flaw, in the eyes of the new people in charge—a flaw that neither ambition nor education nor aptitude could correct. *Religion is the sigh of the oppressed creature, the soul of soulless conditions.*

When she had to give up her life in Višegrad, at thirty-five, she had to abandon her career, her friends, and the possibility of her quiet, beautiful dreams coming true. She lost a place that was full of good memories, success, and personal happiness. Today, she doesn't make up for what she lacks by inventing things, like I do. What's gone is gone. My mother likes a cigarette with her coffee and enjoys having a Twix with it too. Where She Comes From is the flinching when someone in her hometown shouts her name.

I have two favorite photographs of my mother. In one, a portrait, she is eighteen or nineteen. Her expression is—there's no other way I can say it—infinitely gentle. She has long black shiny hair. And her gaze is turned inward. She is complete unto herself. A child doesn't want to see their mother turned inward—they want her turned toward them. But today I find her being sunk into herself insanely beautiful. Especially since I so rarely saw her like that. Mother was always there for me first, then for others, then for herself.

In the second photo she is surrounded by friends. Bell-bottoms, sideburns, alcohol, desires. Father is there, but not yet my father. Mother is smiling while the others are in a serious conversation—frozen gestures from a colorful time. Mother is smiling as though she were outside the picture. She's smiling like she knows more than the others. Or knows less, but is happier.

When the policeman suggested, in April 1992, that she disappear from Višegrad because the Muslims were about to get it, her answer in the life I would have written for her would be: "And who says I'm Muslim?"

Mother didn't say anything like that. Which was smart. She thanked him for the information. She went to get me from Grandmother and Father from work. While we were packing—what were we most likely to need?—the first Muslim houses went up in flames in the mountains.

Mother made phone calls and passed along the policeman's advice. Father and I loaded up the Yugo. My parents hugged in the yard, exactly where—it seemed like only a few days before, and at the same time like a summer many years ago—they'd danced their last dance. Father stood with his back to me, Mother facing me. Her expression, with her eyes wide open, had the same otherworldliness as in the photo. She was physically with her husband and otherwise with herself and her

117

fear—fear for me, for us—but had also already moved on, was already after the goodbye, already now, already gone.

We picked up Grandmother Kristina, who would come with us only to the border; then she would drive back with Father. She wanted to be sure we got out of the city alive. And we did. We survived and left our life—every person for themselves.

HEIDELBERG

In Bosnia on August 24, 1992, there was shooting; in Heidelberg, there was rain. It might just as well have been Oslo rain. Every place you live is accidental: you are born here, exiled there, and in a third place you leave your kidneys to science. Anyone who has any influence over chance is lucky. If you don't leave home because you have to, but because you want to. If your geographical dreams are fulfilled. If you can retire to Florida.

Heidelberg started off for me as an accidental city. I was fourteen and had never heard of it, much less had any idea how nice the Neckar River would turn out to be years later for a stroll with a female philosophy major.

We imagined our Heidelberg home as a short-term escape from the unreality of the war, which had become reality. If we had to flee today, or if the conditions at the 1992 border were as restrictive as they are at the EU borders now, we would never have reached Heidelberg. The trip would have ended at a Hungarian barbed wire fence.

On August 24, 1992, after the rain, the sun came out. Mother wanted to do something nice for her boy rattled by the trip. That she herself had been just as scared, she hid as best she could. I remember a bus ride with her, the rain-blurred windows like a mask with the city like a secret behind it.

She bought us chocolate ice creams at an ice-cream shop. Then, Belgian waffles in hand, we strolled down a long street and alongside a river. We wandered aimlessly through a world where everything was still nameless: the streets, the river, ourselves.

No one understood us and we understood no one. The only thing I could say in German was "Lothar Matthäus," the soccer player. Then came: *"Mein Name ist"* for "My name is," *"Flüchtling"* for "refugee." *"Heidelberg"* and *"šokolate"*—those were easy.

And then the castle:

Schwer in das Tal hing die gigantische,
Schicksalskundige Burg nieder bis auf den Grund,
von den Wettern zerrissen;
Doch die ewige Sonne goß

ihr verjüngendes Licht über das alternde
Riesenbild, und umher grünte lebendiger
Efeu.

The lines would hardly have shone with glory for the tired mother and her son even if they'd heard of Hölderlin and known his famous ode to Heidelberg. On that first day there, nothing in the city was layered with history or foreknowledge or literature. *Heavily down into the valley hung / the gigantic castle, knowing of fate—down to the ground / torn apart by the weather, / yet eternal sun poured / rejuvenating light across the aging, / colossal picture, and vital ivy greened all / around.* For us it was just roofs, façades, building materials. Substances. Men and women in the clear air after a rain. Memories of gunfire. That was all.

But then, unexpectedly, our gaze broke free and soared up to where the eternal sun really was pouring its rejuvenating light on the remnants of the castle resting in the midst of the mountain forest. I had seen more destroyed buildings than I wanted to—but this was my first destroyed castle. Which still, even as a ruin, looked fantastic: fantastic and proud, and somehow once again complete. It looked like it had been mounted there as a pale red ruin from the beginning. As though it could only exist like this, ruined, pleasingly close to the broad river and the now unmasked, doubt-free expression of the old city.

Suddenly we too made sense to ourselves. We were a mother and son standing in a little square in Germany that would soon no longer be nameless: Karlsplatz. Like other mothers and sons in other squares. Like the chocolate taste of the chocolate ice cream. Like stopping in awe beneath an imposing building you're seeing for the first time.

The view of the castle will always taste like chocolate to me. My first happiness in Germany was a tourist attraction. Looking back, I realize that this happiness came from feeling safe for the first time since we'd fled. The city felt foreign, but foreignness wasn't threatening, the rain was just weather, the sun was just the sun. In this strange place where you could be a gigantic ruin just standing around while Japanese tourists scramble all over you, and you're a little arrogant, a little grotesque, and at the same time a little bit "mine"—here nothing could happen to us. Like the castle ruins, we too would endure.

Only cities where olive trees grow are as beautiful drying after a rain as Heidelberg. This image too is a remnant of that late summer, 1992.

SAŠA STANIŠIĆ

Mother thought the war would be over soon and we'd be able to go back home. In our first place in Germany, we shared the bathroom and TV and every door handle with other refugees. We shared with foreign strangers a strange foreign life in a strange foreign land. What belonged exclusively to us were three brown suitcases. That was enough, because it had to be. We started learning a language whose core (*Kern*) was as hard as a plum pit (*Kern*).

Soon we moved to Emmertsgrund, a neighborhood of projects where they hadn't been stingy with the concrete. But in return we got a view of the Rhine Valley, vineyards on the outskirts of the Odenwald Nature Park.

On a mild summer night in my second year in Germany, I lost my heart there to a red-haired girl who wanted to teach me that verbs always go at the end of the sentence in German relative clauses, which I'd already known for a long time, but she explained it so beautifully.

Mostly immigrants lived in Emmertsgrund. That's how it is all over Germany. Immigrants live somewhere in their own neighborhood. Tourists tend to go to Brandenburg Gate first, to look at other tourists, and then to Neukölln to drink coffee and look at the Arabs, and that's not going to change anytime soon no matter how many cross-cultural dialogues for the stage we stay up late writing.

Almost no tourists ever go to Emmertsgrund—there are spotlights on baroque buildings elsewhere. Well, they're missing out on some things. Heidelberg has a slender neck (the graceful Neckar Valley) and delicate arms (the alleys of the old city). Its sandstone façades are always gently reddened—eternally blushing at their own beauty. In this lovely body, Emmertsgrund is the right hand, big and rough and crude and sometimes balled into a fist.

People shook hands in Emmertsgrund: Bosnians and Turks, Greeks and Italians, Russian Germans and Polish Germans and Germany's Germans. Every so often new victims of African wars turned up. We were neighbors, school friends, work colleagues. The supermarket line spoke seven languages.

The institution that did the most for our social integration was a beat-up old ARAL gas station. It was our youth center, drink supplier, lottery-ticket seller, dance floor, toilet. It united cultures in the fluorescent lights and smell of gasoline. We learned wrong German from each other in the parking lot, and learned the right way to reinstall car radios. The only rule was: No smoking near the pumps.

It was especially nice on Sundays. At midday the Poles went to the nearby church and then drank their way slowly through the afternoon. Big-spending blond men still slightly woozy from the blood of Christ, with thin mustaches and sports jackets always a touch too big. Conversations almost exclusively about what had happened in school, tire rims, the Bundesliga, the army, liver-function test results, and always, at some point, procreation. Conversations with a lot of cursing: *kurva, kurva, kurva.* Unforgettable.

That ARAL gas station was Heidelberg's inner Switzerland: neutral ground, on which where you came from was rarely worth fighting over. Anyway, multicultural fist-dialogues rarely took place. The gas station store did get robbed from time to time. But there too, an agreement seemed to exist, so that, say, a German and a Russian German wouldn't come around with gas pistols on the same night.

None of us Emmertsgrunders wanted to work at the ARAL station. That was for the hippies or whatever from Kirchheim, in their fortieth semester of college, studying art history—pitiful creatures that you really didn't want to hurt. Their attrition rate was enormous. But they had a sensational view from the station: on good days you could see all the way to France, on bad days you could see into the barrel of a gun.

Down below the gas station was Leimen, and Leimen is the birthplace of Boris Becker. Sometimes Boris Becker visited his hometown. We sat in the vineyards, drank Leimener Bergbräu beer, and talked about Steffi Graf. None of us became tennis pros.

We became a statistic on the edge of a venerable city in the present still celebrating its past. We became juvenile delinquency, youth unemployment, foreign percentage of the population. The old town—with its Americans admiring the cobblestones, its souvenirs, dog schools, stores open for shopping on Sundays, municipal movie theaters—was a fairy-tale kingdom that we set foot in, if at all, only when school forced us to: ARAL children on a field trip to the Ethnology Museum.

Then the university actually dragged me "down" to the west part of the city. My dormitory had higher ceilings than our Emmertsgrund bungalow was wide. Across the way was the cemetery; the next-door neighbors raised rare varieties of cabbage and subscribed to *Stern*.

After my parents had to leave Emmertsgrund (and Germany), there was almost nothing to draw me back there. I was also in contact less and less often with the friends living on the hill. Anyone who could afford to moved out. The ARAL station belonged to the next generation.

After rough and raw Emmertsgrund, I could then call the old city—the jewelry box—my own. Here it wasn't immigrants who lived in the better hillside houses, but university students in right-wing fraternities. The old city was proud of itself. Proud that it had grown older without looking older—decay was halted or concealed. Proud of the university's place in the latest rankings, proud of having remained undamaged by American bombs. The city was proud of the foreigners in Emmertsgrund, too, as long as we didn't get up to no good.

In Emmertsgrund my being a Bosnian and a refugee was just a sidenote. In academic environments, it was often a main point of interest. I was prepared—I had two or three little war stories ready and waiting; people's attention usually didn't extend to any more suffering than that.

The philosophy department library was open late. During my third semester, I often stayed there and pretended to be reading Adorno. I wore a turtleneck sweater, even in June. The reward was a few strolls along the Neckar with *her*. I voluntarily told her where I was from, what I had been through. I thought: A refugee's fate? Might be worth some points.

She would sometimes quote philosophers; I don't remember whom, or, unfortunately, what. I do still remember what our first kiss tasted like (we'd just eaten kofta).

My first job as a student was bartending at a place called Café Burkardt. What the ARAL station was for the youth of Emmertsgrund, the Burkardt was for the old city: a universe in a nutshell, with paneled walls. Everyone went there: the local chapter of the Social Democratic Party, to drown yet another election loss in pinot gris; diabetic grandmas fanning each other after their second piece of Black Forest cake. Near Eastern studies students spoke Arabic and ate bread dumplings.

Rarely, someone from Emmertsgrund came by too. Some had steady jobs by then; some had started families; but they all talked about the past, about the ARAL station, about being young. About the one Dutch kid among us, Michel, who had once answered a policeman's question, "Born?" by saying, "Yes."

When I visited Heidelberg with my three-year-old son in August 2018, I also stopped by Emmertsgrund. The ARAL station's parking lot was empty, the station itself renovated. I bought a lottery ticket, same as before, and didn't win anything, same as before.

On the way to the bungalow where we'd lived for four years, I ran into the mother of one of my friends from the ARAL time, Martek König. It was hot, eighty-five degrees or so before noon. Mrs. König was sitting on the porch having a soda. She said hello without getting up. "Hi, Saša, how're you doing?" It was like we'd last spoken to each other yesterday, not twenty years ago. "Is that your boy?"

"Yes, he is," I said. "He's mine."

"Martek has three now," Mrs. König said. "I was just visiting him in New York. I was there for three months. Now I need a month's vacation." She laughed.

The crickets chirped. Twenty years ago I ask if Martek's home.

"Yes," Mrs. König says. "Go right on up." With that beautifully rolled Polish *r*. The words I remember. Go right on up.

Martek is reading a comic book.

"Ready?"

"Let's roll."

"ARAL?"

Martek touches his hair. "Where else?"

I said goodbye to Mrs. König and we walked up the stairs to our old bungalow. There was a Turkish name on the doorbell. I had studied vocabulary, and later learned to play guitar, in this little yard. Practiced kissing at the bathroom mirror, "with tongue." Doesn't add much when you've just had kofta.

We strolled through the vineyards. The city gave off a quiet hum of digestion underway in the midday heat. We could hear voices: A girl was teaching a boy German. He repeated what she said to him, clumsily, and she laughed, and he cursed, laughing too, in Bosnian.

"Every city," the English author John Berger writes, "has a sex and an age which have nothing to do with demography. Rome is feminine. Paris is a man in his twenties in love with an older woman."

Heidelberg is a boy from Bosnia having a girl teach him German in the Emmertsgrund vineyards. Who will only much later become aware of the accident that made him a Heidelberg boy as opposed to anything else. Who calls this accident happiness, and calls this city: My Heidelberg.

BRUCE WILLIS SPEAKS GERMAN

You stand outside the door and read "*Ziehen.*" It's a door. Those are letters. That's *Z.* That's *I.* That's *E.* That's *H.* That's *E.* That's *N. Ziehen*, "Pull." Welcome to the door of the German language. And you push.

It's September 20, 1992. You've been in Germany for a month. The door is to your school and today's your first day. You are wearing your new jeans. Your mother bought you these jeans because she didn't want you to go to German school in your old worn-out jeans. She thought they were too expensive and said so in the store. Mother doesn't have a work permit and you don't have much money. These or nothing, you said. It was a jerk thing to say, and you knew it was a jerk thing to say and Mother knew it too and she bought you the jeans anyway.

Sitting next to you on your left is a Finn. His name is Pekka. Pekka has drawn a flip-book in his school notebook. It looks really great. The truth is, Pekka could go right home today and never come back to school and draw flip-books for the rest of his life.

On the right is Dedo, a Yugo like you. Before the teacher comes in, as a precautionary measure, Dedo screams. Dedo will either scream or stay silent for quite a while. Then he'll get better about going with the silence.

No one in the class is from here. No one speaks German. Which is actually perfect, everyone can only barely understand one another and no one has to explain anything because no one can anyway.

Then a teacher comes in. Probably a geography teacher because he sets up a map and points to rivers and mountains and forests and cities. You write down *Rhine* and *Feldberg* and *Odenwald*, and the teacher says, "I was born in Mannheim. Pekka, where were you born?" And Pekka says, "In Odenwald."

So, new jeans for the new German school. New rules too, for playing language and most games. Another new thing is that Father's not with you. Father's still in Višegrad. You and Mother spend hours in the phone booth with the busy signal. Father's voice is perforated with pauses and little coughs. He has no answer to the most important question: When can you come join us?

You scratch your name and the date into the yellow of the phone booth: 10/1/1992.

Father's not with you until six months later. You meet him at the train station and he holds you tight for a long time. He looks the same as always, just with longer hair. He doesn't talk much. Says that it was peaceful in Višegrad. Recently. That Grandmother's doing well. Considering. When it comes to concrete details about *before recently* or *considering what*, he doesn't say anything, and that doesn't exactly make the things you're imagining seem better or less scary.

As for the scar on his thigh, he doesn't tell you anything about that either. You're not well informed enough to be able to say that it looks like a bullet wound, healed. You don't ask about it.

Father brought his brown suitcase with him. The last trip the three of you took with your brown suitcases was to the Adriatic, in summer 1990.

The new language is easy enough to pick up, but it's very hard to carry anything in it. You understand more than you can say. On the baggage carousel of declensions you forget endings; the German words are too cumbersome, the cases tumble together, and your accent always peeps out no matter how you put the sentences together.

You've long since learned the days of the week and the months, although it takes a few before you make any friends. They are easier to find with a shared language. You can understand which soccer team they like. Olli from Eppelheim likes a team from Hamburg. His father takes him and you along to a game in Karlsruhe. It's the first time anyone in Germany invites you to anything. Olli's father screams at the ref. You learn a new vocabulary word: "youmotherfucker." He buys you and Olli bratwursts at halftime. You sing along to "Hamburg boys, Hamburg boys, we're all Hamburg boys." For ninety minutes you're a Hamburg boy. Your team is named Hamburger SV. Hamburger SV loses. You'll get used to it.

The geography teacher gets out the maps again and lists off the German states and state capitals. He asks Pekka what the capital of his homeland is and Pekka says, "Stuttgart."

The geography teacher says, "Very funny."

Everyone laughs, including the traumatized.

The geography teacher asks me what the capital of my homeland is, and I know what I'm supposed to say: "Belgrade and Sarajevo and Berlin."

You don't need much language to play soccer. It's more important that you not be picked last for a team. But your new jeans rip at the knee, and Mother totally flips out, then she cries, then she mends the jeans. While she does, you sit on the sofa and catch a fly. The sofa is from the bulk trash, and the fly's panic tickles inside your fist. First you let it go.

And suddenly: you fall kind of in love. Susanne has blond hair, long and sleek, with a red butterfly in it, a delicate hair clip. Susanne speaks no Serbo-Croatian and no English. Your German is still too bad to fall really and truly in love. How can you talk? You shrug when the other person asks a question and you hold hands.

"What kind of music do you like?"

"Music good, yes!"

Twenty-four hours later, Susanne says, "It's over."

"Over what?" you ask.

"Over, I mean with us. I don't want to go out with you anymore."

"Where go?" you ask. "Outside go?"

"No, you don't understand—I'm ending it."

"Go out to end of what?"

You learn "hold hands" and "kiss goodbye."

Word order. You newspapers deliver. You meet the neighbors and learn a vocabulary word: "tip." Six months later you are still mismaking takes with separable verbs but you've saved enough money for a German scarf *Made in Taiwan* that you give to Mother as a present. Mother cries.

Reported speech. Mother cries a lot. Sometimes from happiness, sometimes from grief, sometimes from fear. She works in an industrial laundry. She says it's so hot there that her heart boils.

You can tell your first joke in German. Only no one laughs, except Pekka, but by this point it's clearly not because of the language, it's because you're not that good at telling jokes.

Relative pronouns. A country whose language you can speak is not necessarily more your country, but it is less relative.

Your family has a small TV set. In the evenings, your war comes on for a little while. You change the channel: *Die Hard* with Bruce Willis. Bruce Willis speaks German. You understand Bruce Willis just fine. But things aren't going too well for Bruce Willis, physically. "Yippie-ki-yay, *Schweinebacke*," he says, and you get out your vocab notebook.

Pluperfect tense. History lesson on National Socialism. You stand up, even though in Germany you don't have to stand up when you want to speak in class, and you shout, even though you don't need to be so loud: "Death to Fascism, Freedom to the People!"

Future tense. Social studies class. You say: "Capitalism will devour itself."

Again you're standing outside the door. You no longer even see that it says "Pull." Knowing something is the best. The suitcase of language gets lighter the more you put into it. All the vocabulary and rules and acquisitions send you off on a new trip: you start writing stories.

Up in a deer stand in the forest. In the Emmertsgrund vineyards. On the bulk trash sofa, paper on your knees. One story is about how your father kills a snake. In another one, you come home from sledding and Grandmother warms your hands in hers. In a third one, your father is shot and wounded. Grandmother Kristina is alone in Višegrad—some of the stories you will finish only many years later. Now.

The 31 bus takes you from Emmertsgrund to Rohrbach South. In Rohrbach South you transfer to tram 3 and take it to Ortenauer Street. From there you walk to school. The route is not especially interesting, or pretty, or dangerous. It's the shortest way. For four years it's yours.

There are similar-looking buildings on both sides of Ortenauer Street. Some have a front yard, some have a backyard. Some have a tree in the yard, some don't. The properties are separated by hedges, and there are white curtains in the windows. All the roofs are brown. The mailboxes are either white or brown.

No one ever accosted you on Ortenauer Street. You have never been starving on Ortenauer Street. You were worried about grades. You had daydreams. You felt hot or cold but it was never that big a deal. You never pissed in a hedge or threw a rock through a window on Ortenauer Street, why would you. One time, in eleventh grade—the war in Bosnia was over—you climbed into a yard after school, just because. There was a little slide, toys were lying around, and a bowl of apples on a table under the apple tree. The doormat said *Home Sweet Home*. The names of a man, a woman, and a girl were on the doorbell. The girl's name had been added in a child's handwriting.

You looked down at your sneakers. Your mother had bought them at Deichmann's. They looked all right, they were simple and black, and the grass was mowed, and yellow flowers bowed their heads in the flowerbeds.

There was a little toolshed in the corner, and you just knew, as you walked over to the shed, that the door would be unlocked. You opened the door and in the dim light you breathed in the air, which smelled of machine oil and cement.

You took an apple from the table and went back onto Ortenauer Street.

TIED HANDS

It is a privilege to work with language, to be a writer. I remember very well how it feels to have *no* language for something. How I'd just break off conversations when the person I was talking to had trouble hiding their impatience at how long it took me to communicate something. How ashamed I felt of my parents' mediocre German after three or four years in the country. When actually, mediocre was amazing! There were lots of people who didn't have the access, the will, or the opportunity to learn the language at all.

At first Father applied for every possible job: both ones he was qualified for and ones about which he said: I learn fast. As long as it didn't involve cooking, he could picture himself doing anything. Gardening, teaching, selling shoes. Any kind of construction. He wasn't often called in for an interview. When he was, he asked me to come with him so I could translate if there was anything he didn't understand.

The fact that an applicant had brought someone with him for support could be a point in his favor: a sign of his high degree of motivation. Or it could be a point against him. I remember the look an interviewer at a trucking company gave me when I said why I'd come. It was a pitying look I was already well acquainted with—the one from Germans who might be sympathetic, but whose sympathy didn't translate into action.

Still, she went through with the interview, even though it was clear to her and to me and presumably to Father that nothing would come of it. She said goodbye to us with the words: "Let me be honest. I like you, but my hands are tied."

That was new, that was interesting: *tied hands*. The interviewer's hands rested on the desk, balled into fists. Next to them was a mug with the company's logo on it, and the slogan: *It's a small world*. Great motto for a trucking company.

Father thanked her. He had learned how to say thank you in Germany very well and very quickly. "Thank you very much!" my father, a thirty-eight-year-old sales manager with a specialty in logistics and a noticeable accent, thundered at the small world.

HANG 'EM!

On August 24, 1992, neo-Nazis throw Molotov cocktails into a residence for Vietnamese contract workers in Rostock, Germany. There are spectators. Citizens of Rostock. Hate-tourists who've made a special trip. Police.

"We'll smoke 'em out!"

"Hang 'em!"

"*Sieg Heil!*"

Fires are started on the lower floors of the building. The crowd sings: "On a day as beautiful as this." There are food stands. You can buy a beer and a sausage and watch the flames. The fire department comes; people have blocked the roads. It's a German pogrom festival.

I didn't hear anything about it at the time. It was better that way. We had just arrived in Germany and were worried about ourselves. Where do you buy sheets, how do you pay for them? Which bus goes where, can you buy tickets from the driver, how do you pay for those?

Three months later, on a Monday in November, a teacher brought a newspaper clipping about Rostock into language class. Vocabulary work. It sounds cynical, but from his point of view it was an opportunity to talk with us foreigners about hatred of foreigners.

SAŠA STANIŠIĆ

We read in silence and sat in silence after we finished. Usually someone would speak up right away because they hadn't understood something. This time everyone understood the basic point perfectly. This time it was about us.

There are twenty entries in my vocabulary notebook for November 19, 1992:

Sonnenblume (f) – sunflower
aufgebracht – outraged
Bürgerwehr (f) – civil defense
Trittbretfahrer (m) – freeloader
Vorgang (m) / vorgehen (-ging) – process / to proceed
Krawall (n) – riot
freisetzen (freigesetzt) – release (released)
basteln (-te) – tinker, do handicrafts
Sprengsatz (m) – explosive device
ersticken (-te) – suffocate
Löscharbeit (f, löschen, löschte) – firefighting (extinguish,
*   extinguished)*
sich zurückziehen (-zog) – withdraw (withdrew)
jmndn das Feld überlassen – leave the field, yield the floor
*   to someone*
jmndn decken – cover someone, shield someone
verkorkst – screwed-up
Einsatz (m) – deployment
Zustrom (m) – influx
mißbrauchen (-te) – misuse, abuse
Einschränkung (f) – limitation
Grundrecht (n) – fundamental right

We looked at where Rostock was on the map. We looked at where Hoyerswerda was on the map. We looked at where Vietnam was on the map. Pekka said, "I don't come from Rostock."

The way home via Ortenauer Street felt longer that day. A German flag—*Fahne (f)*—hung from a balcony. I had seen it before, but now I wondered who'd put it there (*anbringen, -gebracht: to mount/affix*) and why.

Then, back home: What do we Yugoslavs have in common with the Vietnamese? And there I was, rummaging around in the little I knew about Vietnam (I had read about the Vietnam War, tasted Vietnamese food twice, and known a Vietnamese boy at school) to find what about the country and its people was worth hating. The real horror: I tried to weigh what was different, what was *better*, about me as a Yugoslav, to reassure myself to some extent that nothing like that could happen to us, the good ones.

The school library had newspapers out on the tables. I got into the habit of flipping through them during lunch break. At first I could understand only the headlines, later whole articles. I started keeping a news notebook along with my vocabulary notebook. Boris Becker beats Jim Courier. A naval blockade goes into effect against Serbia. In Mölln a ten-year-old girl and a fourteen-year-old girl lose their lives in an arson attack, along with their grandmother.

On May 29, 1993, five people died in a far-right arson attack in Solingen. *Tat (f)*: crime. *Hergang (m)*: sequence of events. *Tathergang (m)*: circumstances of a crime. They're all still there, except the dead people. *Aufarbeitung (f)*: processing.

SAŠA STANIŠIĆ

In 2017, somewhere between 264 and 1,387 attacks on refugee residences were recorded (the number varies depending on
the source). Today is August 28, 2018. Sebastian Czaja of the
neoliberal FDP party tweets, "Anti-Fascists are Fascists too."

SCHWARZHEIDE, 1993

In summer 1993, Father got a job. Now he had to go to Schwarzheide during the week. The place sounded mystical and dangerous (*Schwarzheide–Blackheath*) until Father explained that it was just a city in former East Germany, and now BASF Chemical was there. That was that for the magic.

BASF was building new production facilities in Schwarzheide. Father worked for a Yugo named Haris, but everyone called him Harry, maybe because he wished he were American rather than Yugo, or maybe just because he thought his name was garbage.

It was Father's first job in Germany. He climbed into pipes and did in the pipes whatever he was told to do. The pipes were so big that he could stand up straight in them. By the end of the day, he and his coworkers had sometimes laid several miles of pipes. And when they didn't feel like walking back, they would just lie down and go to sleep, and the early shift would bring them sandwiches in the morning. Yugos have breakfast in BASF pipes in former East Germany.

Today Father says: Nonsense. It wasn't like that at all in Schwarzheide. The pipes weren't that big, and no one ever spent the night in them, and in general: "Just ask so you don't have to make things up."

In fact I didn't know much about Father's time in Schwarzheide. He didn't bring it up much on his own, and I was the

Puberty World Champion in Avoiding-Talking-to-Parents. Only after he corrected me so many years later did I want to know more. Father said he'd write me an email. And he did. Subject line: Life in Schwarzheide.

The email was incredibly strange. *I am living in a former military barracks and I share a room with two other men,* Father wrote, using the present tense. It was like I had gotten a letter he'd sent in 1993. Or like he was still there. *Near the barracks there's a phone booth and in the evening I call to hear how you and Mother are doing, where you are and what you're up to.*

I remember those calls. The phone would ring after dinner. Mother would be waiting. I talked to him briefly, if at all. About school, always about me.

There's a bar here, a döner shop, and a supermarket, so that's what we do in our spare time, Father wrote. Also that the döners of Schwarzheide were the best döners he's ever eaten.

I picture him there. Father had lost weight in Germany— gaunt cheeks, jeans too big. He is eating a döner in Schwarzheide. His hair glows white at the temples under the fluorescent lights.

It's interesting enough, the work here, and life after work too. There's always something happening; every day's different. Beko and another Bosnian have ended up in jail and came within an inch of a long sentence.

Father at the counter in the döner shop is toasting his co-workers from around there. He tells them about Yugoslavia, they tell him about East Germany. They are in full agreement, there in the fluorescent lights of Schwarzheide, that what came after their respective now-nonexistent nations is shit.

The pipes have to be constructed precisely according to isometric drawings. You can't make any mistakes. When you drop a pipe it needs to go exactly into its place. We're always faster than the Germans. They stare at us but what can they do?

Father didn't write what Beko and the other Bosnian ended up in jail for.

Olja is a Serb from the Krajina and a former forest ranger, working in the same pipe group as Father. Coming out of the war, he ended up in Ludwigshafen and, five days a week, in Schwarzheide. In Schwarzheide, starting on his first day, Olja told the same joke—he even liked to tell it multiple times in a row. Sometimes he'd stop, though. He could also talk to you normally.

Here's the joke: The partisans and the Germans are fighting in a forest, then a forest ranger comes and kicks them both out.

It was funny at first, but soon pointless and annoying. That's enough now, Olja, what are you doing? But Olja doesn't stop. Olja would wake up in terror in the middle of the night and tell his joke to the darkness in the barracks, waking everybody else up. No one got mad at Olja, how could you?

But one time, things got serious. An Albanian who also lived in Ludwigshafen, like Olja, and who used to drive him to and from Schwarzheide, went over to him, pipe wrench in hand, and told him: Listen, Olja, I can't take it anymore. No more of that joke. *That.* We can't help you. You've gotta understand that.

An Albanian with a pipe wrench. Maybe sad too, who knows. He stood there and waited for Olja to get it, and Olja nodded, because he got it. And he told the joke again.

For a couple of weeks, he kept commuting to Schwarzheide, but by train—the Albanian wouldn't bring him anymore.

One Monday morning he didn't show up. The next Monday, someone else started, taking over Olja's jobs.

Father doesn't know what happened to Olja.

The partisans and the Germans are fighting in a forest, then a forest ranger comes and kicks them both out.

The partisans and the Germans are fighting in a forest, then a forest ranger comes and kicks them both out.

The partisans and the Germans are fighting in a forest, then a forest ranger comes and kicks them both out.

The partisans and the Germans are fighting in a forest, then a forest ranger comes and kicks them both out.

The partisans and the Germans are fighting in a forest, then a forest ranger comes and kicks them both out.

The partisans and the Germans are fighting in a forest, then a forest ranger comes and kicks them both out.

The partisans and the Germans are fighting in a forest, then a forest ranger comes and kicks them both out.

The partisans and the Germans are fighting in a forest, then a forest ranger comes and kicks them both out.

The partisans and the Germans are fighting in a forest, then a forest ranger comes and kicks them both out.

The partisans and the Germans are fighting in a forest, then a forest ranger comes and kicks them both out.

The partisans and the Germans are fighting in a forest, then a forest ranger comes and kicks them both out.

The partisans and the Germans are fighting in a forest, then a forest ranger comes and kicks them both out.

PHOTOREALIST PAINTING

Special-project week in school. I had signed up for art, for *photorealist painting*—and just to make sure there's no mis-understanding: I chose *photorealist painting* not because I was interested in photorealism or could paint well or even liked painting, but because Rieke would be there. Rieke, tenth grade, Class B-2, red-haired Rieke, green-eyed Rieke, Rieke I liked to look at so much that I was always looking away. I chose photorealism because I wanted to impress her. I didn't know how yet. Or if not impress her, then at least, by spending five days in the same room as her, inform her of my existence. Up until that point all my efforts to strike up a conversation with her had failed, probably because they hadn't happened, except in my head. In there, I'd had hundreds of very nice conversa-tions with her. About the treatment of animals in industrial farms, about Nirvana, about India—all things that Rieke was interested in, maybe.

On the first day of project week, I walked into the art room nervous but firm in my decision. We were supposed to pick a photograph and then paint our picture so that it looked like the photograph, or even more realistic than the photograph, *hyper-realistic*, the teacher said, and maybe it wasn't clear to everyone in the room but it was immediately clear to me that this goal was completely *un*realistic.

I chose a picture of a bicycle leaning against a wall. It seemed like the easiest motif. More or less flat, with the fewest colors. The bike was black, the wall orange.

Only then did I notice that Rieke wasn't there. Maybe she's late, I thought. But she never showed up, not the next day either.

So I had to get through the week without her. Now I had to talk to Andreas about the German Army, because that was the only topic that Andreas was interested in. Andreas wanted to join the force. He wanted to become a general or at least conduct a war at some point. He actually painted worse than I did, something I hadn't thought possible. He complained too, saying painting was stupid. Painting, he said, was "for pussies." I asked him why he was doing it then. Because in the force he would also face situations he hated that he would have to endure, he said. Situations that would ask too much of him, would wear him down.

He painted a fruit tree that didn't look like a fruit tree—the thing in the picture looked like a Golf GTI. I painted a bicycle leaning against the wall of a building and the only hyperrealistic part of the painting was the bell on the handlebars. The teacher painted that, to show me "how to do it."

The work was frustrating. I was the only foreigner in the room. Back then, I thought maybe foreigners in general don't like painting; today I know it was a coincidence. On the first day the handlebars ended up too crooked; on the second day I got stuck on the spokes. But I kept at it, next to Andreas, who was enthusing about fighter planes in his deep voice, and on the third day things started going better. I was more relaxed somehow. I had been painting for three days. The bicycle didn't look that bad at all, if you looked at it from the other end of the room and squinted.

I was also happy for Andreas—his having such a clear dream. And I was happy that he tried a bit in the homestretch. His picture still looked extremely crappy, but he was hunkered down in front of the canvas and the tip of his little tongue peeked obliviously out from between his lips—people look so good when they're concentrating!

On Friday afternoon we were done. We hung the pictures up in the cafeteria, where they would stay for a whole month. Mine up on the wall between the others, like it belonged there: an old bicycle with a photorealistic bell leaning against a wall in, I would guess, Portugal.

Weeks later, Rieke and I found ourselves by chance at the same party in the vineyards. I had started eight conversations with her in my head when suddenly she was standing in front of me starting a conversation (probably no one will believe me, but I'll tell the story anyway).

"Hi. You painted the bicycle, didn't you?"

"Yes!!" I said, very loud, because I was so shocked.

"Cool picture," Rieke said, and—please note—she smiled. "The bell is great."

"Yes!!" I screamed again.

"I like that you didn't do the whole thing photorealistically, just the bell. The heart of the picture."

"YES!!"

"Too bad I was sick, I couldn't come. My name's Rieke," Rieke then said.

"I know," I said. "My name's Saša."

And Rieke said: "With a tiara on the *s*, I know."

Rieke actually was interested in animals' living conditions under industrial farming, she liked Nirvana so-so, and thought tourism in India was just "a subtle way of exploiting the subcontinent."

When it was time to tell her something about myself, again all I could think of was the dumb war. I didn't want to talk about that. Then, out of nowhere, Andreas popped into my mind. I told Rieke that I liked fighter planes, thought paratroopers were cool, and admired the high quality of German weapons, and Rieke said to all of that: "Aha. Interesting. Is that so?"

I painted a picture. With zero talent and not the slightest passion for the fine arts, but with a little time, and peace and quiet, and materials put at my disposal. Together with Andreas. Without Rieke. The second time we met, I admitted that the military stuff was all a lie, and Rieke said, "Good. As long as you like painting, it's all good."

SLOVENIAN ME

Here are some things I wanted after my first year in Germany. I wanted to grow my hair long, both to hide my zits and to look like Kurt Cobain. I wanted fewer zits. I wanted a guitar. I wanted to learn to play guitar and sing like Kurt Cobain. I wanted Rieke to like my songs. I wanted clothes like a male Janis Joplin, and I especially liked tie-dyed T-shirts. I wanted my parents happier. I wanted to learn German better so the Germans I was talking to wouldn't have to try so hard to hide the fact that they thought I was stupid.

Two things I didn't want: to be seen as a Yugo; to be seen as a refugee. So every now and then I would tell someone I met that I was from Slovenia. The Alpine republic was in the headlines the least—they'd be more likely to think I was a skier than a victim, I hoped. And when asked why I was in Germany, I would say something along the lines of: "My father got an amazing offer from BASF and we couldn't say no."

I would sigh and say: "I miss the Alps."

Missing the Alps, I learned, went over extremely well in Germany.

At school, my Slovenianness was obsolete. The International Comprehensive School of Heidelberg (ICSH) was international, obviously, and organized well around the diversity of the student body. Foreigners were neither exotic creatures placed in the middle of class photos so that everyone would be sure to see them, nor did they take our great number lightly.

I was one of the Yugos—one of many. My classmates who weren't Yugos didn't really care which variety of Yugo I was; most of them had enough to worry about with their own origins. And if it did make a difference to someone, that someone would have had a problem. There was zero tolerance for discrimination.

Getting along with all kinds of different people—the need to, the way to—was something almost everyone at ICSH understood. Some managed better than others. That was the main difference. The new arrivals' longings were all very similar, or at least easy to grasp. Learning the language, making friends. Entering into everyday life. Going back home, if there was a home that still existed anywhere. That longing became an urge to belong—somewhere, anywhere.

The German students were in the minority, and being the minority for once when you're otherwise the majority is an extremely valuable experience. Obviously they were well integrated in the life of the school. They let us copy from them and they copied from us. We prevailed or lost for the same school team—*our* team—and decided democratically to buy carnivorous plants for the school garden. Other schools in Heidelberg tended to see us as a wild, anarchistic bunch, which isn't the worst thing in the world when you're between fourteen and eighteen.

As a non-native speaker, I first attended a remedial class focusing on language acquisition and topics related to integration. Material from the curriculum was conveyed on the side so that the transition to regular classes later would be easier.

There was homework help and relaxation time, which most of the students didn't have too often at home.

Most teachers had German as a Second Language certificates and knew what they were doing, or else didn't really know but were motivated, which is more or less the same thing. Most dealt gingerly with the new arrivals. They asked the important questions and not too many of them. You never know what trauma a new student might be carrying or what might be waiting for them at home.

But there were also teachers who finished our sentences for us, and some taught their classes exactly the same way they would have in a private Bavarian Catholic school. That was okay too. We didn't want to always feel guilty for making the lesson drag.

Of course there was also the one teacher who drank in secret, and the one with an uncontrollable temper. One or two were unspeakably boring, and there too it didn't matter if you were from Oberpfalz or the Middle East—dead-boring classes are universal.

The ICSH was a shelter, a place to learn the language; it was everyday life. Plastic trays holding the cafeteria potatoes that were always too soft. I stood in the smoking corner, having never smoked, and chatted about grunge music. I played basketball, monkeyed around. The school paid for a year of guitar lessons. I wanted to learn Nirvana songs and I ended up with Bach minuets. In that place and time it actually often felt like an immigrant kid was a completely normal kid in a completely normal time in a completely normal city. So I gained confidence. Got good grades. In eleventh grade I even decided I wanted a bit more responsibility and ran for class representative. But my class wasn't ready for Really Existing Socialism yet.

Outside of school, I felt for quite a long time that I was readily identifiable as an immigrant and thus vulnerable. As if people could see what I myself was bothered by—the linguistic glitches, the economic precarity. In fact they probably could see it: in my uncertainty, my accent, my clothes. One time, during a basketball game, I cursed in Serbo-Croatian, and the next time I headed for the basket someone brutally knocked me down, and with a stupid comment too. I made both free throws.

Shopping at the Edeka supermarket with Grandfather, talking in line. The topic was how the salami was wrapped in foil: he always thought that was incredibly funny. "A salami must be free!" Grandfather cried, holding the salami over his head with both hands like Dejan Savićević lifting the championship cup. We laughed and missed that the line was moving.

"Hey, wops, you awake?"

I didn't translate that for my grandfather. I turned around and apologized.

Work pushed my parents to the edge of socially and physically bearable life more than school did me. Father ruined his back on construction sites in Ludwigshafen and Schwarzheide and was home only on weekends.

Mother died a thousand melting deaths in the laundry. As a non-German woman, from the Balkans no less, she stood on the bottommost rung of the work ladder and people made sure she knew it.

We were also reminded often that in Germany people have to obey "the rules." As if no one in other countries had ever heard of rules. "Hey, we speak German here," fired at my cousin and me on the tram, was not a rule we had to take seriously, of course, but the intent to intimidate was certainly serious. My parents always spoke Serbo-Croatian preemptively softly in public spaces. Anyone who obeyed the rules, including the ones that weren't really rules at all, could be forgiven in a pinch for being an immigrant. And along with every rule people reminded us of, they were also reminding us: You don't belong here.

Over time we learned the prejudices and learned to fit them, but not *too* much. Aggressive, primitive, illegal. Onions, germs. Emigrated to infiltrate. Basically, we were educating the Germans by behaving the same way we'd have behaved anywhere: as people who, by a stroke of fortune, couldn't be where we wanted to be. We didn't have to disguise who we were.

Today is December 1, 2018. My cousin sends me a picture. In it you can see the garage roof in Emmertsgrund where we used to play soccer. A free, open space, weeds between slabs of concrete, schoolbags as goalposts. The photo shows the sign with the ball in a circle with a line through it, and the words "No Ball Playing." My cousin commented on the photo with: "Childhood in a picture."

We played anyway. Sometimes, not often, someone would say something to us. Can't you read? Then we'd leave for a little while and come back later.

ATOP THE FORTRESS BEFORE
THE ORCS ATTACKED

At seventeen I spent countless weekends with magic spells, Coca-Cola, bow and arrow. Our playground consisted of pen, paper, and a wealth of, as they say, imaginative capacity. Our fates were decided by twenty-sided dice.

What the ARAL gas station was for my socialization in the rough world of Emmertsgrund, fantasy role-playing games were for my initiation into—well, what? Into the battle of good against evil, in any case. Other seventeen-year-olds spent their time on their body, or other bodies, experimented with perception-altering substances, and made themselves one with the world around them. My role-playing buddies and I spent our time, first and foremost, on the advancing orc army in Svellt Valley.

Olli was from Eppelheim; his witch was from a witch's egg. He was in my first regular German class. A calm type: the "I raise my hand only when I'm sure I know the answer" type. One day Olli told me that he and some friends played The Dark Eye on Saturdays. A fantasy role-playing game.

On the computer?

No, in your head.

I was into it on the spot. In your head! I could do that. Olli invited me to join the game, and one Saturday I went over to his place. Jo, Peter, and Seb were already sitting on the rug in his room, up to their elbows in bags of potato chips.

Each of them had a piece of paper with numbers and a badly drawn picture of an armed person on it. These were the abilities and portraits of the characters they were playing. I chose to become an elf from the Shire. My parents had been killed in an orc attack and I'd had to survive as an orphan, which I managed well enough, since I could cast magic spells and was lucky with the dice.

Fulminictus Thunderbolt, strike like an arrow and slay the foe! I cried, hand balled in a fist.

Bannbaladam, your friend I am! I cried, looking my opponent in the eye.

Jo played a charismatic witch. After a few months, she and I got married in a forest clearing full of fairies, high up in the mountains.

Over the phone, I described to Grandmother Kristina what went on during role-playing games. It's like a play, I explained. Everyone has a part that they invent themselves, in a magical world with demons, where creeping vines grow. There are good giants and cool dragons, and it's all without a stage, a script, or a director.

"No audience either," Grandmother guessed rightly.

"Yes, in your head an audience would just get in the way," I said. "When we walk into a room, we don't really walk into the room—or in a way we do, but in a reality that our gamemaster describes. What the room looks like, what's there, and so on."

Grandmother said nothing.

"It's really exciting," I said.

"It is not exciting at all," Grandmother said. She asked if you could at least make a little money with it. At that I tried to steer the conversation onto another topic, her, Višegrad.

We hadn't seen each other for three years and we rarely talked on the phone. The war hadn't destroyed the city but it also hadn't spared the people. The extent of the violence against the Muslim population was gradually coming to light. I didn't bring that up with her. I asked if she was lonely. She said she'd be happy if I came to visit. She said: "But don't come over to my house as an elf, you hear?" And: "When are you coming?"

WHAT DO YOU PLAN TO DO?

In the summers of '95 and '96, Olli and I watched the Tour de France on his parents' giant TV set. The flat stages too.

After running over a pigeon, Olli stopped riding a bike. That was really too bad—he had loved biking. He just couldn't forget the sound of the breaking bones under his tires. I didn't even own a bike. I took the bus and the train to Eppelheim. To be honest, I don't really understand why I suddenly got into competitive cycling, maybe because I liked Olli and didn't like to take my T-shirt off in the summer because of the pimples on my back.

Olli's mother was usually at home but I rarely saw her. She slept a lot; we had to be quiet. When we came to Olli's house for role-playing sessions, his father would make us sandwiches.

While I'm on the topic, here's a little fact about Eppelheim. The Eppelheimers had a thing for crazy mailboxes. I don't know why, or if it's still true, I haven't been back to Eppelheim for a long time. But back then you could see on basically any random street that the Eppelheimers had expended (I don't want to say wasted) enormous amounts of time and creativity on their mailboxes.

They used every kind of material imaginable, the main requirements being that it be more or less weatherproof (not always, though) and as garish as possible. Cogwheels, chains, pipes, matchsticks, coins, moss. I have never seen as many strange mailboxes as I did in Eppelheim during the years when Jan Ullrich was on the scene in professional cycling.

I'm no expert in mailboxes, but maybe this is what was going on: If you live on a street where all the houses look relatively similar, and you're the first person to customize your mailbox, say by building a giant wicker bird with the beak as the mail slot, then that giant bird, let's say an emu, that emu will represent your whole way of being. That emu is a direct and indirect signal to everyone else in Eppelheim that you swim with the current only so far and no farther. That mailbox marks the frontier.

But it's the fate of the trailblazer to attract imitators—you can't very well be surprised if your emu inspires your neighbors to think about their own nature and place in society and set up a correspondingly attractive and imaginative mailbox to express it. Doing that creates an identity, also in the sense of being identical: identical in unusualness. We, says the interesting mailbox in the shape of an envelope to the mailbox being held over a soccer player's head for a throw-in, we are somebody—and in the process, you know what team the latter owner is a fan of without having to ask.

Olli and I didn't watch the Tour de France in 1997, the year Ullrich actually won. I had too much going on: with the threat of deportation hanging over us, I couldn't care about reaching the Alps.

Olli and I graduated. We are smiling next to each other in the class photo. Olli now lives in a commune somewhere in the countryside near Hildesheim. He has two children, and today is September 26, 2018, and the evening paper has the headline "Did Jan Ullrich Strangle a Hamburg Airport Worker?"

My God, Jan.

Martek was in another class in the same grade and he liked to read comic books and in the winter of '93 he didn't go on the school camping trip for some reason, and since there wasn't enough money for me to take the trip I stayed in Heidelberg too. I had to take classes with Martek and three or four other Bosnians and Albanians. We became friends, because after all it creates a connection to miss out together on something awesome.

Martek lived in Emmertsgrund like us. He seemed like the most normal fifteen-year-old boy I could possibly imagine. He didn't talk too much or too little. He wore T-shirts, jeans, and sneakers. He drank apple-juice spritzers with tap water. He didn't read, except comics, but not in exaggeratedly large quantities. He didn't collect anything. His favorite band was called Fury in the Slaughterhouse, whose music sounded perfectly polite. Martek tried out a new kind of hair gel every couple of months. He played basketball in the league and convinced me to join too. He never scored much more than ten points a game, or much less.

Martek's parents were Silesians. I had never heard of Silesia until I met Martek. Martek was born in Germany and had plans to visit his parents' birthplaces in Katowice, Poland, when he turned eighteen. He ended up going to Corfu instead.

Dedo, from the remedial class, had fled his hometown in central Bosnia on a tractor's trailer. The tractor drove across a field. The trailer shook hard. A piece of cloth was stretched between two poles at the place where they drove off the field, warning of MINES in the field. Since that day, Dedo can go to sleep only by shaking his head quickly back and forth, back and forth, back and forth, until he sort of falls unconscious from dizziness.

Dedo brought his musical taste with him from Bosnia in the form of patches sewn onto his jean jacket: *Iron Maiden. Sepultura. Megadeth.* In Germany, the jacket got no other patches and Dedo got no other jacket. I never heard him talk about music.

In my remedial-class report card, it says: *Stanišić has no trouble learning the language. He grasps things quickly and is confident using what he's learned in new contexts. He is especially interested in describing strange things and formulating imaginary stories.*

In Dedo's, it says he's *a quiet student.*

Rahim had curly hair and a curvy name that occasionally resulted in an "Are you an Arab or something?" Actually his father was just a Semitic studies scholar who gave three of his four children Arabic names, all except Melanie, whose name was Melanie.

Mr. Heldau walks into the room, opens a book, rolls up his sleeve, flings out his arm, and reads aloud! For this little man with the big bald head, literature is physical labor, and he likes his work very, very much. Gesturing all the way, Mr. Heldau reads the first sentence, in which someone wakes up as an *Ungeziefer.*

I don't know what the word means.

I ask Olli. Olli says: "Bug." So someone woke up and was a bug, lots of little legs and all. I have to laugh. I can't help but laugh, it's funny for some reason, also because everyone else is listening so seriously and Mr. Heldau just keeps reading as if no one had just woken up as a bug. But now he stops reading and looks at me the way he looks at everyone who disrupts class: his brow and the back of his neck furrowed. Luckily I'm not the only one who's laughing. Rahim laughs too. And someone else, Arkadiusz, who has either paid attention in class for a change or else is laughing because two other kids are laughing.

Mr. Heldau asks what's so funny. He'd love to laugh along with us.

I want to be honest and say: "Mr. Heldau, is funny, someone wakes up, is a bug."

But Rahim is quicker, because his German is quicker, and he says: "Mr. Heldau, the insect. It's funny, you know? I mean the man as this big bug."

The next day, Rahim sat down next to me by choice. Had I read more? I had. "The Metamorphosis" was a wonderful, grotesque story, but "grotesque" wasn't in my vocabulary at the time so I said something else.

Then Rahim asked what I was always writing in class. "You're not taking notes, are you?"

In fact I was taking notes, it helped me figure out later what at the time had just hurtled by as nonsense. But I was afraid he wouldn't think that was cool, so I said, "Just some poems."

Rahim said he wrote too, "just some stories." And that he'd see me sometimes on the 31 bus, did I live in Emmertsgrund too? We quickly clarified who lived where: him in the single-family houses, me not in the big apartment buildings, where you'd expect a Yugo to be, but still in the bungalows just outside the better neighborhood.

Rahim suggested we hang out sometime. "Could write something together even."

"Maybe with Bugman?" I suggested.

"Bugman lives in Emmertsgrund."

"Works at the gas station."

Just-some-poems and just-some-stories stayed a key part of our connection. We both chose German as an honors course in twelfth grade and went to Literature Club with Mr. Heldau. Rahim was a satirical nostalgic suffering from wanderlust; I was a kitschy nostalgic suffering from homesickness. We studied together, shared meals, and planned to take a big trip together someday. But first we paddled down the Jagst in a two-person canoe. Later, our big trip took us to Bosnia. Rahim stayed with my grandmother. Today he's living in Munich and has a little daughter.

Emil lived with his grandfather in Hirschhorn. His parents weren't there and I didn't ask where they were; Emil didn't want to hear about mine either. He liked to read and he loaned me books. I didn't go see him in Hirschhorn much, because Hirschhorn was at the ass-end of the world and because, as a foreigner, I didn't like leaving Heidelberg—especially not to go somewhere where there were more sixteenth-century half-timbered houses than apartment buildings.

The first time I did go, Emil's grandfather immediately showed me his hunting rifles. He was a retiree and a hunter and he said he wished he could always only be hunting, day and night. It somehow felt nice that he steered our first conversation straight to killing animals. In the same breath he revealed that he was born in Danzig and that he knew another Saša, a woman, from the Soviet Union. He said she was beautiful; he wondered what she was doing now.

I asked what she used to be doing, and Emil's grandfather said: Guard in a prison camp. This was all within the first two and a half minutes of meeting each other. I asked Emil if he went on the hunts too, and Emil said he hated hunting.

Emil loved books. He was sixteen and in two reading groups. He tried to convince me to come, but it would have taken me ten times as long as him to read a novel and I didn't want anyone to have to wait for me. The first book Emil loaned me was *Little Man, What Now?* by Hans Fallada. It took me three months to read and I thought it was great.

One time, Emil's grandfather picked me up from the bus station in Hirschhorn. He drove me through town and explained the old houses to me. He spoke of "a skeleton of beams" and "the gentle red of the sandstone." He was especially fond of one large building: the Lords' Hunting Lodge. Emil's grandfather recited its dimensions, its history. "When you're in there, if you're quiet, you hear ghosts. They will stay forever, even though their home is somewhere different." That's what he said, or what I think today that he could have said.

After going to the library and looking up where Danzig was, I asked my history teacher, Mr. Gebhard, what was important to know about Danzig. He raised his eyebrows and said that the explanation would take a while. Poles, Germans, war, minorities, majorities, refugees resettled in Germany. I didn't understand much, but some of it was very, very familiar.

The next time I went over, I asked Emil's grandfather about Danzig directly. He answered in a dry, businesslike way. He said he'd lived in Danzig in a half-timbered house with his parents and three sisters, each one naughtier than the last. His father had been a teacher, his mother a housewife.

Was anyone in the family a hunter?

No one was a hunter.

I waited for him to tell me more but he went off to polish his rifles.

Emil, Rahim, Olli, Martek. Now and then they'd ask me what I planned to do later. I asked them the same thing. The most fundamental thing you need at that age, whether you're a foreigner or whatever, is someone who likes spending time with you.

Dedo didn't ask that question. Dedo had no more easy questions. He was turned in on himself and seemed elsewhere even when he was in class. He wasn't like that with other things, though. What Dedo tried to do, he succeeded at doing. As soon as it went well, he gave it up and did something new. Then his parents divorced too, and he started taking drugs, and then it wasn't about succeeding, but about raising the stakes.

Rock climbing took over. He trained every day, climbed everything higher than a house in the area, from every side. It was clear to everyone who knew him that Dedo was dragging with him something from the past, something bigger and more important than the present. We knew about the tractor and the minefield. Maybe it was just that—having survived that.

When we heard that he was being threatened with deportation, we begged Dedo to go to the doctor. Any psychiatrist

Where You Come From

in the world would have recognized the trauma and Dedo wouldn't be sent back. Dedo said he didn't need any therapy. Always with something in his hand, fidgeting. The eternal jean jacket with the patches sewn on.

In 1999 he was deported to Bosnia. He's not on Facebook, I don't know where he is.

In the summer of 1995, he spent whole days at a time at a youth center near the school playing foosball. Day in, day out. Soon he was so good that it was no fun at all to play with him, or against him.

COMING FROM A PLACE
WHERE WATERS MEET

My history teacher, Mr. Gebhard, was and is a tall, gentle man from Lake Constance with a soft spot for revolutions. The French Revolution, the brave 1848'ers, the Chinese Revolution of 1911—he could talk about any overthrow so vividly, in such loving detail, and with such longing, that it seemed to me like he was telling stories he wanted (or absolutely didn't want) to be the protagonist of. With Danton and Robespierre, rolling the dice. I thought I'd return the favor, so I wrote stories in my history tests until he politely requested that I produce fewer pages and more facts.

In 2016, by which point he had retired, he got in touch with me. He had made an interesting discovery and would like to see me. We met for ravioli and apple-juice spritzers at Café Burkardt.

Mr. Gebhard told me about his father. My former history teacher's father was born in 1916, in Upper Swabia. He grew up poor and lost his mother at age nine. His stepmother was a cold but capable person; she got him an apprenticeship as a merchant's assistant in Tettnang and rarely hugged him.

In 1938 he entered the Reich Labor Service, then the military. He was in the army from the first shot. The army took him to Poland, then to France. In Russia he was wounded (not because he was on the front line but because the front line came to him at headquarters). He was sent to a military hospital in Germany; his comrades in the Sixth Army were sent to Stalingrad.

In 1943, he married Luise Schmelzer in Tettnang. Practically as soon as the wedding bells stopped ringing he had to go back into service, as an officer in the Forty-Fifth Pioneer Battalion, which was deployed to Yugoslavia in autumn 1943. He pushed *farther and farther into the mountains* and wrote tender letters from the field to his wife. (*Picture the little forest railroad, you take the little narrow-gauge train up for a whole day, not that high, past small towns half shot to pieces. Then the tracks stop suddenly because the bridges have been blown up. And there, in the middle of the Serbian mountains running from Belgrade to Sarajevo, I found my comrades.*)

He had found them in Višegrad, of all places. *The city is in ruins*, he wrote to his darling little Luise, *it has already changed hands all too many times and now it's once again under the command of the German soldier, who brings order wherever he goes.* He remained stationed there for several months. Repaired buildings, traveled in the Drina and Rzav valleys, dreamed his dreams *in a bed made of simple boards nailed together with a mattress in a nice neat room in a house that hasn't been damaged yet*, and in January 1944 my grandmother Kristina was a girl of twelve and my grandfather Pero, twenty, had joined the *Communist bands* roaming the mountains, not far from Višegrad. And if my great-grandmother Rumša happened one evening to pass by a nice neat room in a house that hadn't been damaged yet, she might have heard the radio *playing until the lights were turned out.* And if my history teacher's father happened to pass by what was left of Rumša's house at that point, he might have enjoyed her singing and an idea might have come to him: the idea of an evening revue in Višegrad.

Soon, *despite the fact that there were very few undamaged buildings in the little town, a place that seemed suitable for this plan was found: a horse stable, formerly used by bandits, with a good plank floor that was revealed after we got rid of the inches of manure. When Pioneers take charge of something, the result is always good and usable, and so soon there was a clean, well-arranged auditorium for the audience, with fir twigs and walls adorned with original drawings!*

My history teacher and I ordered another apple-juice spritzer each. As we sipped through our straws, we clutched at another straw: the possibility that our ancestors might have met each other. Maybe in the new revue hall, after *the gentlemen in charge took their places on the roughly carpentered benches and the band opened the performance by playing some spirited Schlager music.*

And maybe a local singer could put on a little singing number? Sometime before the main attraction: *"Erich," the clown and animal tamer, taking the stage and enthralling the crowd magnificently.*

Excursions around the region are also mentioned in the letters. The marches cost *not a few beads of sweat,* which reminded me of my grandmother's story about the sweating soldier in her village. The officer who always drank milk.

My dear wifey! A radiant Sunday morning is laughing through the window at me. The high mountain peaks are glittering white in the morning sun and the water of the Drina is flowing cheerfully down the valley. So far I have been leading a restful life here.

In the photographs, the young soldier is in places in Višegrad where I too have been at some point. The Drina is always there, unruffled, indisputable. A temporary boardwalk connects the white piers of the partly destroyed old bridge.

When the couple wanted to make sure that at least some people wouldn't be able to read what they were writing to each other, they used shorthand.

A thousand sweet heartfelt greetings go with these lines today, and a kiss for my dear wifey.

How wonderful to get a kiss from you now.

GRANDMOTHER AND
THE REMOTE CONTROL

Grandmother is trying to turn off the TV and she finds the volume control instead. Sandra Afrika thunders:

Nije tvoja briga moj život, moja igra,
dok za nekim ne poludim biću ničija.

My life is my affair, it's none of your business,
until someone drives me crazy I'll stay all alone.

Father takes the remote control out of her hand and turns down the volume. I think it's intrusive that he took it without asking, and I would have done the same thing if I'd been sitting closer. Grandmother seems happy to see Father and thanks him. "The buttons are so tiny."

Father hands her back the remote.

"When did you two get here?" Her gaze wanders from him to me. Father disappears into the bathroom; he doesn't want to be welcomed again. Grandmother turns to me and smiles. I sit next to her. Her nightgown is soft, white. She yawns. In front of the sofa is the eternal coffee table. One of Grandmother's eternal doilies, crocheted an eternity ago, with a plate of glass on top, and a glass of water on top of that.

I hand her the glass. She doesn't want it. Her hair is reddish, thin. With a hair comb in it, decorated with a little bird.

"When can I go home?"

"You are home, Grandma."

Grandmother runs her fingers over the glass edge of the coffee table. Stands up. Her embroidery and our photographs are on the walls. Grandmother strolls casually in front of them as if visiting an art gallery.

She sees me in Paris, I'm brushing my hair aside—an old picture, vain and peacocky, I picked it out specially for her. Because I hadn't grown a beard yet, and I knew Grandmother didn't like beards.

Next to that photo are her sons, my father and uncle, as schoolboys. Their teachers had made them look thoughtful and serious—they'd combed their hair.

She sees the sideboard, which holds receipts and jewelry and medicine and prescriptions for more medicine. She opens a drawer and closes it again.

She sees the stove and turns the temperature gauge.

She leans out the window and says: "No. I want to go home."

"Where is your home, Grandma?"

"In Višegrad, my little donkey."

"We're in Višegrad, Grandma."

"This isn't Višegrad."

I'm inclined to agree—for me, too, this Višegrad isn't my Višegrad. But she doesn't mean it in a metaphorical sense. She means: "Can you drive me there? I want to be in a room of things that belong to me."

"All this is yours, Grandma." I spread out my arms.

Grandmother doesn't even look. "I have nothing."

I go over to her and this time she takes the water glass I'm offering, but she doesn't drink any. She gestures out the window with the glass. "There's a house like that one there across from my apartment too."

"That is the house across from yours, Grandma."

"That's not the house."

"What hill is that? With the house on it?"

"That's Megdan, you donkey."

"And where's the house that you can see from your apartment?"

"On Megdan." Grandmother suddenly trills a little la-la-la, a child's tune.

"That's Megdan, Grandma. And this, right here, is your home," I say. Fictions occupy my home, I think.

Grandmother shakes her head. The next moment, she pours the water out the window. The splash bounces up from the yard. Grandmother holds out the glass to me.

"Get me some water, please, my son."

I'm Saša, I want to say, but I don't. I get my grandmother a glass of water.

I think that there's almost nothing worse than knowing where you belong and not being able to be there.

Father comes out of the bathroom. I suggest buying a new remote control, with bigger buttons. Father agrees and wants to leave right away, get out of here. Grandmother is standing at the window, with her back to us, in Višegrad, not in Višegrad.

My grandmother doesn't drink enough water.

DR. HEIMAT

When anyone asks me what *Heimat*—home, homeland, native country—means to me, I tell them the story of Dr. Heimat, DDS, the father of my first amalgam filling.

I met Dr. Heimat on a hot day in the autumn of 1992, in his yard in Emmertsgrund. I was level with his yard on the other side of the street when I heard someone calling, heard a greeting. It was an old man with a mustache, in Speedos, watering his lawn with a hose and waving at me.

Must one be skeptical when a senior citizen in Speedos says hello to one? I said hello back. He was looking for conversation over the fence, but didn't find much—my German was abysmal. But giving me a friendly greeting across the street was good enough for the time being.

Dr. Heimat's mustache was a thin little Clark Gable line, that breed of facial hair you so rarely find anymore, alas. At fifteen, I was a bit scared by the thin mustache but at the same time I trusted it—it matched my image of Germany.

The street on which his lawn looked so soft, his house so big, and his Saab so old in a good way, was the nicest street in Emmertsgrund, with the most alarm systems. Dr. Heimat didn't have a family, which I thought was too bad, given his good manners, mustache, and teeth.

He discussed my teeth with me the following spring. Up until then we had never exchanged more than a few words over the fence. He must have somehow seen the apocalypse in my mouth with X-ray vision through my cheeks. He suggested I come by his office. I could come by anytime, but he recommended: very soon.

I had no health insurance, but Dr. Heimat didn't care. He treated all our cavities—the Bosnian cavities, the Somalian cavities, the German cavities. An ideal *Heimat* cares about the cavities and not about what language the mouth speaks or how well.

I had to go several times. During my fourth or fifth visit, I told him a little about me and my family from the examination chair. Not because Dr. Heimat was curious. He was only unbelievably nice. I mangled some sentences about Mother, slaving away in the laundry. I said that as a Marxist she was actually kind of an expert in exploitation, and now she was being exploited.

Dr. Heimat smiled, stuck a horrible-looking implement into my mouth, and unburdened himself of the adage: "Karl Marx probably had bad teeth, but good ideas." He started scraping away at mine and said absentmindedly: "Workers have no fatherland."

At some point later I told him about my grandfather Muhamed, too. That I thought he was the least happy of any of us here in Germany, yet much too friendly and grateful to admit it. Dr. Heimat asked me if there was anything in particular my grandfather liked doing.

When anyone asks me what *Heimat* means to me, I tell them about a neighbor's friendly greeting from across the street, over a fence. I tell them how Dr. Heimat invited my grandfather and me to go fishing on the Neckar. How he got us fishing permits. How he brought sandwiches and juice as well as beer, because you never know. How we stood by the Neckar for hours, a dentist from Silesia, an old brakeman from Yugoslavia, and a seventeen-year-old schoolboy with no cavities, and how for a couple of hours none of us was afraid of anything in the world.

GETTING UP TO NO GOOD

We felt like getting up to no good. We went to the railroad yard—Piero, Martek, Dule, and me—and climbed into the freight cars. Their beautiful copper. Later we climbed a fence to get to the wastepaper dump. That's how getting up to no good usually starts: with a climbed fence. We lie down in the giant paper containers full of newspapers, magazines—left over, unsold, it'd be a real shame if no one read them, Piero shouts in Italian. Maybe that's what he shouts, we don't understand what Piero's saying, but he's right.

The most important things there are the music magazines, because when you're sixteen music says everything important. But there's more: sports magazines, bundles of the *Süddeutsche Zeitung* or *Der Spiegel*. I dig into a photography trade journal. I'm saving up for my first camera, and I read that digital cameras are coming soon but that they'll be a passing fad.

Heidelberg smells of printer's ink and Martek's hair gel (apple). Our fingertips get darker with every magazine, and Piero shouts: "Well I never!" Lying in the words and the pictures and the forbidden, looking up at the bright sky or, like Piero, down into the bright breasts of a sailoress on the cover of an illustrated magazine—it's like vacation, but a good kind, without parents, with friends.

Dule lights one up even though it's obvious that that's an idiotic thing to do in a giant container of paper. The smoke is soon not in our imagination, and it's like a movie the way we race out of there, flying over the fence in slow motion, and that's how getting up to no good usually ends, with dashing away over a fence, this time it's a happy ending, since the fire isn't anything serious, and the only one of us who remembers in the panic to bring a magazine with him is Piero, and we're pretty happy about that.

LETTING EACH OTHER FINISH

Rahim's parents are atheists and scholars from Franconia. They have four children and a spiral staircase.

I was never exactly clear on what Rahim's mother's specialty was. Maybe she wasn't a scholar at all. We never talked about it. She finished her sentences as if she'd known in advance how they should end.

Unlike her, Rahim's father often spoke about his job. He was a professor of Semitic studies and often traveled to regions where noteworthy dialects were whispering against their extinction. He brought them back as proseminars.

I spent a lot of time with Rahim and also saw his parents a lot. Now and then I'd stay for dinner. The way the dishes were served! The sauce on the plate like a lacy arabesque. Everything tasted like a Michelin-star chef had *conjured* it into being. It wouldn't have surprised me to see someone actually come out of the kitchen one day, bow humbly, and wish us bon appétit in Aramaic before disappearing in a cloud of saffron smoke.

I enjoyed the recklessness, occasional adventures, and camaraderie of the ARAL clique, and I enjoyed the comforting thematic organization of the bookshelves and the way everyone let each other finish talking and really listened in the spacious living room at Rahim's house.

One time, there were two guests over for dinner besides me: two vivacious lesbians, both named Andrea. Both were veterinarians in the Palatinate, one practicing, the other a researcher. I must have mumbled my answer to the question of where my accent came from, in any case Andrea the researcher thought I said "Boston" instead of "Bosnia" and laughed with extraordinary delight, as if I'd just given her a gift. She started telling the story of her lectureship at MIT and what a good time she'd had in Boston. She spoke English with a very English accent, which I recognized from a British wrestler, the British Bulldog. She did it even though she'd heard me speak German. Maybe she thought I'd feel more comfortable talking in my native language.

I let her talk, nodded when I understood something, and answered her questions honestly—what I was doing in Germany (*school*, I said in English), where I lived (*near the river*), when I was planning to go back (*soon I hope*)—in my best Bruce Willis accent, and she accepted the answers like they were perfect. It was magical.

The Semitic studies professor chuckled; Rahim helped himself to more bread dumplings. Every sentence from the sympathetic cattle expert made me feel somehow . . . more there. One misunderstanding had taken the burden of where I came from off my shoulders. It was so much easier to be an exchange student from Boston than a Bosnian with a temporary residence permit.

Have you ever been to a Celtics game?

Here I even ventured a counterquestion: *No, you?*

I sure have! she cried. *It was fantastic!* And then, when Rahim's mother came in with the salad, she unfortunately also brought a pause, and our host put his hand on Andrea's arm and quietly said, "Not Boston, Andrea. Bosnia."

"Oh!" the researcher said.

"Oh!" the practicing veterinarian specializing in industrial farming livestock said.

The delightful dishes were served onto plates amid the misunderstanding, and the role-play with the other self was over. Everyone laughed, of course; naturally Andrea apologized, I apologized. We toasted (Rahim and I with our glasses of iced tea), and Rahim's father—turning toward the veterinarians, and as though telling a joke more than asking a question— cried, "So, how's life in Kaiserslautern!"

Around fifteen years later, in 2010, I was at MIT myself. I was teaching German literature and creative writing. Living not far from the Charles River. When asked where I came from, I would sometimes say "Višegrad," sometimes "Europe," sometimes "Kurpfalz," the Electoral Palatinate. Kurpfalz went over best. When you're abroad and say "Kurpfalz," the person you're talking to is never quite sure whether it's a city or a speech impediment.

I said my parents were scholars. I said my grandfather was a hunter, resettled from Danzig. I said my mothers were lesbians. I said where you come from is an accident, again and again, even when not asked.

In the NBA Semifinals, the Celtics were playing against Orlando. I was there for the third game. My Celtics won big.

VISITORS

My first year in Germany I rarely had people over. I always came up with some excuse why it wouldn't work out just then. In the place where we were staying in Wiesloch, we slept six to a room. The house was full of strangers. They would pop up and disappear again—there was no point in introducing yourself, much less inviting a school friend into this industrial park hell.

In Emmertsgrund there was more room, but peace and quiet was still a matter of luck. In the afternoons, everyone was at home. My cheerful little cousins, ex-Yugos, would drop by unannounced the same way they would have in Yugoslavia—as a sign of a culture of good neighbors. But quite annoying if you had a math test the next day. I sometimes studied at the living room table, sometimes on the floor. At some point my father bought a table for the room I slept in. At least I wanted to believe it was bought.

Even now I tell myself that I had only good reasons for not wanting visitors over. There wasn't room and it was too loud, that was one thing, and my friends understood that. But did they also know I was ashamed? I was ashamed of the old furniture, of not owning any games, or a PC, or almost any music (I had a few albums copied onto cassettes: Metallica, Nirvana, Smashing Pumpkins). I was ashamed that we ate off nonmatching dishes, and rarely together. Using knives with bent blades.

I hated that feeling but couldn't do anything about it. Outside the house I had almost no trouble anymore with the roles I had chosen or which were imposed on me. At home it'd all come out. People would see *how we were really doing*.

Mother and Father toiled away unhappily. In 1994, Father spent a whole month in a rehab clinic—his back had gone out. The first day after he got out, he went right back to the construction site to keep doing the work that his back hadn't wanted to do anymore. He feels the effects to this day.

My parents didn't spare themselves but they spared me. They kept their most serious worries and problems from me, rarely talking about them. I've only recently started to understand their hardships and defeats. What it really means to leave a settled life in your midthirties and have to fight with the landlord over whether we were allowed to plant tomatoes in the garden.

They'd both had to give up careers they enjoyed and were good at. In Germany they would have taken pretty much any job to survive. That's how it was everywhere in our circle of Yugoslavian friends. Employers knew how to take advantage of desperation too. Wages were low, overtime largely involuntary and unpaid. Was it discrimination? My parents couldn't say. Was it miserable? That's for sure.

There was rarely enough money coming in for extra training or further education. And for the fundamental thing—language courses—there was not much time or energy. Still, there were not a few people who would spend another two hours after work with blisters on their feet vacuuming up German verb forms. Even then it often wasn't enough to break out of dependency, or else it came too late—deportation came too soon.

Looking at my own successful case, I can see how wide-spread the structural disadvantages were that refugees faced then and face now. But my own refugee status removed the practical hurdles. I was given an education and I could work while in school. The more opportunities I was able to take advantage of, the harder it became to push me aside or make me a victim. I never had to feel the existential pressure my parents were exposed to.

I can't say whether or not it was good not to know at the time what was worrying and tormenting them. Or to put it another way, whether it was good that I assumed they were in a better position than they really were, in terms of their fears, and our finances, and, ultimately, happiness in this German life. I knew some of it, but didn't really want to believe it. I spent as much time as I could outside the house. And I was not often there for them.

I wanted space, and freedom, and my parents let me have it. With their encouragement and affection and a little pocket money, they increased my chances of having a more or less normal teenage life, despite all the hurdles of an immigrant's existence.

Things changed a bit with Rieke. Rieke was my first girl-friend and my first German visitor. She came and went freely, candid, well raised, bothered by absolutely nothing that I had assumed, reflecting my own prejudices, a German would necessarily be bothered by. She asked me if we didn't hang pictures on the wall because we thought art was dumb, and I must have looked at her like she was crazy. She laughed and said it was a joke. I was constantly underestimating everyone.

Rieke and Mother got along well. She helped Granny in the garden. Grandfather took Rieke's hand in his, hundreds of times, and held it, smiling, as though this hand was the most precious gift. Rieke ate from the colorful mismatched plates and taped records for me.

At some point, Father got me a little boom box with a CD player at Media Market (or was that from the trash too?), and I bought my first CD, a CD single by Bob Marley, since Rieke liked reggae (I, unfortunately, didn't like it so much). Rieke didn't like to eat meat (I, unfortunately, did), so at some point I became a vegetarian. Mother probably wanted to strangle me with a scallion over that.

Rieke is sitting with Mother on the floor of the living room watching *The X-Files*, I am studying on the patio, and Granny comes into the living room holding a tuft of hair in her fist. Could she throw it away? Saša's brush was always so full of hair, she wasn't sure, was he maybe collecting it?

Mother clears her throat. Rieke asks what's going on and Mother translates. The two of them discuss it in German, which Granny understands not a word of, then Mother says: "Yeah, leave it for him. Saša's using it for voodoo."

From then on Granny would lock the door when she went to sleep. She stared at me strangely and made mysterious gestures. Cast the beans for herself. I had no idea what was going on.

Weeks later, at breakfast, she blurted out: "Why do you want to do magic? What are you missing?"

Mother burst out laughing and cleared everything up. Granny muttered some curses. Rieke hugged her.

I wasn't missing much. Some language. Some courage. I decided to work up the courage to invite someone over *for my parents*. Rahim's parents seemed like the best candidates. I wanted to wait for their answer before telling Mother and Father about it. They would be happy and say yes, I was sure of it.

I had never felt uncomfortable at Rahim's or with his parents, in their life that gave off the scent of curiosity from a hundred books, of successful time management from extended mealtimes. Every member of the family had their own room. Rahim's father had a study, too, in the basement, along with a collection of Syrian cooking utensils, or weapons, who knows.

At the end of the day, husband and wife told each other at length about the beginning of the day and the middle of the day, and listened too. I found it immensely therapeutic, this listening to each other at the end of the day, even as a complete outsider who happened to be there as though he weren't— there at a conversation that belonged to just the two of them.

In general, they treated me with a lack of demands that I found exceptionally comforting. They rarely asked me anything that went beyond the worlds I shared with their son (school and sports). That was honest, and right. I was a friend of their son's, a guest.

One time, we talked about dealing with small children. They had raised four children, and I was saying I found my two little cousins a burden. I don't remember what they said; I remember that the two of them sat across from me, one leg crossed over the other, wine in their glasses, and that they seemed to be seriously considering how they should respond. Basically that's enough to make something a good conversation—that someone thinks seriously about how they should respond to you.

After they found out that I had fled the Bosnian War, they neither told a story about vacationing in Croatia in the eighties on the island of What-was-it-called-again nor launched into a discourse about the mentality of "the Serbians." Rahim's father said: "I'm sorry you had to go through that, Saša. I'll be happy to read up on it and we can talk about the conflict more the next time you come over. If you want to?" Or something like that. I didn't want to. Much later, when I had more language under my belt, we did discuss it after all. Legs crossed, glasses of wine and iced tea in hand.

A good host is also a good guest, as a Bosnian proverb says. Rahim's parents were good hosts, and I thought a million times about whether it would work to have them over as guests. How my parents and grandparents would feel; how I would feel. I wanted us to do something as a family that went well, even something as simple as having dinner with new acquaintances.

I especially wanted it for my mother, who had so liked hosting people in Yugoslavia, much more than she'd liked being a guest. When she was a guest she went straight to the kitchen after arriving, to help; she offered other guests drinks; it was touching. With her own guests she was so effusive that you got the impression she was about to write them into her will.

How would Rahim's parents react to her friendliness? Or to our life without saffron, without the curtains it was hardly worth buying since we expected to be deported at any moment?

I hoped that they would be as nonjudgmental at our home as they were at the dinner with their lesbian friends from the

Palatinate. My parents would be excited; they would be happy. We would ask each other questions (until the food was served), thoughtful, friendly, legs crossed. "What did you plant there in the garden?" Wouldn't that be a wonderful question to ask a refugee in Germany!

Then we'd eat and discuss the ingredients. Our guests would not immediately trot out their ideas about Balkan cooking. They (or their Michelin-star cook) served a wide range of international cuisine; for them, Balkan cooking would be neither unusual nor suspect. Definitely. My parents would tell them that kidney beans were the only thing I didn't eat. Even though they were the basic staple of our cuisine. When they said goodbye, Rahim's parents would thank us for the lovely evening, and that would be the absolute best: for someone to thank us for something nice.

The next time I had dinner at their place—something made of just three ingredients, none of which I recognized, and it was Franconian, not Middle Eastern food—I uttered the invitation: Do you want to come over to our place too sometime?

They both put their silverware down on their plates and dabbed their lips with their napkins. Rahim's mother said that that would be lovely, and his father also thanked me and said, Really lovely, we'd be delighted. They said it in a friendly way, and a little surprised, too, and a week later I was back over there and this cuckoo clock was on the wall of their dining room. The bird came out at seven and gave us all a hearty greeting.

At a minute past seven, the split-pea stew was on the table. The meat was extremely tender, from cattle from the Palatinate. I learned a new vocabulary word: "free-range." There was the cuckoo clock, and there was an orchestra—playing from a tape, maybe, but maybe from inside the wall: Haydn or Mozart. At the time I would have given a lot to be able to recognize the difference and say something about music.

I didn't tell my parents about the dinner invitation, and I didn't have the courage to mention it to Rahim's parents again. Obviously they didn't remind me of it.

"Free-range," the professor of Semitic studies had said on the evening with the split-pea stew, "up to the fence." Everyone chuckled.

My best friend's family never visited my house and my family were never guests at his. Our parents never met. The cuckoo clock came from this place in the Black Forest, I forget the name.

THAT'S JUST WORDS (VISITORS, 1987)

We had visitors coming and going constantly. What'll we play tonight? Drinks and dice are at the ready, notebooks and pencils. Kosta is over, Berec too—the former a passing acquaintance of my father's, the latter a good friend. Kosta chain-smokes, Berec chain-smokes. Berec has a mustache with blond tips and a glass eye. He shuts the other one when the smoke bothers him. Father and Mother smoke too. This Saturday evening in November of 1987 smokes.

I am sitting behind Mother on the sofa. The back of her neck smells good, even through the cigarette smoke. The dice clatter brightly, and my father says: "Genocide against the Serbian people?" and Berec says, "That's just words," and Kosta says, "High time for someone to say them," and Father says, "You're nuts," and Mother says, "*Alea iacta est*" and rolls a Small Straight. What did Mother's neck smell of?

A year later, Kosta storms with the Serbian White Eagles into the building where we're hiding in the cellar. Then and there he is transformed into literary fiction. Camouflage on his cheeks. How calmly he says he's hungry, while the children whimper around him. "I'm hungry, what's going on?"

Berec is a Serb like Kosta. He is not drafted, because of the glass eye; he enlists by choice with an outfit that accepts glass eyes. He's stationed in Varda, and then Varda is largely shut down, and Berec is first unemployed, then a fishery foreman.

189

The long inspection rounds up and down the riverbanks. In the afternoon shadows of a plane tree, sheltered from the wind by a cliff, on the grass, on the dirt, on concrete: Berec rests during work. Berec peers around with his one eye and smokes. And if he ever catches you, for instance, fishing for Danube salmon beneath the reservoir dam, and if he says, "You know there's no fishing here, Dušan," you'll say, as Dušan, "Berec, how's it going, sit down and have a smoke with me." With a little luck and half the fine, or a fish, that smoke will have been a peace pipe and Berec will turn a blind eye with the one that isn't and move on.

A few days before we left Višegrad, Kosta came biking toward me on the bridge. You're supposed to move aside for people on the bridge, but he stopped in such a way that I couldn't easily get around him. He gave a friendly smile and tried to ruffle my hair; I ducked. The camouflage on his face had peeled off and was hanging in flakes of green and black from his cheeks. He asked how I was doing. How my parents were. I didn't know what I should say, so I said good, good, and Kosta said good, good.

I saw him only once after the war, in 1998, again on a bicycle. He was riding slowly along the Drina, as if he owned not only the right to interpret history his way but the river itself. Berec steered into shore in front of him. Kosta approached. They talked. It looked like they would both just nod at everything the other one was saying, or else wave it off. There was nothing between them that looked like Maybe. They each smoked a cigarette and went their separate ways.

I don't know what Kosta is up to today. No one I ask says they knew him too well.

Berec is still smoking in Višegrad, his mustache still blond. He speaks softly and asks no questions. Every evening he goes for a walk, stops here and there, chats. He knows lots of people in the city, lots of people know him.

Father and I ran into him in April 2018. I turned the conversation toward the game nights from the old days. I asked if they missed them.

"Yeah, let's organize another one," Father cried at once, "as long as we're here."

Berec took a puff and tipped the ashes onto the sidewalk. "Not with me," he said seriously and softly. "I can't win here anymore."

Father and I cleared our throats.

Berec smiled and looked past us and said: "That's just words."

GRANDMOTHER AND
GET OUT OF HERE

She wakes up. Where is she? The sheets feel damp. Wallpaper. Probably a bedroom. Her feet feel hot. Slippers on. She pushes them off. Carpet. Ugly, ugly carpet, she has the same one at home but it's much nicer. Bookshelf. Brown and white, gilded spines. Books. Tito's biography. Then Meša Selimović, Abdulah Sidran, Saša Stanišić, and *Healing with Tea*. Ach, books.

Confusing dreams, confusing, confusing. There was a soldier. A girl. A man who loves her. A gravedigger. All mixed together. Dreams are something alive—and as such fleeting, like the mind. Where did that come from?

Doilies everywhere. On the radio, on the nightstand, on the coffee table. Nice, nice. It's been a long time since she's crocheted. At some point the eyes just wouldn't play along.

What if whoever's apartment this is comes back? She buttons the top button of her blouse. What is she wearing, anyway? It looks like her own nightgown.

She carefully opens the door. Now she hears something like singing. A kitchen with three doors. Behind the first is the stairwell. Behind the second, the bathroom. She needs to go. Behind the third, the singing. She opens the door. A living room. It's like she's been here before. The TV set is singing. A sofa, under a pink blanket, like it's cold.

192

The woman on TV isn't singing very well. They always have to sing and wear high heels. Bad for the hips. How do you turn that thing off? Ach. Take care of the cord, problem solved.

The best thing would be to just go home. She just has to change first. The clothes in the closet fit. Pack a few things. She knows there's a suitcase somewhere, here it is.

Home, the best thing. Yes. Money might be a problem. She opens a few drawers, doesn't find anything. But there's a little box with nice jewelry in it. She takes it.

Get out of here. Wait. Almost forgot the comb.

Back home, yes. The key fits. Outside the name on the doorbell is *Kristina Stanišić*.

But that's me, she thinks, going down the stairs. This suitcase sure is heavy. Everything's hard when you're disoriented. She wants to turn on the light in the stairwell, but there is no light. What day is it today? Doesn't matter. The important thing is that it's not yesterday again.

Catching her breath in the yard. The fresh air feels good. Where to now? Everything's right and wrong, everything's possible. She closes her eyes and spins on her axis. Once, twice. She laughs, You child! Opens her eyes again. There is a building. She recognizes the grayish-yellow façade. She lives in that building! She wants to turn on the light in the stairwell, but there is no light.

On the fourth floor her name is on the door. The door's open. She goes in. Puts the suitcase down. Time to unpack, in a minute. First, a coffee.

LAMBS

On May 1, 1990, we grilled a lamb in a forest clearing at the Višegrad health spa. The lamb's mouth was wide open in a faded scream. Teeth sticking out of the jaw at all angles. Its skin glowed and bubbled. It gave me the creeps, so I laughed. Father suggested I scrape the fat off the skin with bread. I did. I ate the bread. It got stuck in my throat. Here, wash it down. Father handed me a bottle of beer. Was he serious?

I kicked the ball into the fire. Kind of on purpose. Father got it out and said that's a nice big potato. No one was mad at the ball or me.

Lamb, bread, salad.

Grandmother Kristina was sitting between her sons. She'd had her hair done—the all-powerful roller curls, a shining red in the forest green. Someone shouted: How untalented this family is! No one can play an instrument! We hummed The Internationale. I decided to learn guitar.

We played hide-and-seek, the grown-ups too. I ran into the forest until I couldn't hear anything except the forest and myself. I sat down on a tree trunk. No one in the whole world knew exactly where I was. I scratched around in the moss. And since no one found me, it got a bit boring.

On my way back I found Mother and my uncle's wife behind a rock. They were giggling over a wine bottle. I eavesdropped unseen. I don't remember anymore what they were talking about. I hope I thought it was all harmless and nice. Two years later dozens of Muslim women would be taken to the Višegrad health spa, raped, and killed.

Višegrad is hardly a happy, carefree place for me anymore. Hardly any memory is just personal; almost every one comes with a postscript, a footnote, of perpetrators and victims and atrocities that took place there. What I once felt has had what I now know about the place mixed into it. I know court decisions about the events in the area during the war. I've read about the pain that was scratched into the walls with the fingernails of the women held here in the spa hotel.

There are no stories I can tell of my childhood except dissonant ones. A ball in the fire isn't just a ball in the fire. People hid in the woods and it wasn't only a game. I chose these motifs on purpose.

My mother feels and processes this dissonance more intensely. She's a different person in Višegrad. Jumpier, moodier, never silly. Mother sleeps badly in Višegrad; Mother doesn't giggle in Višegrad anymore.

I don't need to explain to anyone why I'm no longer where I come from. But I feel like I keep on doing exactly that. Almost apologetically, too. Explaining to myself too. I feel like I owe some kind of debt, because of the history of this city, Višegrad, and the happiness of my childhood there, and like I'm trying to repay it with stories. I feel like my stories are about this city even when I'm not trying to write about it.

On May 1, 1994, Father parked his company's VW bus in front of our Emmertsgrund bungalow. In it was a lamb on a spit. The mouth, the crooked teeth. The plan was to go to the grilling shack. I said, "I'm not coming, I need to go."

I ran into Martek at the ARAL station. Martek was sitting on the curb playing his Game Boy.

I said, "My family's grilling a lamb."

Martek looked up from his device and touched his hair, which was gelled up in a stiff rectangle. His skull looked like a Roman castle, with Martek constantly plucking at the stockades to make adjustments. Martek said, "That's cool."

"In the grilling shack," I said.

"Cool," Martek said. "I'm hungry." He put away his Game Boy and stood up.

It was strange. I had revealed to him something I was ashamed of. Eating preferences, constriction, hardships, bulk trash sofas—I didn't mention any of that. I just didn't want to grill an animal on a spit! And most of all, I didn't want other people to know that my family did such things. That's exactly what the Germans expected of us: that we grill lambs and commit nasty fouls in basketball and sleep with brass knuckles under our pillows.

"Well I'm not going," I said.

"Well then I'll go without you," Martek said.

The animal was roasted by the time we got to the grilling shack. Martek saw the spit, the picnic table with the generous salads, rice, and potatoes, my uncle on a tiny stool with a tape player between his legs turning the spit, Herbert Grönemeyer was belting out some song or another, and Martek touched his hair.

Granny Mejrema looked up from her knitting and waved. Martek saw Grandfather Muhamed, who now said "Hello" and would later say "Thank you." Martek touched his hair. Martek saw the sword and the wreath in old ink on my father's forearm when Father shook his hand. He saw sweat suits and T-shirts from C&A with pictures of things on them. Granny was wearing one with a surfboard and the words *California Dreaming Waves Diamond* on it, with a long, colorful dress.

Father introduced himself. Mother offered us drinks from a tray. Grandfather took a Fanta, Uncle a Campari Orange, Father a beer. Martek and I looked at each other. I reached for a Fanta; Martek had misinterpreted my look and took a beer.

Father said, "You don't want one too?" Meaning me. My parents didn't know I drank alcohol, I thought. There were so many things we didn't talk about. Almost always because of me.

I drank my first beer with my father, with my good friend Martek, with lamb, and with Herbert Grönemeyer.

Everyone spoke German because of Martek. Hello and thank you. Grandfather smiled. Father and Martek talked about cars. That was simple enough and interesting to both of them. Father liked to look at the used car ads in the paper on weekends and didn't buy any; Martek was just getting his driver's license. Father would name a brand ("Opel Astra"), Martek would blurt out a critical comment ("It's shit"), and Father would finish with his two cents ("But cheap, Opel Astra"). "Mercedes!" Father said, eyes shining, and Martek had no choice but to just cry "Mercedes!" too. They clinked bottles.

I was proud of Father, I had no idea why.

Martek touched his hair and ate his second bowl of *lukmira* (scallion yogurt). Later I gave him a suggestion: "Scrape up the fat from the meat with your bread. Like you mean it. Your bread can't be dry." Martek did it. Then he did it again.

ARAL LITERATURE

I knew Yugos who fit the Balkan cliches (a bit aggro, a bit antisocial, with a bit of a chip on their shoulder). They confused belligerence with confidence, insults with free speech. Carried with them the sewn-on symbols of the old days. They were Croatians and wanted everyone to know it. And the first time we met, they sorted out what I was: not-Serbian. Further details held no interest for them, they left me in peace, and I avoided them. These types came to the ARAL station just to get gas. None of the Yugos in the ARAL crew overestimated the value of where you came from. There was a joke here and there. If Zoki had tried to make us all put our names on a list here, Adil would have forced him to eat it, with the pen too.

Adil with the scar running across his cheek like a second mouth. Dule, the nerd, with his speed-demon sister, Ines. Sometimes Dedo would come around too, to spend a while saying almost nothing before leaving again. The ARAL Yugos were generally considered clever, nimble-fingered, and a bit lazy. A car topos was established very early. One of the legends was that Dule could fix absolutely any car in no time flat. Another, that Adil could break into any car in no time flat. A third, that Ines could drive across the Bierhelderhof in any car faster than you could in yours.

None of these was true, but it's not the worst thing in the world to be the hero of a legend, so no one corrected them. I was the exception—it was clear to everyone that I didn't even really understand how a car was able to move.

We would have been friends in any life. Our parents knew one another; we celebrated birthdays together; today, we have each other's current email addresses (except Adil's doesn't work, I just tried it).

I didn't want any contact with Yugos from milieus I found uncomfortable, not in Emmertsgrund and not in school contexts either. I avoided them, offered no help unasked, and preferred to see the ARALs for hanging around or the Germans for studying with. I observed the social differences that fleeing the country didn't erase; I considered myself better. It was downright shabby how opportunistically I parceled out my affection while in the same breath criticizing the unequal treatment we all received equally as refugees in Germany.

The legend common to everyone who watched the sun go down over France from the ARAL parking lot—whether from the Balkans, from Silesia, whether a Turk from Leimen or Michel from Holland—was that we liked to tell stories. Young people with no smartphones gathered under the blue neon flame waiting to hear the next story. All it had to be was excellent. Whoever told it had to be part of it. And an unbelievable amount of spitting went on during it.

ARAL Literature is a teeny bit exaggerated but otherwise definitely realist. The hero's motivation: proving yourself or proving something to someone else. Getting up to some mischief to pick up a little extra money. Barely escaping. Winning without deserving to. School, training, parties. Bets, misde-meanors, traffic incidents. There were no tragic heros—after all, the hero was still there to tell the tale. Defeats galore, though, including tragic ones.

First-person narration with little in-depth examination of the inner world of the narrator. Elliptical, pointed, no digres-sions. In German sprinkled with the mother tongue, which was really nice. I would have loved to be able to tell stories like that, but never managed it nearly as well as Ines or Army-Wojtek.

Or Please-not-with-the-feet-Krzysztof, who stole Fatih's chrome tire rims. Before long, everyone knew that it was him. Even Fatih knew that it was Krzysztof, his neighbor!, who'd stolen his tire rims. But everyone kept their trap shut, including Fatih, and Krzysztof just couldn't stand it: the fact that everyone knew what he'd done, and everyone knew that he knew that everyone knew, but that no one said anything.

Eventually the universal unspoken knowledge wore Krzysz-tof down so much that he gave Fatih the tire rims back. And not in secret or anything, he just rang the doorbell and had the things with him. Fatih, the kickboxer, was super-friendly and thanked him effusively and asked Krzysztof if he had a minute. He walked with Krzysztof a little ways, asked after Krzysztof's family and so forth, and then stopped and said, "But now I need to hurt you a little, *lan*, you can't pull that kind of shit with neighbors."

Krzysztof totally understood, of course. Stood there, legs in a wide stance, and said one thing, quietly: "But Fatih. Please, not with the feet."

And Ines bolts out of the bus to avoid the ticket inspectors, sprints into the train station with the inspectors hot on her heels, leaps into an express train as the doors are closing, falls right into the conductor's arms, and says sorry, old man, didn't have time to buy a ticket.

"And what is your destination?"

"Yeah, where's this train going?"

She laughs, he does too, it's almost romantic, there on the line to Bensheim, but she has to pay anyway.

She gets out in Bensheim, waits almost an hour for the train back, misses her appointment.

"Where were you going, Ines?"

"Open call at Rhine-Neckar Public Transit. They're hiring ticket inspectors."

DIDJA HEAR HOW WOJTEK ARMY-CRAWLED UP TO EMMERTSGRUND?

From Rohrbach South to the last stop of the 31? It went down around midnight, he was holding a stick in both hands about the length of a rifle, then off through the vineyards—all to prove he could still do it a year after his stint in the army. And fuck me if it wasn't really impressive. It was. Honest!

We went with him, at a snail's pace—Krzysztof and Fatih (they're friends again), Dule and Ines, Piero, two bags of Elephant beers, and the new moon. What Fatih had said before it started still ringing in our ears: "Yeah, but will you be able to do it in your underpants?"

The climb took two hours. What a crazy awesome stroll through the vineyard! The mild night! The silent sky! Taking time for a pleasant saunter like that at our age!

Piero was the most talkative. He'd had to read Hermann Hesse during the week for an ambitious German teacher at the trade school. He said: He liked it. *Steppenwolf.* "From start to finish," Piero cried. "In three days!"

I asked him what made him think of that just now.

Because the book was like Wojtek's army-crawl: exhausting but cool!

It was the first grown-up book that Piero, age seventeen, had ever read. He was excited. He was thrilled. Happy to be alive.

He asked, "Do you know any others like that?"

"Piero, buddy, what? Whaddaya mean?"

"So . . . knowing? There were things about me in that book, things I didn't even know. Like how I'm totally different at home than I am with you guys. You can't always be just a boring guy, you're also, like . . . a wolf."

What did I reply? Probably told him a couple of things I'd liked reading. Maybe not in German yet. Kafka, Brecht, Fallada. The main thing was I liked that someone in the crew thought I was an expert in something, even if it was just books.

Piero cried out, to no one in particular: "Everyone has their own fate, and none is an easy one, right?"

Anyway, Wojtek pulled it off. He got to the top dead beat but of course didn't show it at first; instead he yodeled into the starry sky, for some reason. That went off well too, it sounded good, you had to admit it, especially when you think he'd probably never practiced that.

"Let's just relax for a bit," he said, letting himself sink into the grass. "And if I fall asleep," he sighed, "don't forget me."

"Just like that!" Piero cried. "He's just like that!"

"Who is, Piero?"

"Hesse, man! He lies around the house and he kind of doesn't want me to forget him. And I can't! It's right here, right here!" Piero knocked on his forehead. He blabbed for a bit and then the world was quiet. A writer could have heard our hearts beating.

Now, twenty-five years later, I crack open one last beer in the night with Piero and Wojtek and all the rest. I have us drink to the big Silesian with the scraped knees and the little Italian who got through Hermann Hesse.

"Friends!" I have Saša cry. "To Wojtek! To joy! To experience, to ecstasy, to elevation!" And we drink.

And no one that night is forgotten.

DIPLOMACY, 1994

A grilling shack in Emmertsgrund. By accident, two groups are there at the same time. The other group is eight young men from Bammental—a bachelor party in the field with the net-less soccer goals. Pork neck on the grill; cooking aprons with tits printed on them. Imperative announcements from the buddies, getting louder and louder over time. All their T-shirts have your name on it: Sven.

Sven's Boys
Bye-bye Freedom!

On the other side: us. Ines drove her Golf onto the grass, and the trunk is open with an Argentine tango or Dr. Alban turned up full blast. Giant campfire. Women are with us and the better soccer players. We didn't care about the shack itself, and without alcohol I'm sure nothing would have happened, no one would have shouted that we should piss off, I would think of the comment "This is a German forest, assholes" as an effort to bring Joseph von Eichendorff into the present, and we probably would have just mingled playing soccer when everything was still peaceful.

When the comment came, Wojtek said at once: "All right then" and hiked up his pants. He marched over to the bachelors with the others behind him: our Silesian army boys, plus Fatih, who smelled nervousness and loved it, and Rahim, who smelled an argument and loved it. I hung back; I always hung back during scenes like this.

When they got to the other side, there was diplomacy. Listening, hearing out. Hands on shoulders. Looking in eyes. No one laughed, which was a good sign. Laughing is tricky in delicate situations—psychiatrists might have a different opinion about that but they're wrong. Laughing is tricky when people are deciding whether something's going to go down or not.

After ten minutes or so, our delegation came back. Wojtek turned down the music. "Listen, people," he said, and we listened, but he didn't say anything else. Didn't have to. We finished our drinks, put out the fire, packed up, and drove to the ARAL station.

I hope your marriage is strong and that it's made you both happy, Sven.

PIERO, FROM LUCERA IN APULIA

And then Piero crashed his motorbike. Not long after his eighteenth birthday. It was a truck. The driver didn't see him and made a turn, or Piero overestimated himself and slipped, doesn't matter. Piero was on his way to the ARAL station, that's what counts. We knew he was planning to come, didn't think twice when he didn't come, didn't wait for him.

The following day everyone's answering machines said: Piero got wiped out. Meeting at ARAL. Everyone brought something—cigarettes and a lighter, a Discman and CDs, a porn magazine. Everything you need in a hospital. I brought a book, poems by Gottfried Benn.

The ARAL crew headed off for the multi-bed room as a group. There he lay in a cast. "Mummy, *kurva*." Where you could see any skin, it was blue. Blink once for Yes, twice for No, three times for Fuck you.

Piero was a good fixer-upper, a bad student. A heavy metal guy who learned precision mechanics. None of the ARAL boys had long hair except Piero and me, and somehow it had been easier for me to have long hair because he had it first.

For a while we'd played *UFO: Enemy Unknown* on his computer almost every day after school. Aliens were landing on Earth and they weren't in the mood to talk. We ate cheese with the games, no bread. Piero's parents were overworked and

SAŠA STANIŠIĆ

invisible. When they did talk, it was in Italian, obviously. To me too. I thought that was great. I learned a few words of Italian and forgot them again over the years.

We stayed in the hospital room for an hour. I took the book back with me—Piero was so battered, how could he read? He had to piss through a tube for weeks. But then it was okay and Piero could piss normally again.

I rarely saw him over the summer. That was when Piero would drive to Italy with his family. Would go home, his father said. Would go to Apulia, Piero said. Nine months after his accident, Piero took the same route on his motorcycle. He decided to buy a candy bar at a rest stop in South Tyrol and married the attendant's daughter the next year. Makes sense when you think about it, for someone from ARAL.

The wedding was in Schwetzingen. The South Tyrol rest-stop attendant's daughter's name was Anna. She and Piero dropped by the ARAL station once. She was nice, pretty, and of course there were two or three jokes from our side about gas stations.

There was a second, bigger wedding ceremony in Lucera, the birthplace of everyone in Piero's family for the past three hundred years. And a third one near Merano, where Anna was from.

Piero's grandmother lives on Via Mazzini. It's a sixteen-minute walk from her apartment to the Castle of Lucera, but she has never once been to the Castle of Lucera. What's she supposed to do at a ruined fortress?

Frederick II was crowned Holy Roman Emperor in 1220. During his reign, he decided to take under his wing the Saracen (Muslim) rebels of Sicily who at some point had settled

208

in the area around Lucera in Apulia. He founded a new city of Lucera next to the old one, a fortification built on the rubble of a fortress of the Normans who had settled there before. Barracks and military training grounds were added, mosques and numerous craftsmen's workshops. The emperor granted the Saracens in Lucera wide-ranging autonomy and freedom to practice their own religion.

As a result industry flourished, Arabian horses and camels grazed on the meadows outside the city, falcons and leopards were trained for the hunt. The Saracens repaid the emperor's generosity with manpower and military technology. Their warriors were superbly trained, their archers on horseback widely respected and feared. Frederick II's bodyguard at one point consisted mostly of loyal and capable Saracens; the light cavalry rained down poison arrows on his foes. For a short time, Christians and Muslims lived peacefully alongside one another in Lucera. But of course none of that was in harmony with the desires of the pope. He withdrew his support from the Hohenstaufen emperor, that *godless heathen, the Beast of Revelation.*

In 1246, Frederick II wrote to his son-in-law Vatatzes: *O happy Asia! O you happy rulers of the Orient, who need not fear the weapons of your subjects or worry about the contrivances of your bishops and clergy.* By that point, *Satan's son and pupil, the ambassador of the Devil*, had already been deposed.

In 1300, under pressure from the pope, King Charles II of Anjou destroyed Lucera. A majority of the local Saracens did not escape with their lives.

THE KEY PLAYS OF THE GAME

In 1994, Father came for the first time to watch one of my basketball games. I made only three of my seven free throws. Three rebounds, none of them offensive. I finished with a measly eight points. We barely won.

Father waited for me outside after the game. When I got there, three other men were talking and Father was smoking off to the side. I noticed that. Of course I noticed it.

On the way home, Father went over the key plays of the game with me. He wanted to discuss a bad pass right before the end of the first half: too risky on offense. About the three-point shot I'd surprisingly made, heaving it up from my waist, he laughed. But: I shouldn't make a habit of that.

Why hadn't I invited him to come to any games before? He would have loved to come. I admitted that it didn't feel quite right to me. I said that with him in the stands I'd be less focused. The truth was, I didn't want him to shout encouraging words in Serbo-Croatian, the way he'd done today after I missed an easy layup. And I also didn't want him to see me miss easy layups. Then, during the game, neither had actually bothered me. I was annoyed at my mistakes on my own. My mother tongue wasn't embarrassing anymore.

Father asked who the next game was against.

Ladenburg, an away-game, I said. On Saturday.

Father didn't come. We lost in a total rout.

My tenth-grade German teacher caught me not paying attention. I was writing poems while he was talking about poems.
He told me: Go ahead and write, just not in class. And: Write
them in German! He'd help.

We set up a time to meet during lunch, sat next to a skeleton in a biology classroom, and talked about metaphors. He
was my first reader, but also the first person in Germany who
thought that something I did was good. Who set aside time
for me.

I started by translating from Serbo-Croatian, then, with
his encouragement, I wrote my first poems directly in German.
He suggested having the class interpret one of the poems. I
should pick a pseudonym. I thought about it for days. We were
covering poems by Hilde Domin and Rose Ausländer. Refugees, loss of homeland, my poem fit well. I eagerly raised my
hand for every question, trying to improve my oral grade. My
pseudonym was: Stan Bosni.

And that's where the anecdote ends. I've told it in this form
a hundred times, and the listeners always chuckle. I didn't actually raise my hand. I listened more closely than I ever had
before. I heard my class, my friends, talk about a poem, and the
poem was mine.

That day on the way home, on Ortenauer Street, I had an
idea for a story. I had to write it up at once, so I sat down on the
curb with the paper on the knapsack on my knees. A few weeks
later I showed the story to my German teacher. We talked about
dialogue and allegory, across from a shelf holding a kidney, a

heart, and a brain in some order I couldn't figure out. Maybe they weren't in any particular order.

In the story, Father has come for the first time to watch one of my basketball games.

Mother and Father at my graduation party. I was playing guitar in a little band formed of people in my grade especially for the party. We were playing country music. Mother cried a little. She'd been very sick that day but had, of course, come anyway.

Maybe Mother was crying because she was seeing me in a public context for the first time—not at home, not among Yugos. Maybe she was crying because I was feeling confident enough to do something and I could do it and get applause for it too. Or because I was wearing a suit for the first time. Or maybe just because she was sad that all this had any meaning and weight at all in our life, where so little could be taken for granted.

There were four of us sitting at a round table: my parents, Rieke, and me. There were three courses. Olli joined us after dessert and I introduced him to my parents.

I talked with Dedo, insofar as one could. I talked, he hemmed and hawed and fell silent. It was our last conversation, although neither of us knew it at the time.

I talked with Emil. Emil wanted to do civilian service in an old-age home instead of his military service.

I said: Are you joking?

He said: Yeah.

I asked how his grandfather was doing.

He said: Yeah.

I talked with Rahim. He was planning to major in Slavic studies, learn Russian, and travel to Russia. Learn Polish and travel to Poland. We daydreamed for a minute about a book we'd write together about all the trips we were looking forward to taking.

At some point my parents left and I didn't notice. They didn't want to bother me, they said the next morning. Six months later, the Germany chapter of their lives was over.

STORY GLUE

In 1998, my parents had to leave the country. Heidelberg, to this day, is one of their favorite cities when they imagine what it could have been for them if they had been able to have a normal life. The world is full of Yugoslav-fragments like them or me. The refugees' children have long since had children of their own, who are Swedish or New Zealanders or Turks. I am an egotistical fragment. I cared more about myself than about my family and our cohesion.

Literature is weak glue. I realize that from this book too. I invoke the whole and paper over what's broken; I describe life before and after the convulsion while in reality I forget birthdays and neglect wedding invitations. I have to think to remember my cousins' kids' names. I have never once lit a candle at the graves of my grandparents on my mother's side.

I don't blame my alienation from my family on the war and on distance. I put stories between us as deflections, displacements.

As for the fact that I can, and want to, write these stories at all, I owe that not to borders but to their permeability—I owe it to people who didn't compartmentalize but listened.

I wasn't deported in 1998 because the case worker at the foreigners' registration office did more than follow the letter of the rules. He listened to me, and paid attention when I said I wanted to study in Heidelberg. He reviewed my options.

"Bring me your enrollment documents," he said, "and then we'll see what happens."

I was able to see what happens in Germany. To start with, only as long as I was still at university. After that I needed a job that my studies were relevant for. I wanted to be a writer, so I had to prove that literary studies were relevant for being a writer. Next, that being a writer is a job at all. Finally, that this job could feed a grown man.

Another case worker, at the Leipzig foreigners' registration office, told me straight out that it was practically impossible for freelance artists—especially (a) writers and (b) clowns—to make an uninterrupted and sustainable living. To thank her for the information, I brought to our next meeting a copy of a story that a literary journal had paid me forty-five euros for.

She said she wasn't allowed to accept any gifts.

I said: "In that case, do you want to buy a copy?"

She said: "I don't read much."

I said: "Doesn't matter, I don't either."

She looked at me pityingly. Maybe also because I had printed out the story on paper that had something else printed on the backs of the pages. She accepted it after all, but didn't pay anything. "Contracts." She said. "Bring me contracts. The law needs proof that someone wants to pay you for what you're doing. The more money, the better."

A few months later, I'd signed the contract for my first novel. I phoned up the case worker and told her the sum. She laughed.

I said: "Now that's not nice."

She said: "Wait, is that per month?"

"If everyone buys the book, I'll be rich!" I said.

"Immigration law," she said, "doesn't include anything about *ifs*." And, after a pause: "Ach, bring it by."

That "Ach" was it! A few weeks later, I could go pick up my visa.

RESIDENCE PERMIT
*Expires upon termination of independent
activity as a writer and related activities*

I wasn't allowed to have any other job. That was fine with me. I didn't want any other job.

Olja, Olja from Krajina, Olja the joke-teller from Schwarzheide, had lost two brothers in a single day in a forest near Knin. He was the only survivor.

I rarely talked to the Yugos in Heidelberg about the fractures in our biographies. How often had I seen Dedo! Only once had he mentioned the tractor in the minefield, laughing off his survival. A lot of people mentioned nothing at all. Either way had to do.

We talked about Germany. The present. What worked. Setbacks too. Humiliations. Turning it into a story made the shitty things absurd and somehow more bearable, maybe—I don't know, I wasn't often in that situation. We collected experiences of discrimination the way hikers collect stamps from the destinations they've been to. But at the ends of our roads, there was no circle of chairs under a wooden shelter with a picture of Mary and a pleasant view of a beloved German mountain, just a random racist with Thor's hammer, rage in his belly, and the unpleasant likelihood of trouble.

Most of them had been through worse than me. In the Balkans and in the Palatinate. The violent images of my war were bearable, and I never got beat up in Germany. Ortenauer Street looked the same as ever, and at the last stop on the 31 I picked up Rieke and took her to the deer stand in the woods once, which I otherwise only shared with books. I read. Studied. Played Bach on the guitar and practiced headbanging, and sometimes just shut my eyes for a long time to find myself.

Ines from Bijeljina and Wojtek from Bielawa got together at some point and got married. They wanted children, and planned to give them international names, but it didn't work out at first. The doctor said: Wojtek, you smoke too much pot and you drink too much booze, your sperm count is low and they're not fit for duty, it's not going to happen.

So Wojtek went on a cure. In the Odenwald. He was the only patient younger than, I don't know, sixty. I went to visit him. Took a train, then a bus, with a kilo of tangerines in my backpack. The day I walked into his rehab room, Wojtek had gone three weeks without a drop of alcohol and two weeks and six days with no drugs.

He was surprised to see me. We weren't that close. But okay, he was happy I'd come. Happy about the tangerines too. "Tangerines, you faggot, that's awesome!"

We went for a walk. Ate over a pound of tangerines each. Just talked. Topic: Tropical fruit. Topic: Nurses in aprons. Topic: ARAL. "Do the guys miss me?"

"No," I said, "everyone's glad you're gone."

Wojtek laughed and said, "You know, *kurva*, you would've made a good Silesian. A little soft, but we'd take care of that."

"Wojtek, I wouldn't want to be a Silesian."

"*Kurva*, I wasn't asking if you wanted to."

Wojtek, Piero, Rahim, Rieke, Olli, Emil. With them and thanks to them, I wasn't lost in Emmertsgrund and in Heidelberg. We made something of our time and our place, even if what we made of it was mostly nonsense.

Here's one way to sum it up, but I need to think for a minute about what kind of mushroom begins with *M* so the sentence will sound better: My German friends lived lives of paper and plastic recycling, poppy-seed cake, and picking morel mushrooms in the Odenwald; custody battles, collection agencies, and crime shows on Sunday night TV. There was more or less all of that among the ex-Yugoslavs too, with less poppy seed and more plums, except find me a single Yugo who ever watched *Tatort* and liked it. But fine.

Here's one way to sum it up, in which I try to bring together my scattered experiences, when I write: I once got into a canoe with the ARAL crew in an outdoor pool, for a little nighttime canoeing in a pool. The next morning, Olli and his father took me to a medieval market, where we witnessed a horseshoeing.

Here's one way to sum it up, in which there's the sentence: Conformity was my rebellion. Not conformity to the expectations people in Germany had of how immigrants should be, but also not intentionally against it. My resistance was directed against the fetishization of where a person came from, against the specter of national identity. I was for belonging. Wherever people wanted me and I wanted to be. The lowest common denominator was just fine.

My great-grandparents from Oskoruša had not been migrants. Unlike Wojtek's parents, who came from Silesia, Piero's parents from Apulia, Rieke and her parents from the GDR, Kadriye and Fatih from Turkey, Emil's grandfather from Danzig, Dedo from the nightmare of a minefield.

Here's one way to sum it up, in which I find a way to bring it all back to Oskoruša.

I remember leaving there nine years ago. Grandmother and I were standing in Gavrilo's living room, dressed to leave, when the old man thought of one last thing. He ran out the room and came back with a piglet. He proudly held the animal up high, and the animal was proud to be held up high by Gavrilo. Gavrilo wanted to give it to me as a present. I refused the piglet, which made Gavrilo ask me if I'd prefer a chicken. "Take it to Germany with you!" he said. I thought he was joking, but just in case I answered seriously, with regret: "They'll never let either the piglet or the chicken through customs."

It wasn't a joke. Gavrilo cried: "Yes they will, yes they will! We just need to think how to pull it off."

FATHER AND THE SNAKE

I write in our WhatsApp group:

> *I want to go back to Oskoruša.*
> *Do you want to come with?*

Father writes:

Yes

> *Mom too?*

Yes
When were you there before

> *In 2009*
> *At the cemetery a poskok was*
> *lurking in the tree above us*
> *the whole time*

I think it's probably gone by
now

:) :) :)

I hate snakes

> *You killed one that got into*
> *the chickens once*

I definitely did not

> *In the henhouse? The poskok?*

I'd remember that. I would
have run away.

> *I'm sure of it*

Can I call you?

> *Busy right now*

Father calls anyway. "There's a really high mountain near Os-koruša," he says in place of a hello. "You know the one I mean?"

"Vijarac. Grandma keeps mentioning it."

"Below the peak there are the fire cliffs. I was thirteen or fourteen the first time I went up there alone. It's a steep slope covered with red rocks. I picked some up and threw them so they'd roll downhill, picking up other rocks as they went. I was an avalanche god, Saša!"

"What are you talking about?"

"Listen! Then I remembered a big boulder. Dark red. It was loose, tipping. Sending that one down would be amazing!

SAŠA STANIŠIĆ

I found a thick branch. Braced myself and heaved. The stone moved, it started rolling down the hill, and I lost my balance. There were snakes in the hole! It was a nest of horned vipers! All those heads! All those eyes! Scared, angry, their bodies all wildly tangled together. I fell toward them and their tongues licked at me. I pulled back even while I was falling and—flew. It was like something had grabbed me by the neck and carried me over the hole! I landed, fell. Skidded down the mountain like you wouldn't believe. Ran the whole way through the forest till I got home, somehow. Grandmother was cutting onions, and she was startled at how dirty I was.

"'*Poskok!*' I shouted. 'A whole nest of them!'

"'Did any of them get you?'

"'No, I got away somehow.'

"'They jump at your neck, spray poison in your eyes,' Grandmother whispered, biting into an onion."

Father has high blood pressure. Like Grandfather. Like I'm going to have. I hear his heavy breathing over the phone.

"If it wasn't you with the snake, then where did I get it from?"

Father has no idea. I'm afraid he might say: Maybe you just imagined it. But I can see the pictures clear as day. First, two people dancing; then, one person dancing with the snake.

"The fear is still with me," Father says. "When should we go?"

GRANDMOTHER EATS A PEACH
AND DOESN'T GIVE THE
GRAVEDIGGER ANY

Grandmother is tired of waiting for Grandfather. First she puts on a dress, then changes to just pants, they're not going to a dance or anything. She packs food: a peach for herself and polenta just in case, because everyone likes polenta.

In the light of dawn, she starts off to climb Vijarac to look for her husband. After a few hours, she is found in front of the church, eating a peach.

The gravedigger is who found her. He, like all gravediggers, has a disability. He can't hear with his right ear. Which is due to the fact that he has no right ear. It fell off when he was little. No one knows why anymore.

He sits down with Grandmother. He knows her—who in this city doesn't know Kristina Stanišić? And she knows him. Because when you're old you know who puts the dead in the ground. She asks what the devil a gravedigger's doing on Vijarac.

Then the gravedigger has to ask what she means. Half of it he hadn't heard, the other half he hadn't understood.

Grandmother offers him some polenta. No one says no to polenta.

"A mountain," she says, "near Oskoruša."

The gravediggger doesn't know where that is, but there's one thing he knows for sure: this is his mountain, his Megdan, his cemetery, his church.

"But what does that really mean, *mine*?" he adds. He clears his throat, and Grandmother sees something like pride and fervor in his eyes. And that—these two emotions in the gravedigger's large eyes—leaves Grandmother in no doubt that she isn't where she wants to be. Anyone who talks fervently about something he's proud of, and then tries to hide his fervor without being able to suppress his pride—he's not lying.

Grandmother must have already sensed that she'd gone the wrong way. This is what happened: In the dawn light, the Drina coming down from Megdan doesn't look like a river; it looks like a very, very good idea. No river in the world looks like that.

Should he bring her back home? the gravedigger asks.

"Yes, that would be nice."

"Where is it?"

And Grandmother apparently has to think it over, or else she's in no hurry, because she stays sitting there and proceeds to finish her peach.

IT IS AS THOUGH YOU HEARD OVERHEAD A BOLD BRISK BEAT OF WINGS

What kind of book is this? Who is narrating? A thirty-nine-year-old in Višegrad, Zurich, Split is writing it. A forty-year-old on a balcony in Hamburg is writing it. It's spring, summer, autumn, winter. It's today.

There is no word for all words. If there were one, a word for all words, it could only exist for about three seconds. A new word is invented about every three seconds, on average, and it influences the totality of all words and makes the one word for all words invalid. The word for all words is obsolete after three seconds, robbed of its meaning by the constant pressure of new word creation. New word creation! And just like that, it's gone, already gone—the word for all words.

A snake in the Oskoruša cemetery? The horned viper in the fruit tree? The Natural History Museum in Vienna says that horned vipers are absolutely terrible climbers. So it has to change. Shed its skin, as if taking off a mask, no longer be a *poskok*. It needs a new name: Josip Karlo Benedikt von Ajhendorf. Not to be confused with Joseph von Eichendorff the Romantic poet.

So, Ajhendorf. He, the snake, is no longer just a necklace for the fruit tree and the story. And he also can no longer be a link in the chain of motifs around Father and his encounter with the viper, which in fact only happened on these pages.

(Father raises the stone high above his head: strength, decisive action, seriousness; but then the war came and was stronger than him and etc.) I am sick of the betrayals of memory and am gradually getting sick of the betrayals of fiction too.

The wound in his thigh, why?

How thin Father was by the end in Germany, how thin.

Don't let yourself be distracted by wounds. Instead, imagine the snake. Imagine it not as a poet. Tailcoat. Stand-up collar, wide lapels. Mustache. There he is, a poet after all! At rest, sighing and eccentric, in the crown of the tree, tempting itself.

> *And all your merry comrades—*
> *Larks and woods and springs—*
> *Are rustling again, inviting you:*
> *Journeyman, won't you come soon?*

I like the poet in the tree better than the reptile in the tree. Eichendorff and flora are well acquainted with each other. The poet in poetic dialogue with the fruit, why not? A serious, contemplative middle-aged Upper Silesian shouts down lines:

> *Suddenly, here and there, a stirring—*
> *Whatever might it mean?*
> *It is as though you heard overhead*
> *A bold brisk beat of wings.*

Now what is this image? Is it of a bird? Is Ajhendorf out hunting? Do horned vipers hunt in trees? The Natural History Museum in Vienna says: I don't think so. But a bird could have its nest in the hollow of a tree, and the horned viper, just trying to sun itself, might happen to notice. Yes, and if it's there already . . .

The bird needs a name too, ideally a meaningful one. What about a wryneck? Now that's a great bird, Bird of the Year in 2007. Woodpecker family. Neck twists and turns. A migrating bird, and so potentially tragic, since every migrant is either heroic or tragic. So, Josip von Ajhendorf is looking for a brood of wrynecks. Wait a second. Do wrynecks ever nest in southern Europe? Do they nest at this time of year, late spring? It's possible, according to one ornithologist in Bucharest.

The wryneck won't come. Ajhendorf, the snake, will wait in vain. Eichendorff, the poet, will be rather sad about it. That's not so bad, Romantic poets can be rather sad, it makes them write better.

I want more Eichendorff. I decide to spend a whole week reading nothing but Eichendorff and Focus Online news. The first morning, I read three of his "Wanderer's Song"s in bed. I make breakfast, crack some wheat for my muesli with cracked wheat, and sing as I grind the wheat mill:

Down in a cool valley
A millwheel turns and turns,
My darling girl who lived there once
Is gone for evermore.

After breakfast I get the child ready to destroy things. I clear the table, put the laundry in the washing machine, brew myself a pot of coffee, and read Eichendorff poems on the balcony for two hours, shirtless and half-loud or, if I really like it, very loud, so that the retired neighbors can hear and see from their balconies someone from the Balkans reciting Eichendorff's poetry to them, shirtless:

> *Gentle rustling in the willows—*
> *A little bird flying away,*
> *Burbling brooks from silent peaks—*
> *Tell me where my country lies?*

I bellow, then I hang up the laundry.

I make another pot of coffee and translate the whole poem into Serbo-Croatian. It's called "Memory." I call Grandmother and read it to her over the phone. She calls me a donkey and hangs up.

Meanwhile I go read Focus Online once and instantly give up my plan to read it alongside Eichendorff, since after all when you're having vanilla ice cream you don't pair it with cold chicken soup seasoned with ashes and sucked in through your nose.

On Tuesday I read Eichendorff's novel *Memoirs of a Good-for-Nothing*. Now and then I take a note. There are two kids with worms in the nursery school. I check my son's stool—no worms there. I talk to my parents on the phone. They need to leave Croatia for three months soon. Back to the authorities again. Uncertainty again. Not having health insurance. The sentence: "We're not young anymore."

On Wednesday, throughout the course of the day, on the Elbe, I read some thirty or forty poems and order drinks. Two cases of carbonated mineral water, one case uncarbonated. Eichendorff lies in the sand, sunning himself.

My son is with me today—I didn't want to take him to nursery school, to the worms. I read Eichendorff's biography. The child builds streets in the sand. The streets he builds lead to a hospital, a police station, a kindergarten, and several machine shops and construction sites.

The child says: "Daddy, we have a new choo-choo trainee in school."

I dig a hole with the toy shovel and bury Eichendorff's poems in the sand. I eat nothing all day. I drink a half gallon of coffee.

Can't sleep. It all comes together—the tongue of the snake, the language of the poet. That Grandmother is no longer losing just names and dates but words and will. Grandmother consists of gaps—uncompleted sentences, vanished memories—while here I intentionally, artificially put gaps in.

I get dressed and wander around the neighborhood. I wander through the silent night, the moon above so gentle and still. And so on. It's three o'clock, I want larks. I stand in the middle of an intersection with no one in sight.

> *Oh wonderful song of night:*
> *From far away the rivers' course,*
> *Soft shuddering in the dark trees—*
> *The thought whirls through my mind*
> *That my crazy singing here*
> *Is like a birdcall, but from dreams.*

My crazy singing here. Go to bed, donkey.

In his best portrait, Eichendorff is looking around—high collar, dark coat, hair thick. So much hair. Mustache, gold chain. He looks like a drug dealer or a hipster. My crazy singing here.

I go home and, that night, start trying to formulate what I like about Eichendorff. I call the project: HUGE DIVERSIONARY TACTIC BEFORE GRANDMOTHER IS GONE. I like that so many things send him into raptures: the night, the woods, the eagle, the hunt, a woman named Luise, another woman named Venus, plus the lark, the Saale River, the lark again, always the lark, autumn, spring—well, every season—half-light (dawn or dusk, doesn't matter). I like that he doesn't just say "Good morning" like everyone else, but that this comes out of him:

Morning, that is my joy!
In the silent hour I climb
The highest mountain in sight and greet you,
Germany, from the bottom of my heart!

I appreciate how Eichendorff pays court to the world. How kind he is confronting it. Facing it, the mystical aspect of it too. How he plunges into Nature with all his senses, and then writes about it clearly and insanely.

I like his quaintness. His biography moves me. It moves me that he was a civil servant, hunting insects that crawled across his desk in his office, but still carried this wanderlust in his heart.

Among the files, between dark walls,
Longings for freedom enrapture me,
But the severe obligations of life,

> *And from the cabinets, heaps of files—*
> *The affronted Muses laugh at me,*
> *Right in my office face.*

I have been spared so much.

    On Friday I read yet more poems.

    "What are you doing?" my son asks.

    "Working," I say.

    "That's not how people work."

    "How do people work?"

    "On cranes or something."

The wryneck makes its nests in hollows. Only the wryneck sings the way the wryneck sings. The wryneck sings the most when it's reproducing. Its song consists of eight to fifteen rough-sounding *veed* or *vawd* sounds. It utters warning with *dekk* or *tawp* sounds.

    My grandmother, who calls me *donkey* and *sunshine*.

    My grandmother, who sleeps with slippers on her feet.

    Where I come from, what came out—no heroic tales.

    Huddling here in Hamburg, alliterating pontificating and quoting Eichendorff on Saturday morning before a family trip to Wendland: O ye quiet, cheerful joy!

    Confidently confronting being considered foreign (in language, too). Family, woodpeckers, Eichendorff, my son, Twitter, the Višegraders, the Brothers Grimm, computer games, Grimm's *German Dictionary*. The possibilities for telling a story are basically endless. So find the best one. And: Didn't you forget something? You've always forgotten something.

GRANDMOTHER AND THE BIRTHDAY

It was Grandmother's birthday yesterday and I forgot. I call to wish her happy birthday at least belatedly. She says hello and calls me by my father's name. She asks me to help her find her glasses.

I say, "They're on top of your head." A joke, but Grandmother is embarrassed when she laughs, because her glasses really are up on her head. She thanks me and asks me to stay on the line. She shouts for her sister: "Zagorka!" I hear her rummaging around the apartment, then a door opens and closes. After a while, when she hasn't come back, I hang up.

Later I remember why I'd called her. I dial the number again. Grandmother doesn't answer the phone for the rest of the day.

Grandmother saw her sister in the inner courtyard. Zagorka is jumping around and laughing, like she's hunting good dreams. Grandmother shouts out the window for her to come up. "Zagorka!" she cries. "Little Sister!"

Zagorka doesn't hear her or doesn't want to. She spins and spins in a circle. Grandmother heads out. Later someone talks to her at the supermarket, when she can't find the exit.

Grandmother is looking for the exit.

Grandmother is looking for her comb.

Grandmother is looking for the electricity bill.

Grandmother is looking for her sister and her husband.

Grandmother gets the key to her neighbor's apartment so she can water the flowers when the neighbor's on vacation. A brave choice. All the flowers survive though. But Grandmother polishes off everything edible she can find. The neighbor says that's all right. My grandmother is eighty-seven years and one day old.

THE YOUTH RELAY

Event planning was, without a doubt, one of Really Existing Socialism's strong suits. All the festive holidays, parades, and receptions—all the stagings of the People's love (for the Party, for the President)—they were good, big and colorful, with giant military caps and medals, truly nothing to grumble about. All right, they always went on much too long, but who are you going to complain to about that?

One of the most important Yugoslavian holidays was Youth Day, on May 25, garnished with the fantastic tradition of the relay run. Specially chosen young men and women carried the wooden baton through every region of the country and, in the final meters, pressed it into Tito's hand. On it was generally a symbol of some kind—flame or star or some agrarian product. The Youth Relay took place every year, starting in 1945. At first it was to honor Tito, until Tito generously said: Nah, you should honor the youth instead. After his death, the baton was handed off at the end to another president, whose name no one remembers today.

Everyone taking part in the relay knew what they had to do. Arrival times, departure times, route, where the baton should sleep: everything was regulated and regimented. The most important rule was: Do not UNDER ANY CIRCUM-STANCES drop the thing! No one knew what would happen if you did, since this had never occurred. Ninety-nine years of drought? The return of the dinosaurs to Yugoslavia? Or even . . . capitalism?! Something of that magnitude definitely seemed possible.

Before the baton-bearer arrived somewhere, there would be music and speeches. While the baton was waiting on site to be carried farther, there would be music and speeches. After it had been carried onward: music, speeches.

At night the baton would sleep in a safe place in the city it had reached that evening. Once, it was in Višegrad. Father was on the planning committee for the sleep of the baton. It spent the night in the House of Culture. Outside the House of Culture, young comrades kept watch. It was uneventful.

One time, I myself was a baton-bearer. It was in 1986 or 1987. At the time, I thought it was because I was good in school and wrote poems about partisans dying heroically. Now I know that it was because Father got me in.

I was well aware of the significance of the act—as momentous as my fear of doing something wrong. The night before the baton arrived, I had a dream of a soapy wooden stick that slipped through my fingers, landed at my feet, and instantly turned into a fish with a mustache.

At breakfast, Father reminded me of my role: to take the baton from Comrade Precursor, raise it over my head like a trophy, rejoice, and pass the baton onward. He asked if everything was clear. I saluted.

He hadn't mentioned the most important thing, because there was no need to mention it: *Do not under any circumstances drop the baton!*

It was due to arrive at the sports center at 1:00 PM. I was there three hours early. The accompanying program started at eleven with the official entry of the Pioneers. A column marched in through some applause, with me at the head. We were led to a place in front of a soccer goal where we were to stand and wait for two hours.

What year was it exactly? I do a little googling and find out that 1987 was the last year the baton underwent its pilgrimage. That would suit me very well, symbolically—to be one of the bearers of the Last Baton—but I also find out that the 1987 baton was made of glass and plastic, unlike in my wooden memory. It was a casing with eight white rods sticking out the top, with eight red dots, to symbolize the blood of the eight peoples of Yugoslavia. With hindsight today, it's not hard to see a foreshadowing of the bloodshed among those peoples that was soon to follow.

In my memory, the baton is a wooden cudgel with a five-pointed star on it. So maybe it wasn't 1987? The 1986 baton wasn't made of wood either. Anyway, whether it was in 1986 or 1987, I wore my Pioneer's cap, I waited for the symbol of unity and brotherhood, and the time came when I desperately needed to pee. I so unbelievably desperately needed to pee—what is it about children and memories of needing to pee? It was urgent, uncontrollable, in the middle of the crowd of freshly showered Pioneers and perfumed functionaries and teachers happy about having a day almost off. I was Tito's Pioneer! Self-sacrifice and commitment! I was a resistance fighter! I didn't move from the place assigned to me.

Then it erupted: cheering, marching music, a big commotion—the baton was finally here, and all I could think was: Please, no speeches. That's all I ask. Please, comrades, I'm begging you, I can't hold out much longer! And in fact no one spoke, and then I saw it, I saw him: an athletic young man in a runner's shirt, running toward me through a lane of flower children, beaming and sweating and looking healthy and happy; he looked fantastic, really, I wouldn't have been surprised to find out that he'd run direct all the way from Ljubljana to hand the baton off to me.

He looked me straight in the eye. A half generation separated us; this thing in his hand connected us again. As object, as symbol, as duty. We had grown up with the Baton, we knew its story, and now we were becoming that story's protagonists. It was an honor, we felt pride, and we were scared. The biography of the country is based on these three feelings. They reward and inspire and paralyze, all at once.

At the handoff of the baton, pride won out. I could see it in the eyes of the man facing me. Actually that's bullshit, I'm just saying that now—I didn't see anything in anyone's eyes, I was totally fixated on the baton, so that I would take it WITHOUT DROPPING IT.

Its wood was warm and smooth. I raised the Baton of Youth over my head like a champion raising a trophy. I didn't drop the baton, I didn't run off with it, I just handed it quickly to the girl behind me and shot out of formation to go piss in the quiet, still Drina.

WE'RE NEVER HOME

I write in our WhatsApp group:

> *Hey*
> *Is there a photo of me with*
> *the Baton?*

Mother writes:

Yes there is
I don't know if we still
have it
Maybe in Split
We're never home

> *Was it wood?*

I don't know, maybe

> *In 1987 the baton was glass*
> *or something*
> *But I remember a wooden*
> *one*

You were in third grade
or so
I'll ask Dad
He was on the org committee,
he'll know

                                        Ok

He says the baton thing was
in 1986
And it was wood
He's sure because it was made
by Varda

                            His company made it?

Yes that's how he knows
There were always local
batons as well
From local companies and
clubs and so on
Along the route as well as the
main baton

                                     Wait

Varda had one
Alhos too

SAŠA STANIŠIĆ

You're saying I never held the
Baton of Youth, the real one,
that went to Belgrade?

Never

Mother sends me the photo showing me with the false baton.
I'm a little beanpole holding up a stick with a red star. The same
red polygon on my cap. My expression: tortured.

I show my son the photo. "Who's that?" I ask.

My son wants to keep playing machine shop.

I nestle back into the past. It doesn't have to be actual fact.
I didn't drop the Baton of Youth—the one turned on a lathe,
made of wood, the real one—into the glassy form of a blown
ideology. I was happy, on my Youth Day, with my Baton.

MUHAMED AND MEJREMA

Granny Mejrema read the future from kidney beans only once in Germany. It was in the winter of 1998, on a snowy day, a few weeks before my parents had to leave the country. Everyone in the house was feeling tense. My parents were facing a new beginning in the US; my grandparents were expecting, every anxious moment, that they too would be deported; my older cousin was having problems in school. I had just moved out, and I came by for visits (not often enough).

We gathered in the living room. Granny had spread out a cloth on the rug and was sitting in front of it, smoking. A lean woman, sitting crisscross. Swaying her upper body back and forth. I handed her the ashtray.

First up was my cousin. Granny didn't even look at the beans but just said: If you don't study, you'll get nowhere.

She threw the beans for her husband and hugged him without saying a word. She didn't reveal what the beans had said.

She said nothing to my mother either. These beans are broken, she cried, and she threw them out the window. Then she sent me out to gather them up from the snow. When I came back to the living room, Mother was pale and Father was talking softly to her.

Granny threw the beans for me and said: "Do you remember how I once told you about an older woman who would fall in love with you?"

I did remember.

Granny said: "Forget it."

I said: "Rieke's older than me."

Granny said: "That's what I'm saying."

When I left, Granny advised me not to take the bus. I ignored her and the bus got stuck in the snow.

Then Granny Mejrema and Grandfather Muhamed were deported too. Their homeland needed labor for the reconstruction, was the line. They couldn't go back to Višegrad. So they joined their daughter's family—my aunt Lula's—and got a tiny apartment near them in Zavidovići. They didn't know anyone else there, but that changed quickly, at least for Grandfather. He painted walls, went shopping, watched kids. Shaved just beautifully. He was unchanged—good and unchanged. There were trout in the Bosna River. He went fishing, went to bed early.

Granny sat by the window and grew more and more serious. Something was choking her. She waited for her husband to come home; at some point, she asked him not to go out so often. He promised he wouldn't and kept his promise.

I went to visit them once and spent a week in Zavidovići. Granny was sick; her husband and daughter took care of her. I would have loved to go fishing with Grandfather but didn't want to ask, under the circumstances. Alone I caught nothing. I watched a movie with Granny and we fell asleep in front of the TV set.

Granny wasn't getting much air. Something to do with her airways. Something to do with her lungs. A doctor tried this and that. Granny got even less air. Granny died. Something to do with breathing.

Grandfather went downhill after she died. Hardly ate, rarely left his bed. He asked people to leave him in peace. His children wanted none of that. Aunt Lula downright dragged him into the fresh air, shoving him around the city. Day after day after day. Mother traveled there, talked with him, shaved him. They didn't leave him alone, not even alone with his grief.

Uncle had the idea about the river. He took him to Salzburg and the Salzach River. He fished, his father looked on, and at some point wanted a try. He couldn't get the fish out of the river with his own strength. The next morning, he shaved himself for the first time in weeks and wanted to go back to the river. When he got home after a few weeks, he had recovered.

My grandfather Muhamed had five more years. He went fishing and helped people out to the end. The approach of death was no reason to stop. If his legs wouldn't carry him one day, he'd wait for the next day.

One frosty morning in December 2011, he shaved, threw on his railroad worker's coat, and went out into the yard. He offered to chop wood for a neighbor, his voice soft. He tried to do it but was too weak. She thanked him and later brought by some flowers, and found him lying feverish in bed. Aunt Lula was with him. My grandfather died helpful and well shaved on a burning cold day in December 2011.

GRANDMOTHER AND
THE TOOTHBRUSH

Grandmother doesn't brush her teeth that much anymore. In her rare moments of hearty laughter, you can see yellow spots, remains of food. She probably forgets. Doesn't remember that it's time to brush her teeth and that it would be good to do so. If someone reminds her, she does it.

Grandmother's toothbrush used to be blue; now it's light blue. The bristles are splayed. When we brought her a new toothbrush and threw the old one away, she got it back out of the garbage and threw the new one in. She wasn't going to let people just boss her around, she said.

We agreed that she was right. But it was also true, we said, that you can't take something that people have bought for you and just throw it in the garbage.

She agreed that we were right. And threw the new toothbrush out the window.

Another time, we tried it with arguments. She listened closely, and said: "My toothbrush or no toothbrush."

We didn't give up. Someone had the idea of replacing the old toothbrush with a nearly identical new one. Light blue for light blue. The color was almost exactly the same, the handle a tiny bit longer. We dabbed toothpaste on the brush so that it would look less new. The only really noticeable difference from the original was the straight bristles, but we counted on

Grandmother's bad eyes. We hid the old toothbrush, deciding to get rid of it only if Grandmother didn't notice the swap.

Grandmother noticed the swap immediately. She bent the new toothbrush in rage, the plastic bent but it didn't break. She wanted her toothbrush back. Fine. We said that she should also use the new one though. And we left Post-it notes saying *Brush your teeth!* in the bathroom and above the stove.

What was it all for? We wanted control. We cleaned out Grandmother's closets and drawers and threw away the junk, which likewise made her furious, because for her it wasn't junk at all. Since we usually weren't there, we wanted to feel useful when we were there. We kept leaving for a couple of days and Grandmother would be alone again. We wanted to prove to ourselves that she could count on us.

Rada, the neighbor from the third floor and a friend for many years, helped us as much as she could. She cooked and did the laundry, gave Grandmother her insulin shots, kept her company. Grandmother took care of the cleaning herself: no one was going to scrub the bathtub after her.

Rada also would just drop by sometimes, check in, after all you never knew if. She left her own apartment door open to hear if Grandmother was setting out on one of her excursions into the past again.

In spring 2018, while Grandmother was recovering from her pneumonia, the toothbrush disappeared and couldn't be found. My parents bought a new one. Grandmother didn't care. Her teeth, when she gave a hearty laugh, had yellow spots. She didn't clean the apartment anymore; she was too weak, or else forgot, or she wasn't interested in cleaning. She could no longer wash herself. When she wasn't talking for a while, her head would drop until her chin almost touched her chest.

She needed professional care, preferably round-the-clock. There was no one who could do it in Višegrad. Anyway, Grandmother had become difficult with strangers; there was one doctor who tried to take her blood pressure and Grandmother had almost bitten her on the nose.

The pneumonia was serious enough that when Grandmother was in the hospital, no one said out loud what everyone was thinking. Mother and Father came from Croatia and took care of her for two whole months. Mother took on most of the work, took on more than she could handle.

Grandmother couldn't find her watch anymore.

Grandmother couldn't find the front door anymore.

Grandmother couldn't find her husband.

My grandmother needed diapers.

Mother gave her insulin shots, did the shopping, cleaned, cooked, forgot to eat anything herself. Sometimes Grandmother knew who this woman washing her and holding her hand was. She patted her cheek. On some days, the woman badgering her about this and that was a stranger. Grandmother wanted to brush her hair herself. And she couldn't find the brush.

Father stayed up by her side during the nights when she didn't want to dream. Mother took her on walks during the day. Mother, who didn't trust the city, walking around the city. On the alert. Because she didn't know many people there anymore. But also because she did know some.

Grandmother recovered. She wanted to wash the carpet. She repeated her wish over and over until Father and Mother washed the carpet. The next day, she wanted to go see her husband in the mountains. The day after that, she was furious because a man and a woman she didn't know were standing in her kitchen. She ate a chocolate bar while Mother and Father were out shopping. When they got back, she wanted to wash the carpet.

MAYBE A TRAIN'LL COME

Today is March 29, 2018. The morning smells of urine and cherry blossoms. Mother is changing her mother-in-law's diaper, making breakfast, and watching how her mother-in-law eats. She asks: "Do you need anything else?"

Grandmother screams, "If I need something I'll get it myself!"

Mother clears the table, washes the dishes, and is planning to get dressed when she sees her mother-in-law kneeling in front of a suitcase.

"Where you going?"

"Little Sister's."

"Where's Dragan?"

"Who's Dragan?"

"Your son."

"I don't have a son." Grandmother thinks it over. "Where's Little Sister? Where's Zagorka?"

Mother hesitates. "I'll help you."

Mother and Grandmother pack. They pack dresses, blouses, underwear. Mother puts a winter coat in too. "Who can say how long they'll be on the road in this life," she says, and both of them laugh for the first time in days. They pack shoes, boots, and sandals. They pack more blouses. Shower gel. The toothbrush. Grandmother wants to bring the broom, and a quart of milk, and that's okay too. They pack three brown suitcases.

The suitcases are much too heavy, so they leave two of them in the courtyard right at the start. Grandmother seems so happy at the prospect of leaving, or arriving, that she doesn't care. She takes her daughter-in-law's arm.

The house where Mother was born is near the bridge. Its yellow façade is covered with age spots—bare bricks where the plaster has come off.

"Why did we stop?" Grandmother asks.

"I don't know," Mother says.

Grandmother wants to cross the bridge, Mother doesn't.

Mother wants to go to the high school. She peers through the windows. Standing there in front of the blackboard, she expounded on theories with no future for her students. *The ruling ideas of a given time are always just the ideas of the ruling class.* The gym looks new. It's strange: something new. Something whole.

Grandmother has already crossed the street and seems to want to get to the Drina. Mother catches up to her and steers her toward the market square. When Grandmother gets there, she says: "But we're too late to get the good *kajmak*." The market is a miserable chimera of Chinese schlock and smoked meat. The shoemaker there is still the same one, three hundred years of a bent back on this footstool.

"Are we taking the train?" Grandmother asks, and Mother thinks that's a good idea. The bridge over the Rzav has been closed for months, due to risk of collapse, so they have to take the long way to the station. The suitcase scrapes along the sidewalk; one of the wheels is stuck. People stare, but people always stare here.

The station is a ruin. Trains haven't stopped here since 1978; bus service was cancelled a couple of years ago. A girl is crouching in a corner of the waiting room. It's the little beggar girl, the Roma with the blue eyes. She takes a shit and gives the two women a friendly wave.

Mother wipes off the bench with a handkerchief. Grandmother sits down. Pigeons land, dance with each other, fly off.

"Gosh, it looks terrible here!" Burning nettles are growing out the window openings. A cat washes its encrusted eyes.

"This is how it looks," Mother says. She doesn't want to stay sitting. She counts the ants on the wall. She counts a hundred and seven ants, then stops counting ants.

One thing that belongs to Mother, five decades later, is: Standing on the rails in the din of the arriving train, waiting for her father. There he is, the heavy coat, the sooty face.

Across the street from the station, she is a child again. The house is sand-colored, bare and angular like a barracks. A pack of dogs is asleep in the morning sun. Can't have a ruined city without a pack of dogs. A washing line with no laundry on it. On the stairs, she tries to be quiet, why? The lights don't work anymore. The door to her family's apartment is the same door, just more rundown.

Knock?

It's not ours anymore.

THIS WHOLE BROKEN THING

THIS SAD CRUMBLING PIECE OF SHIT

Out of there. Grandmother is still sitting on the bench. Mother wants to take her away. Grandmother protests weakly—she wants to keep waiting for the train. Mother is more decisive: no more trains are coming.

Almost every window in the former turpentine factory is broken. There's one whole pane, on the top floor, third from the left. Mother picks up a stone. Grandmother too. Birds' nests, a rat. It's still a home for animals.

"Now for a coffee," Grandmother says, satisfied.

Inside the bookstore on what was once Tito Street, the light is too dim. It was always like that, always. Mother wants to finally be done with that, she wants to complain about the darkness, wants to tell someone how uninviting the store is. Books need light! She walks in and buys her grandson a dinosaur coloring book.

Mother let go of Višegrad the day her life was threatened there. Now she finds shelter in the city, but no rest. She comes only because her mother-in-law needs her. She sees: the joyless, the broken, the half-done, the nepotism, the collapse, the eternally twilit, the eternally outdated. She hates. Hates that the last owner of Alhos left his office one morning with plastic bags full of cash and came back twice to get more bags of cash each time, walking right past the silent workers at their silent sewing machines. Nothing would have changed anything, they said later. This city will never be what it once was.

Grandmother takes Mother's arm again. They walk past the sports center. There is no more sports center. Emir Kusturica, the filmmaker, had it leveled to the ground. On the spit of land between the rivers, he had an unimaginative, kitschy fantasy of a fake town named Andrićgrad built. Seventeen million euros that piece of shit cost.

Grandmother says: "Isn't that nice."

Mother says: "It's incredibly stupid."

In Café Intermezzo, Mother orders an espresso for her mother-in-law and a tea for herself. She gets a slice of lemon in a little lemon squeezer with her tea. The waiter says something to Mother. Wasn't she his political science teacher, ages ago? He is honestly happy to see her. They talk. How it's going. Mother smiles. The next time he comes back to their table, Mother compliments the lemon squeezer. How practical. The next time, the waiter brings her the lemon squeezer wrapped in a paper towel. He wants to secretly give it to Mother as a present. Mother can't accept that. But please, do, you have to, please, Comrade Professor. Mother pays and hugs her student. Mother puts the little lemon squeezer in her bag.

Grandmother is back on her feet. Mother lets her lead the way. Grandmother goes home. The suitcases are still standing in the courtyard. She opens the apartment door herself. It takes a really long time, but she manages it. That's what counts.

Mother runs a bath. Grandmother likes the water hot. Maybe because then she can feel her body and because the body as a concrete fact is a welcome change from her fading memories.

Mother scrubs Grandmother's back with a sponge and sings. The song is called "Little Ants." An ant disappears down a young woman's neckline, a man watches, oh how he wishes it were him. Dreadful song. Grandmother and Mother close their eyes.

IT ALWAYS KEEPS GOING
ONE WAY OR ANOTHER

The phone calls with my grandmother have recently gotten even shorter and more absurd. At some point she stopped answering the phone; at some point after that, the line was dead. We call Rada. The neighbor reports that Grandmother locks herself in the apartment and screams terribly. On other days, someone else has to lock her in because she wants to leave and go see her Pero. It's almost impossible to stop her. In a frail voice, Rada admitted she couldn't go on. Neither she: taking care of my grandmother. Nor Grandmother: continuing to behave like this.

The nearest old-age home is more than thirty miles away, in Rogatica. My uncle and father drove there and were sold on the rosebush hedges and the bright rooms, and that the nurses were regularly paid their wages. When they mentioned the old-age home in front of Grandmother, she said they should stop talking such nonsense.

"We want to take you to a hotel," they said the next day. "A vacation."

"Do you think I'm crazy?"

We were all pretending something to ourselves. The sons wanted to believe that her condition wouldn't get worse. I, that Grandmother would still be able to answer my questions. Grandmother, that she could make it through the day without a dose of insulin: she fell into a diabetic coma. The neighbor found her almost unconscious and called the emergency doctor.

Today is April 24, 2018. I get into the streetcar in Hamburg to go to the airport, but this streetcar doesn't go to the airport. I realize my mistake too late, run out, hail a taxi. The driver says, "Don't worry, I know shortcut." Anatol says "shortcut" with an uncompromising Russian *r* and drives uncompromisingly too. I tell him—to give him even more motivation—that I'm trying to go see my grandmother who is sick with diabetes and can't remember things. I say (and only then do I consciously become aware of it myself as a real possibility) that this might be my last trip to see her.

Anatol lets me talk, then reaches into the glove compartment and hands me a bar of chocolate. "For emergency," he murmurs. I break off a row and give him the rest. I don't make the flight. And while the airline checks my options, I think: What if Grandmother decides to march off somewhere precisely now, and gets lost forever on the way home in her head?

"I haven't seen my grandmother for thirty years," Anatol told me. "She has nothing. With nothing the Germans don't let you in. And the Ukrainians don't let me in. Grandmother is a tough woman, very religious. So she has lot of love and lot of anger," Anatol said. "And even so I'm scared for her."

I am rebooked onto a flight that afternoon and arrive in Sarajevo five hours later than planned. But really I'm months late, maybe years. What I still wanted to talk over with Grandmother has long since left her.

My parents pick me up at the airport. We chat about the dilapidated tunnels on the road to Višegrad. About the soaring prices of Apple stock. Father strictly stays below the speed limit and drives extremely slowly when there's no speed limit visibly posted. The traffic police here take their job seriously. The Croatian coat of arms on his license plates guarantees that we'll be stopped in Serbian territory, if any cops are lurking, and also that they'll find something wrong with the car.

On the Romanija karst plateau, darkness catches up to us. On the Romanija we're stopped. The policeman asks if Father knows why.

Father rolls down the window and cool air streams into the car. Father says, "Because of the license plates?"

"Because of being twenty kilometers an hour over the posted limit of sixty. License and registration, please."

That is a lie of at least twenty kilometers an hour. The "please" is a lie too.

Father hands him the papers. "My speedometer must be broken then. Are you absolutely sure?"

The policeman says: "Who can be sure of anything nowadays?"

Father says: "Have you written it up yet?"

The policeman says: "I'm cold."

Father says: "When do you get off work?"

The policeman looks at his watch: "It's dinnertime soon."

Mother shouts from the back: "We have a cheese sandwich."

The policeman sticks his head all the way in the window, like he wants to see if it's true, about the sandwich. He is clean-shaven and a bit plump and the smell of booze on his breath is not unpleasant. Mother holds out the sandwich for him. The policeman hesitates, maybe considering if he's in the mood for cheese. Or considering something else. What his family's doing right now (he has a wedding ring, tight around his finger). Maybe he, like me for that matter, was surprised to hear the word "sandwich" among the dark karst mountains, and he's figuring out how it fits in. Is it inappropriate? Or—as an offer to share food—is it just nice?

"Where are you from? I can hear you're not Croatians," he says to the sandwich.

Now that's tricky. Any answer might be wrong.

"From Višegrad," Father ventures.

"From Višegrad? Are you shitting me? Why didn't you tell me before?" The policeman's eyebrows start doing a jolly dance. "Me too! My name's Mitrović," the policeman cries, as though everything's all taken care of now. "I almost wrote you guys up. Man!" He snatches the sandwich, relaxes, leans against the car door, wants to chat: "Which branch of the family are you from?" he cries into the night on the legendary Romanija plateau.

And nearby, a factory, unfinished for a decade, coughs uncomfortably; it doesn't like that EU currencies have been embezzled for its fake construction.

And not far away, my uncle drove his car into a ditch during the Olympic winter of 1984.

And somewhere up here, Grandfather Pero was wounded in 1944.

And in the hills to the east, partisans liberated the village of Kula from the Ustasha in February 1942.

And once there used to be bears in these woods.

And everywhere on the Romanija plateau there are *stećci*, medieval gravestones, and on one of them, far to the west, it says:

Bratije, ja sam bio kakav vi a vi ćete biti kako i ja

Brother, I was once like you and someday you will be like me

If you damage a *stećak* you'll be hit by lightning.

And the policeman takes the sandwich out of the tinfoil and sniffs it. "What kind of cheese is this?"

"Trappist cheese," Mother says.

"Is that a cheese from Croatia?" the policeman asks.

"No," Mother says in a friendly voice, "it's a cheese from cow's milk."

And everybody laughs. The policeman takes a bite of the sandwich, chews, and swallows. "Mitrović," he says at one point, between bites. "I'm sure you know us."

ALWAYS BE NOBODY

The apartment door is unlocked because it's so late. Grand-mother is lying on the sofa, with the pink blanket, in the living room. She's pale. Is her chest moving?

My parents will spend the night there; I've rented a small apartment on the Drina. There's a wedding party going on in the hotel next door. Turbo-folk music, screaming, the usual. No chance of sleep. An hour later, I'm wandering the streets again. Teenagers stare and spit. I never learned that—this clean, com-pact, precise spitting.

The Drina, mute and black. Somewhere there my great-grandparents' house once stood; there's the weeping wil-low under which my grandfather liked to go fishing. A man is pissing in the river, cursing, calling someone a whore. He throws his shirt in the water.

On the way back, I climb down onto the riverbank near the old bridge. Under the first pier is a group of people sitting around a campfire. I get closer; two stand up. I understand. I raise my hands and shout in English: "A friend, just a friend!" I say my name. The two men sit back down, keeping their eyes on me.

Where are they from?

Afghanistan. And me?

From here.

Can you help us?

They're trying to get north. They show me photographs of their families standing next to rubble and ashes. I think about whether Stevo might be able to drive them. I stupidly offer them some money, but they don't take it. The bridge over their heads is four hundred and forty years old.

What was the worst thing about their trip? One laughs. Another says, in English: "Always be nobody."

In the morning, Grandmother recognizes all of us. She's happy we came. At lunchtime, Grandmother recognizes only her daughter-in-law. In the afternoon, she shyly asks my parents: "Who is that nice young man with you?"

Before dinner I go back to the bridge. The Afghans are gone.

Mother has cooked stuffed peppers and I can smell the sauce from the stairs. The stairs store up bygone smells too. Of the little plastic ball that we kicked from one side of the hall to the other as children. In socks and not too hard, because of the glass in the doors.

Sometimes there's the smell of the soldiers too—a mix of gasoline, metal, and screaming. In the autumn it's corn on the cob. That one's deceptive: when the stairway smells like corn on the cob—unlike the ball or the soldiers—I don't know if it's my memory or if someone's really cooking it, and if so, who? I want one!

Mother's in the kitchen and the peppers are almost done. Grandmother is sitting in the living room, watching TV with the sound off and the picture off. The TV's broken, she cut the cable but says it was someone else who did it, not her. I sit down with her. She takes my hand and looks at me.

"We want to go to Oskoruša," I say. "Do you want to come?"

"Oskoruša?"

"Yes."

"Pero wanted to climb Vijarac, but it's such bad weather. He's . . ." Grandmother breaks off. The plates clatter nervously. Father is setting the table. He keeps asking where things are—where's the salt, where are the napkins.

"If only my Pero had known you were coming! He would've waited for you and not gone up alone." Suddenly she sounds angry. "It's because you never let us know in advance! Pero left days ago."

"Where was he going?"

"Into the mountains! Up Vijarac!"

"To do what?"

"I told him at least wait till the weather's better." Her voice sounds frailer and frailer with every word.

"Who am I, Grandma?"

"You're a donkey is who you are, to ask something like that."

"Should we wait for Grandpa together?"

"A donkey and a joker." Grandmother leans back. It's as if the sudden worrying about Pero lost in the mountains has robbed her of all her strength.

"Have you had enough water to drink today, Grandma?" I give her a glass of water but she doesn't touch it. Mother has put the pot on the table and she serves us all. I help Grandmother to the table. Grandmother likes the food. She slurps up the sauce. Mother asks if she likes it. Grandmother says: "No."

Grandmother isn't allowed to eat everything but in secret she eats everything.

"Are you thirsty, Grandma?" I push the water glass toward her like she's a child and I have to draw her attention from there to here. "Grandma, have you had enough to drink?"

Grandmother puts the spoon down. Wipes her face all over with the napkin. There are pale little hairs above her lip. She brings the plate to her mouth, tips it, and drinks up the sauce in great gulps.

"I remember," Grandmother says, "this and that in Oskoruša."

Today is April 25, 2018. A Serbian motorcycle club is visiting town. I am sitting at a café with Grandmother. Leather vests swagger down the streets. Patches with Chetnik slogans and symbols from the Serbian nationalist guerilla forces in World War II.

With Faith in God.

Skull and crossbones.

Freedom or Death.

The Serbian cross.

Lots of selfies in front of the bridge. (*Some were killed on the bridge, some thrown into the river and shot from the bridge.*)

Grandmother says: "You know, around here it's always the person with the least scruples who has the most stuff."

I remember my grandmother's clear thoughts. Her firmness toward what she considered unjust. Her indulgence toward me. I think she was alone a lot, after we—first Grandfather, then my parents and me, then the neighbor women, one after the other—left, each in our own way.

I take her hand. It's cool and dry.

"You came too late," she says, and lets her head drop.

"Too late for what, Grandma? Grandma?"

In 1996, during my first visit to Višegrad after the war, the city was full and desperate, aggressive and unemployed. I wasn't coming back, I was coming to a new place for the first time.

I was traveling with Rahim. We were supposed to drive my uncle's car to Bosnia. Kind of illegal, I think, and I think that only our enormous, naïve luck let us pull it off—that and what my uncle paid us for the job, which we paid out as bribes.

I had a permanent bad conscience in Višegrad. When I ran into former schoolmates who'd stuck it out here while I was riding a canoe in the night in a swimming pool in Heidelberg. When I exchanged my German marks. When Rahim wanted to know something about the city and I couldn't answer him. When almost everyone was talking about how bad they were doing and I thought: I'm doing pretty well.

The one really great thing that actually felt like being back home was Grandmother. So healthy, so indomitable. How determined she was when she talked to Rahim, as though he must be able to understand the language. And how he did in fact understand that she would strangle him if he didn't eat up all her pita.

Grandmother carried the carpet down all the stairs, alone, scrubbed it clean and let Rahim and me carry it back upstairs. She helped the neighbors with the vegetable garden, made sure that the building got electricity back. She came with me to city hall, where I had to get my birth certificate; shoved her way to the window past the people standing around; spoke softly to the clerk, who waved us through; and we could leave city hall ten minutes later, our business accomplished.

Today I bring my grandmother to the woman who cuts her hair. She asks: "Same as always, Mrs. Kristina?" And my grandmother has to laugh, a very loud laugh.

"If it looked good," she says, "then yes, please, same as always."

OSKORUŠA, 2018

The sky is clear this morning: April 27, 2018. We load up provisions; Rada will look in on Grandmother. At eight we're on the road. The route leads through eastern Bosnia, considered the stronghold of the Serbian nationalists. The Croatian coat of arms on the license plates is again an issue. "We should have guns when we're driving around here," Father quips.

Mother's not in the mood for jokes.

About halfway there we pass a forested area just when some hikers come out into the open. They're about two hundred, maybe two hundred and fifty feet from the road, carrying rucksacks but also shopping bags. One of the women has a child on her hip. I ask Father to stop. When we open the doors, they run off as if by command, ducking into the shelter of the trees. The last one turns back to look around—a serious young woman pale with worry.

Mother lights a cigarette and moves away from the car.

A woman and her son were walking along a country road late in the evening. A rucksack was pressing down on her shoulders; she was pulling a brown rolling suitcase after her. The boy was almost as tall as she was. A red-and-white scarf around his shoulders braved the hot, humid air.

Scenery: Dust and farming.

The woman turned around when she heard a car coming. She waved, shouted, stuck her thumb out—every car drove by, some of them honking. It sounded like curses.

Hours went by. Drinking water, eating bread.

A city. Sidewalks, streetlights, families around tables eating dinner. An old man behind a window. The boy stopped and stared. The old man brought a spoon to his mouth. Chewed. And again. Lit a candle, making a pleasant light for himself. So much to say. The boy hesitated. Then he caught up to the woman.

To the bus station. Five parking bays. No police. The waiting room: ashes on rancid tiles. Back out. At the kiosk: "Do you take German marks?" Cookies, potato chips, water, tissues. Keeping the luggage in sight at all times. The bench: the bed. It's not that cold.

A bus pulled in. The driver, the only person in the bus, stepped out. A fat man. His silhouette smoking in the headlights. The woman called out, in a thin voice: "We want to cross the border."

The driver's face, a surface of shadows. Please, be friendly, that's all we're asking.

"We're from Bosnia," the woman said. "We can pay. Maybe you know a place where it's possible to cross without attracting attention?"

The bus driver stepped on his stub and came closer. "Why not try it on foot?"

"We were sent back."

"I'm off for the night."

The woman said nothing.

"Look at that thing." He gestured to the bus. "How could anyone cross in that without attracting attention?"

"The boy's tired."

"I'm not tired," the boy said.

The woman looked harshly at the boy, but dropped the harshness in less than a second. Out came: "We don't know what . . ."

The driver rubbed his eyes. "Where are you from?"

"From Višegrad."

"As in Ivo Andrić?"

"Ivo, Ivo Andrić." The woman lowered her eyes.

The boy shouted: "They took a giant hammer and knocked the head of his statue right the fuck off!"

A pause. The driver snorted or coughed or both. Mother grabbed the boy by the wrist. He immediately broke free. The boy wasn't just a boy anymore.

"I can drive. That's it. I can't promise you anything else. Most people are sent back and end up here again. I can drive, that I can do."

Now he was standing in front of the bench and holding his pack of cigarettes out to the woman. She sat up and lit one. The woman and the driver smoked; the sky was clear and starry.

It is August 17, 1992. Mother gets into the bus and I follow her.

It is April 27, 2018. Mother stubs out her cigarette and gets back in the car. We keep driving.

Never trust Google Maps in rural areas. We stop at a bus stop where a young woman surrounded by shopping bags is putting nail polish on her fingernails. She has this to say about Google's alternative route: "If you take that, the mountains'll swallow you up." And: We need to go to Uvac first; from there we can go up to Oskoruša. And: She was going in that direction too, and the bus might come today, might not. "Take me with you?"

Of course we can hardly say no. She asks if we could let her finish painting her nails. Now to that we can say we're in a hurry. But we don't. Almost as soon as we drive off, she asks about our license plates: "ST—that's Split, isn't it?"

This time I'm quicker than Father. "We're from here," I say. And, after a pause, "ST stands for Stanišić." It was obviously a joke but I felt it sounded totally convincing: "Stanišić."

I think about the refugees in the woods, the refugees under the bridge in Višegrad. Their routes across the Balkans take them through places we've fled from ourselves. I open the window. I'm here voluntarily.

"I know some Stanišićs," the woman says. She recites their full names, often the name of their father, the name of their village. It's like a refrain to a song with no tune. Only one of them is not a farmer—a tire dealer in Uvac.

Mother has opened her window too. Before her eyes the Serbian hinterland speeds past, and graffiti written in Cyrillic letters, so Serbian:

For king and fatherland.
Give not what is holy unto the dogs.
Our blood, our land.

Written in a language she understands, in any case. *Ours* means *not yours*. Mother is not addressed, and at the same time is.

Our passenger gets out in Uvac, at the border between Serbia and Bosnia. A strange place. Tiny shops, packed tight together: shacks of corrugated steel, a little supermarket, peppers, plastic. A stand with tomatoes; a stand with tracksuits and

Adidas slides; a stand with toasters and hair dryers. Boys with severe haircuts and "Franck Ribéry" or "Messi" on their jerseys are hunting each other barefoot, armed with plastic guns and fresh vegetables.

An absurd number of tire dealers has set up shop here: there are warm tire pyramids everywhere, with cats on them, sunning themselves.

Father, over Mother's protests, wants to go right over and ask about the prices. He parks in front of one of their businesses.

Mother says (for her this is very serious): "You're crazy."

The dealer—stocky, crew cut, undershirt, jeans—asks if the tires are for the Renault out front. Father says yes.

The dealer—clean-shaven, with a lot of hair on the backs of his hands—asks: "How come you have Croatian license plates?"

Father decides on a new approach with a counterquestion: "We're going to Oskoruša. Can we get up there from somewhere around here?"

"Who're you going to see there?" The dealer—tattoo on left forearm: sword and shield—leans over the counter. My father has a similar one: sword and wreath.

"Gavrilo Stanišić," I say.

"Stanišić?" On his right forearm is a three-headed dragon.

THE SUNNY SIDE TASTES SWEET, THE SHADY SIDE BITTER

"Gavrilo is family. I'm a Stanišić," the tire dealer said, stating the price for a set of four tires. "Dirt cheap." Smile, gold eyetooth. Father couldn't say no and bought the tires, and the dealer insisted on changing them then and there. He said he would take care of it himself and then shouted for someone somewhere to come change the tires.

A young woman in overalls and headphones did it and we were ready to go in ten minutes. But the dealer also insisted that we follow him to the intersection to Oskoruša; he wanted to make sure we took the right road. He drove a black BMW. He waited in the car and watched us until we turned off into the mountains.

The approach to Oskoruša is uphill, through a forest, on a winding road. Dirt side roads with family names, not street names, lead off to buildings and yards. In open areas, there's a clear view down into the Lim valley. Green of the river, brown of the fields, red of the exposed brick walls. Fertile in some places, empty in others. Farther up, every curve seems tighter and steeper than the one before, and then the pavement stops. We pull over on brand-new, dirt-cheap tires.

Now where? I don't recognize anything. Father's last visit here was fifty years ago. Trees, ferns, whatnot. The sky gives nothing away, nor the woods. In the dips in the road it smells cadaver-sweet.

We decide: continue uphill. There's rustling, humming. Leaves sighing, woodpeckers knocking, insects chirping. A toppled fence, as if someone had gone along its whole length plucking it up out of the ground. It was somewhere around here that Gavrilo had waited for Grandmother and me.

I try to picture Grandfather as a young man on these paths. In his sports jacket. On the donkey. I can't do it—there is nothing there, there's just me, using photographs.

The first intersection. A narrow forest path runs downhill: light-colored dirt between bushes. No, keep going uphill. "You get to the top by going uphill," says Father, the geography whiz. We follow him. When no one knows what to do next, you follow the first person who wants to do something.

A cabin crouches at the peak. An old man steps out the door, sees us, saunters toward us, and stops halfway from the house to the new arrivals. Cap, wool sweater vest, low-slung pants, and a giant ham sandwich in his hand.

He shouts: "Who's that wandering through my forest?"

Mother says quietly: "Call me Marija." She is skeptical enough to prefer a Serbian name to her own.

We introduce ourselves and Mother smiles, showing her teeth, when she says, "Marija."

The lord of the forest starts walking again. His eyes are dark brown. Like mine, I think at once, because I don't want to think it.

"Which branch of the Stanišićs then?" A nod at *Bogosav*, a "Good, good" at *Kristina*. "So, you want to go to the cemetery?"

"Yes," I say.

"And so what are you doing here?"

"We want to see Gavrilo too."

"How do you know him?"

"I've been here before."

"Well then you should know the way. Gavrilo's down in the valley. We have a cabin there. Just follow the loudest snoring and you'll find him. Let me get back to tending his sheep." The old man shakes his head and grins. "My name's Sretoje," he says, putting the sandwich in his left hand to shake ours properly. "Gavrilo's my brother. Although sometimes—I don't know . . ." He grins, so we grin, and during this grinning Sretoje Stanišić feels the need to lay out the family relationships and orient himself in that landscape.

"Kristina is your mother," he shouts at my father, and says now he's really curious about us, "about why you're here." He'd actually been planning to get back to the sheep but now he invites us into his house. "So that we can get to know each other properly. You can go to the cemetery later, everyone'll still be there."

He says again that he's curious, and starts telling stories. First, he apologizes for the sandwich: he hasn't had breakfast yet, he says, and the house here is the school and it has a refrigerator. His own hasn't been working for a few weeks.

"When I was in school," Sretoje says, not taking a bite of his sandwich, "there were seventy children here. Now there're three. I had a teacher who, let's just say, not everybody liked. Danica. Young and smart. Some of the parents didn't like her, I mean. What was the problem? She wasn't from here. Not from here and she'd brought her own ideas and all that from where she was from, you know.

"Ratko complained the loudest. He had three sons, each crazier than the last. Danica kept the sons under control, and Ratko didn't like that. Week after week he'd turn up at the school. Say he didn't like this and didn't like that. Home ec! Why should they study that? And so on. Well, one day Ratko fell off his horse pretty bad, broken bones and everything. The worst thing, though, was that he'd bitten his tongue so badly that they didn't know if he'd ever be able to eat again without a straw.

"And Danica, the teacher, was the first one besides the family to go see him in the hospital. With bananas! There were stories about that for a long time—that she'd brought him bananas. And also that she'd said to a doctor, right above Ratko's head, 'I hope you fix him up, but please, leave his tongue out of commission.'

"Yes, well, Ratko had to laugh. There were seven letters of the alphabet he could never pronounce again, but they weren't the real important ones, and he gave Danica a lot of credit for coming to see him. You never heard another bad word out of him about her. Danica went back to the city later, too bad, well, wha'd'you expect, and we ended up back with a male teacher, complete with discipline and cane."

We are still standing below the school, and Sretoje says: "What are we doing standing around here. Let's go to my place, have a seat like human beings." He leads us straight through the woods. "Your people have always been good to me." He looks at Mother. "Where do your folks come from, Marija?"

"Višegrad, all from Višegrad," Mother says, and she keeps talking—she has to distract him so that he doesn't ask about her family tree. We see a house at the edge of the forest and Mother asks who lives there.

"A cat. The man who built it was a volunteer in the army. Came back from two wars but was fatally wounded in the second, he just absolutely wanted to die here. His children died here. His grandchildren'll die somewhere else." Then, to me: "Don't stare like that. Of course he didn't come back here to die! He spent five years or who knows how long getting on everybody's nerves with his war stories."

Sretoje stops in front of that house and I think: Now, now he's going to take a bite of that sandwich, but he doesn't, instead he raises his voice like it's important for others, not just us, to hear what he's saying: "Build a house where your house stood! The land is yours, it's all yours!"

In the yard outside Sretoje's house, a sorb-apple tree is in bloom, a sow is wriggling into a pile of manure, a table is fading in the sun. He sometimes sleeps on that table at night during the summer, he says. For his back. For the stars.

He brings us over to his smokehouse, to his black dog, his black horse. "I keep him for riding, but now it's also to have someone to talk to," Sretoje says, adding that he misses his wife. "She spends almost all her time in the valley too." Then he laughs, and says: "Sometimes. I miss my wife sometimes."

He invites us in. After we take off our shoes, he says: "Marija, be so kind as to make us a coffee."

Mother tenses up.

Sretoje gives her the jar of coffee and sits down, invites Father and me to join him, and puts the sandwich down on the table. Mother looks around the room. She wants to ask something. Doesn't ask, doesn't say anything, opens cupboards. Father and I don't say anything either.

Outside, the grassy hills and the world curve in every direction: down into the valley, across meadows and fields and villages, and up to the imperious peak of Vijarac. This is Oskoruša.

"Don't hold it against me that I'm living here so ... that the house is so messy. I'm alone, I didn't know you'd be coming for a visit," Sretoje says, and Mother has found the coffeepot and is harrumphing.

"Don't get me wrong, I'm not trying to put on airs. We were the first ones in the village with an icebox," Sretoje says, and Mother busies herself about the stove.

"Thirteen kids and six grown-ups, we were. Mountain of shoes outside the door. You tripped over them coming in. You can't live around here without well-soled shoes, that's for sure. Mother cobbled and mended all day. If you needed new shoes anyway, you sent a letter and a couple days later the commune would bring you new shoes. Or flour. Or medicine. That was under Tito. The commune took care of you. But you were in trouble when the commune decided to take instead of give. Then there wouldn't be anyone standing in front of your door like Santa Claus with a sack full of shoes, but three or four people brandishing their IDs and not wanting to break bread with you," Sretoje says, and Mother presses buttons and holds out the palm of her hand to see if the burner is getting hot.

"Where I'm sitting right now was my father's place. At breakfast and at dinner. During the day he'd eat something in the field. He only ever sat here, always here," Sretoje says, and Mother pours water into the pot and puts it on the stove. She has turned her back to us and she briefly puts her face in her hands.

"All right then. Now for a drink," Sretoje says. "Marija, would you look there on the shelf, there's the bottle. Bring a glass for yourself, too, they're in the glass case." And while Mother pours the schnapps, Sretoje, at last, bites into his sandwich. He chews, and behind his back Mother tosses down her drink.

"Every one of us children had one God, one father, and one carpet," Sretoje says. "This one here is one my mother wove and dyed. To her soul!" He raises his glass.

Mother hesitates. Hers is empty, but she wraps her fingers around it and raises it to her lips again. We drink—Sretoje doesn't. He pours one drop into his hand, rubs it, and smells the spot.

"I want to make sure you understand," he says, taking a blister pack of pills out of his vest pocket. "It's my back. I'm not supposed to lift anything heavy, haven't been allowed to for six months. Couldn't even if I tried. Me! And I can't drink with you, I'm truly sorry. Don't hold it against me," Sretoje says, and Mother goes and stands by the stove again. The water's not even steaming yet.

"I've been to three hundred and seventy-four weddings," Sretoje says, and Mother waits for the coffee to boil.

"There were good times and bad times here. But never really terrible times, and that's the most important thing, right? I'd go down to the valley for a few weeks at a time during the winter, at most, and otherwise always be here. We used to need ten whole days to plow our fields. Ten days! Today all I have left is a potato field and a little clover," Sretoje says, and Mother waits for the water to boil.

"All that time, though, in all those years and decades, I never imagined that someday I'd be alone so much," Sretoje says, and Mother waits.

"I could go away. Could leave it all behind. But how. This here is what life gave us. I inherited it from my father, and he from his. It's not magic. What you get from your fathers—take

275

it! That's what they say. I don't say that. I tell my children," Sretoje says, and Mother waits for the water to boil, "if you're doing better somewhere else and you don't need this here, great—don't use it. But put a fence around it. The neighbor's cattle shouldn't get onto your land," Sretoje says, and the water is still not boiling.

"Let's not misunderstand each other," Sretoje says. "I'm not here because I need anything. I'm here because without me everything that's ours will fall apart. And I'd just as soon go with it, to be honest." He dabs schnapps on his palm again and sniffs it.

The water won't boil. Mother's hands ball into fists. Mother is furious that she has to wait for this water in this world. She's been standing at this ancient stove for ten minutes. She's furious, but at the same time definitely worried that the coffee's not done. And she's pissed off at us for letting her feel this anger and this worry. And she's right to be.

Sretoje takes a bite of his sandwich. Behind him, a giant, ancient telephone is hanging on the wall.

"Does that work?" I ask.

Sretoje picks up the receiver, listens, hangs up again, and says: "No."

Mother opens and closes various parts of the stove. Pours out some of the water. A censer is hanging above the stove. The top of the refrigerator is loose, not lying flat; a box of salt on top is about to slide off. On the door is a magnet shaped like the head of Irinej the First, Archbishop of Peć, with beard and funny hat and everything. Sretoje pours us another glass. In the bottle, I see for the first time, there's a wooden cross.

"The priest," Sretoje says, "blessed my still every year. Then one year he didn't come, and no one could taste the difference, so I stopped asking him to come."

Mother is pacing back and forth in front of the stove.

"Čajniče is the next big town around here," Sretoje says. "Had a spa in the seventies. Hotels you couldn't get into without a tie. Today Čajniče's a dump. The war took care of that. Forty-nine percent Muslim before, today it would be a hundred percent if it weren't for Kornjača and his troops, I'll tell you that straight out. The best thing though would've been if there hadn't been a war. I was a soldier, I won't deny it. Personally I never divided people by religion, never! I am what I am," Sretoje says, and Mother kicks the stove. Father and I look up, Sretoje takes a bite of his sandwich and keeps talking.

"In this country there are three criminals for every good man. I never went hungry, never went naked. But that happens nowadays, it does happen," Sretoje says, dabbing his palm with schnapps, and Mother goes outside.

She's back after maybe thirty seconds. With a stick, pretty thick, long as her arm. She stands in front of the coffeepot with the stick and winds up, holding the stick with both hands like a baseball bat.

There's a picture of a saint on the door to upstairs: Saint George, framed in gold. The dragon is snapping at his horse's flank. The horse shies. The saint's eyes are wide open, lance pointing to one side. Mother wipes her mouth with her sleeve.

"Let me ask you something," Sretoje says to me. "I'll believe what you say. A used car. If you buy it where you are and drive it here, plus customs and so forth. Say, three years old?"

I know the life cycle of the beaver better than I do used cars. I look at Father, but he's staring at Mother and not listening, so I mutter a few random numbers. Sretoje nods at everything, and now he's talking about his tractor, I can't follow what he's saying, there's a bang—

Mother puts the stick down. She looks around. Her cheeks are red. She takes the coffee jar, unscrews the lid, and pours some into the boiling water.

"My great-grandfather Milorad," Sretoje says, "lived to be a hundred and eighty-three. Until his hundredth birthday, everybody had to listen to him, the whole family, which meant half the village. He spent the last eighty-three years just thinking. When his youngest son, my grandfather, had killed a cop on the fire cliffs and had to run away, my great-grandfather went looking for him. Found him too. They talked. And my grandfather turned himself in."

"Why did he kill the cop?" Mother asks.

"Why does anyone kill anyone," Sretoje says. "They let him out after a couple years and he never killed anyone again, as far as I know." Sretoje stands up.

"Kristina Stanišić is a good person. Took good care of the gravestones in our branch. She did her part. Above and beyond what she needed to. Tell me, how's she doing? Is she alone much? Yes, it's on you to make sure she's not alone too much, that's on you. When I tell you about Kristina I need to stand up. You can't stay sitting with a woman like that."

Mother brings in the coffee. Pours us cups. We drink strong black coffee.

Father asks Sretoje about the fire cliffs.

"What do you want up there?" He coughs.

Father tells him about the snake pit. What he or we actually want up there isn't exactly explained. Before I can think of anything, Sretoje says that it's not a good idea to go up there. The paths'll break your leg and your heart, if you're not careful. And the weather—the weather's going to change in the afternoon, the sunshine now is just a trick. "And now I need to go check on the sheep, make sure they're not getting into my clover." Sretoje leaves the room without having finished his coffee.

Mother sits down and takes a sip.

"Did you see that old phone?" I say to her, just to say something. Then the dog outside starts up. He barks and barks. It's the only sound. Sretoje doesn't come back and the dog doesn't stop. We go outside, Mother in the lead.

The dog is baring its teeth and barking through the fence. But there's nothing there. The air like rosemary. The mossy table. Sretoje talking to the dog. Mother kneels in the grass next to Sretoje. The dog is going crazy, slobber running down its jaw. Mother sticks her hand through the fence. The dog snaps at the air, howls, shakes, and falls silent. Sniffs Mother's palm. Mother looks like she wants to whisper something to the dog. It yawns.

"Well, time for you to get going," Sretoje says. He keeps his eyes on Mother. "And if you really want to go to the fire cliffs," he says, "better not it too late!"

When we're out of sight, Mother stops. The forest is in front of us. The path slopes gently uphill and disappears into the underbrush. Vijarac looms overhead.

Mother says: "I don't want to go up there."

"I'm sure it's not far," I say.

"What? What's not far?"

I have no answer for us.

"What do you want up there, why are we here at all?"

"Nothing specific," I say. No snake turning into words and vice versa, I think. And I think: I know how to make coffee too. And I think: Something's missing. Someone's missing.

"So, now we'll go to the cemetery," Mother says, "then we'll drive home. There really is a storm brewing back there. I don't want to be stuck here in the rain too."

I agree at once. Mother doesn't seem anxious anymore, just annoyed, with good reason. This could have been simply a family nature hike, we haven't done anything nice together, just the three of us, for ages. Father goes a few steps toward the woods, but then turns back.

Yes, to the cemetery, to close at least one circle. The grass has recently been mowed, and fresh flowers are lying on one Stanišić. We pull out weeds, light candles. The first white flowers are budding on the sorb-apple tree. One sentence from my research has stuck in my mind (the remembered word), and I feel compelled to say it out loud: "The blossoms are in terminal corymbs in young brachyblasts." Father asks what that means and I can translate it only roughly.

I'm hungry. The flowers smell okay.

I look at my great-grandparents' dilapidated house, and there are so many things I don't understand. Not how knees work. Not seriously religious people, no more than people who put their money and their hopes in magic, betting offices, homeopathy, or clairvoyance (except Granny Merjema). I don't understand how anyone can insist on nationalist principles or how anyone can like sweet popcorn. I don't understand how where you come from is supposed to bring with it certain qualities, or how some people are prepared to slaughter others in the name of those qualities. I don't understand people who believe they can be in two places at once (but if anyone really can, I wish they'd teach me). I would rather be in two times at once. I like asking my son about his favorite things. "Purple's my favorite color," he recently told me. "And yours too." That I understand.

I stand under the Tree of Knowledge, and the tree's roots dig down into the grave of my great-grandparents, and up in the branches there is no snake hissing, no symbol left. There's just flowers in the branches.

We get back to Višegrad that night in the rain. We buy beer and a loaf of warm bread. Grandmother is sitting on the sofa when we walk in. I want to say something cheerful, but nothing cheerful comes to mind. I hug her and ask if she's had enough water to drink.

"You didn't find my Pero," she says hoarsely.

"No," I say.

"You didn't look hard enough."

Mother brushes Grandmother's teeth and we bring her to bed. We sit next to her, drinking beer.

Father asks if I'm glad I went back to Oskoruša one more time.

"Are you?"

He shrugs.

Mother says: "I'm glad. The landscape's glorious."

"Strange guy, Sretoje," I say.

"Not strange at all," she says.

Grandmother has shut her eyes. I put my hand on her cheek. We didn't look hard enough.

EVERY DAY

Grandmother never asks me how I'm doing. I always liked that. She says how I am: "You're hungry," she says. "You're tired."

Today I'm leaving again. Grandmother says: "You're upset."

That came as a surprise, because it wasn't true. I had been hungry when she said I was, and cold when she brought me a sweater. I am not upset today. Tense, maybe. Sad. I'm sitting across from her—another goodbye. She grabs for the spoon to stir her coffee; there is no spoon. Her movements are impetuous and slowed down like those of a child who's learning how to do things.

I'm not upset.

She drinks her coffee on the sofa with the pink blanket. The blanket is not nice. It's old. The hands in her lap are old. I am not upset.

I don't like how little she drinks. I am constantly offering her water. Sometimes I forget that she already has a glass and I bring her another one. You're thirsty, Grandma, you're tired.

That the neighbor locks Grandmother in the apartment when she goes out bothers me. But I agree it's the right thing to do, as long as there's no other solution. That we as a family still can't find another solution annoys me. Her chin on her chest.

Grandmother raises her head. "Don't be upset! It'll all fall in line, here and here." At the first "here" she puts her hand flat on her chest. At the second, she taps her finger against her forehead.

It bothers me that she doesn't say that. It bothers me that I imagine her saying it. In reality, she just sits there without moving, as though her sip of coffee has used up her strength.

I'm not upset. Nothing has to fall in line as far as I'm concerned. I can't make Grandmother younger or healthier. There is no story I can tell against her chin on her chest.

She drinks a little water. "Should we go for a walk?"

"I have to go," I say.

"Nonsense, no one has to go anywhere today."

"What day is today?"

"Every day."

YOU NEED TO PROTECT
YOURSELF FROM WHAT WANTS
YOU TO REMEMBER

Uncle sends a photo in the family chat: Grandmother huddling on a bed, chin on her chest. The wall behind her is turquoise. The sheets are a purée of yellow and green. Her broken arm the color of ripe plums. Grandmother in a strange bed.

Uncle writes: *She's not doing well.*

She's not doing well.

Those aren't her sheets.

Does she know where she is? I write.

Uncle doesn't answer.

Today is June 23, 2018. Uncle has taken Grandmother to the old-age home in Rogatica. A couple days ago, at home, she climbed up onto the stove to take down the curtains to wash them, and she fell. Rada found her moaning on the floor and took her to the hospital. They put her arm in a cast. Back home again, Grandmother hacked at her cast with a kitchen knife.

Rogatica is a small town surrounded by mountains. The mountain panorama is beautiful. But who decides what's beautiful? Grandmother can see the hospital from her window. Rogatica is even sadder than Višegrad. Who decides what's sad? During the war years, a farm at the edge of town was turned into a concentration camp for the non-Serbian population. On August 15, 1992, Dragoje Paunović Špiro's unit took twenty-seven prisoners to the front as a human shield. They survived the battle

and were then shot by Špiro's men. Armin Baždar was fifteen years old; he survived with two bullets in his arm.

On July 12, 2018, I visit Grandmother for the first time. She is lying in her room, on her side, legs bent, slippers on her feet. Her hand is sticking out over the edge of the bed, her glasses hanging loosely between her fingers. I take them so they don't fall on the floor. Grandmother doesn't move.

In the other bed, a very little, very old woman all in black is eating a pear. A tatty suitcase is waiting between her knees. It's hot. The air in the room reeks of plastic and pear. I want to open the window but there's no handle. I ask a nurse why. I already know why but I want her to say it. There's no handle so that the women don't open the window and jump out. She doesn't say *jump out*, she says *fall*. She brings me the handle, I open the window, and I stand in front of it.

Grandmother lies there unchanged.

Her roommate drags herself out of the room with the suitcase and the half-eaten pear. A nurse brings her back, without the pear. The old woman lethargically curses at her. Grandmother doesn't move. The nurse pours orange juice into two plastic cups. The old woman drinks hers and sits back down on the bed, suitcase between her knees. I take my grandmother's cup. The nurse says her name is Ana. I can't manage to pretend that I care what her name is. She leaves again.

A fly is looping around Grandmother's head, as if it's whispering something in her ears. There is a stud in Grandmother's earlobe, a simple round thing. Hairs in her ears; hairs on her upper lip. Birthmarks, age spots, I can't stand it. I grab her shoulder and call, "Grandma?" She opens her eyes, which are dull.

In Germany lots of older people spend the twilight of their lives in places like this. Is that what they call it, *the twilight of their life*? There are discussions with the family early on, agreements with friends to live in the same place once they can't live alone anymore. Who will supply the food? How's the view? Is there Settlers of Catan available? Questions like that.

In Bosnia, there aren't many senior facilities. Grandmother would probably have fallen off the stove every day rather than voluntarily gone into a home. The family, if it's intact, takes care of the eldest at home.

"Grandma?" I hold out the glasses to her. She puts them on and she scans my face: her look is serious, almost angry.

I've read up. You're not supposed to ask dementia patients too many questions. So I don't ask if she knows who I am. She doesn't smile—that'll have to do.

She wants to stand up, so I grab her elbow and she makes a face. It's her broken arm. I apologize and she gets up. Takes tiny steps. Stops in front of the wardrobe, leans against it. Those little steps. I have never seen Grandmother so weak.

"We're too late."

Don't ask questions.

"I waited all day."

"I'm sorry."

"The funeral started a long time ago. I wanted to see her but now she's definitely in the ground already."

"Who died?" Now I ask a question after all.

"Yes, this . . . woman! Where's my brush? Do you see how I look?" She grabs her hair; it's thin, the pale skin of her skull glimmers through. She opens the wardrobe and there's the brush.

I don't know anything about any funeral. I don't even know what year Grandmother's in at the moment. I don't know what she believes, where these walls around her are, what her turquoise means. Uncle told her that she had to spend some time in a convalescent home because of her arm. In a hotel. It's possible she's long since seen through the lie.

She roughly brushes her hair. "What time is it? Maybe we'll make it to the funeral meal."

On the patio, old people are sitting in the sun. One man in a wheelchair has no legs. Another man is rocking himself back and forth in a rocking chair but doesn't like the motion and is grumbling. One bald toothless lady says her tea tastes like orange juice.

I help Grandmother into an armchair.

"What are you doing? Why are we stopping here?"

"Grandma, I forgot where the funeral is happening."

"You know, there."

"Where?"

"I can't go like this. I need my watch. I need my shoes." She slides her slippers off.

"Grandma, please, whose funeral is it?"

"This woman, who's being buried."

Maybe she means herself.

She nudges me; she wants to keep going. I put her slippers back on. She looks for the exit. It's hidden by an overgrown rosebush hedge. I steer her farther into the garden. The old-age home is a civilized place. Turquoise façade, turquoise chairs, turquoise flowers. Whoever's in charge here likes turquoise.

In the garden, someone wearing no T-shirt under his overalls is mowing the lawn. The window from the common room is open and the TV is so loud that the bad folk songs are audible over the sound of the lawn mower. An old man passes us and gives an insanely loud fart.

Hell, I think. This is Hell.

Grandmother sways and has to sit down. The lawn mower falls silent and someone has turned off the TV. The only sound is of the crickets, when Grandmother says: "I so wanted to talk to the family, we see each other so rarely." She sounds inconsolable.

The sun shines hot.

There is no funeral Grandmother can go to. There is probably nowhere in the world she can go where she'll be safe, consistently happy, without this dull gaze.

I take her head between my hands. "Grandma, you won't believe what happened!" I look in her eyes. "They were getting the woman's coffin out of the chapel this morning and one of the bearers said, 'Do you hear that? Someone's knocking inside!' They took the lid off and there she was, alive and fresh as a daisy! And not too happy. 'Hey, what are you doing to me!'"

Grandmother repeats: "What are you doing to me?"

"She is arisen, the woman! I mean, she stood up! She wasn't dead at all! They almost buried her alive!"

I am one hundred percent sure that what I'm doing is wrong. But Grandmother smiles.

"It's totally crazy!" I cry.

"Not dead at all," Grandmother whispers.

"No one noticed."

"Or no one wanted to notice . . ." Grandmother raises an index finger in warning.

"The doctor didn't say anything either."

"Well that's no surprise."

"Right," I say.

"Crazy," Grandmother says. "Hey, what are we doing talking here without any coffee? Go get us some already!"

Right next door is a little café; you place your order from the garden, over the fence. When I come back with the coffee, Grandmother greets me and says a name, and it's my name. She's glad I'm there. I'm glad I'm there. My grandmother and I drink coffee in the sun.

"Crazy," she says softly. And then: "I don't want to die like that."

"Like what, Grandma."

"Not all at once."

EPILOGUE

Back in Višegrad that night. The apartment is strange without Grandmother. I sit on her sofa. The blanket on it is pink and clean and old. I drink water from the glass with the crack. Photographs everywhere: Grandfather Pero's face, Father's face, Uncle's face, Mother's face, my face, and my son's too. I no longer know what I'm doing here. I lie down at eight and wait for sleep.

In the morning I drive back to Rogatica. Grandmother is eating well; she drinks tea, talks about her family, especially about Zagorka. She's a little worried about her little sister who left with the goat at dawn and hasn't come back by dinnertime. When the worry gets painful and Grandmother gets loud, I make up something about Zagorka.

I brought a photo album with me. We page through Grandmother's biography. In the oldest photo, a young woman is sitting with friends on the grass at a picnic. In the newest, an old woman is sitting alone on her sofa. I don't know what bothered my grandmother in her life. What she would have wanted different. Now everything is different every day.

She looks for a long time at one photo, showing herself, her husband, and me between them. We're in her apartment. The embroidery above us like icons. Grandfather in his good jacket. I'm wearing a sweater vest that Grandmother probably knit. She is wiping her thumb tenderly on her husband's face.

"Do you remember him?" I point to myself.

"A little boy," Grandmother says.

When I first set foot in the Oskoruša cemetery, I assumed that Grandmother and Gavrilo wanted to show me the place to get me excited about its stories, my ancestors, my origins. They wanted me to drink water from Great-grandfather's spring and I felt pushed into a confession of belonging.

I'd been wrong. No one had expected anything from me. They were sharing with each other. On their own initiative, from their own pleasure in the burdens of family and the rigidity of time. There was pride in there, too, for everything that had been accomplished and inherited, irrespective of whether or not it had been theirs. None of it was mine, and it wasn't supposed to become mine. I just happened to be the chance witness to their taking stock together—not too late in a family affair for once. They were not alone but they knew they soon would be. Except death had another social surprise ready.

Furrows. Fences. The cross in the liquor bottle. Polenta for the parents-in-law. Vijarac. Gavrilo and Grandmother—now also Sretoje—told stories to commemorate all that. They put in a good word for their dead. The taste of the spring water is made of language. The language will keep flowing. Someone will survive to tell it. To say: My life is incomprehensible.

Gavrilo has a bum knee. Sretoje has the bad back. It comes from climbing, over the decades—from digging out and carrying off the mountains, in the right posture your whole life long, always bending from the knees, but sooner or later you'll need pain pills anyway.

On my third day in Rogatica, it's time to say goodbye to Grandmother again. I am flying to Germany in a couple of hours. We look at the photo album. Play dominoes. The photo album again. Eat rice with something. When Grandmother opens the photo album for the third time, I hug her and stand up. The other old people buzz around us. She pages through her past. Points to one photograph and says: "Is that me?"

I leave her with the question. We'll tell more stories soon, Grandma.

In the airport waiting area, a girl is clambering around next to an old man reading to her. At first I can't follow the story, but then I can, and it has a happy ending, and I would have preferred it if it ended differently. Travel, all the bright lights, the announcements. The seasonlessness of airport waiting areas.

I don't get on the plane. I cause a huge commotion over my suitcase, which has already been loaded onto the plane. I go to rent a car and have to wait hours for one to be free. I can't leave until evening. I drive back to Rogatica.

I get there an hour before midnight. In the glow of a hurricane lamp a man is cutting the rosebush hedge outside the old-age home. I park the car across from the gate. From here it looks like branches are growing out of the gardener's back. Like he's part of the hedge. His shears are giant; he must be strong to use them.

I walk through the gate into the garden. The hedge is overgrowing the path. The gardener surveys me with one eye; a patch covers the other. He is tall and hunchbacked. He shines the lamp at me. I squirm through the hedge, the thorns catching on the fabric of my jacket. Something, some animal, scrambles out of the sphere of light and the hunchback curses. Then I'm on the other side.

I say: "Thanks for the light."

He clearly recognizes me, because he asks if I've forgotten something. There's a wreath of branches around his bald head. His voice is raw; I try to find an image, and he snips off a tendril of thorns next to my ear. I duck under the sound and hurry toward the building.

"Yes," I call back, "I forgot to wish my grandmother good night."

DRAGON'S HOARD

WARNING!

Do not read this book in order! You decide how the story should continue—you create your own adventure.

You are the son of a sales manager and a political scientist specializing in Marxism. Grandson of a Mafia Godmother and a man who died too soon, a—well, a what, exactly? Great-grandson of farmers and a singer and a raftsman. You are me.

You have come back to the old-age home to wish your grandmother good night. But maybe you've come back so that Grandmother won't go to sleep.

The Slavs love danger. Countless dangers lie in wait for you! Your decisions may lead you to success, whatever success might be. Or to ruin.

Good luck.

YOU ENTER THE OLD-AGE HOME. The fluorescent lights flicker at you. On the walls in the hall are pictures. The residents made them. Paintings, pencil drawings, watercolors.

A house with a lawn.

A field of clover with a mountain backdrop.

A Mercedes-Benz.

A wrinkled face.

You cautiously open the door to your grandmother's room. She is sitting on the bed, and the light from the hall turns her into a silhouette.

"Is that you, Pero?" she says without turning around.

Do you lie? If you say, "Yes, it's Pero," turn to page 345

If you tell her the truth—"It's me, Grandma. Saša"—turn to page 301

YOU FORGET EVERYTHING you know about the Sirens' song, you throw all your experience with role-playing games where forest creatures lure travelers into traps out the window—you're sure nothing will happen to you. As soon as you take a few steps toward the water, a dozen leaf-clad beauties swirl around you, and when one of them touches you, seemingly by accident, your tongue is filled with the taste of honey or strawberries or steak, whatever your favorite food is. You get thirstier and thirstier—now you're running to the spring at top speed, while the forest women tease you, singing:

> *If a man only knew what it meant*
> *to lie on his belly drinking,*
> *he would never drink on his belly*

Your throat is dust. You have to drink. One of the vilas scoops up some water and holds it out to you in her hands.

You accept her offer and drink. Turn to page 346

You drink directly from the spring, lying on your belly in the grass. Turn to page 343

YOUR GRANDMOTHER SAYS IN A FLAT VOICE that she's glad you've come. You sit down next to her. Grandmother takes your hand.

"You've come too late."

"I'm here now."

"If my Pero knew you were coming, he would have taken you with him. He wouldn't have gone up alone."

"He's up on Vijarac, I know."

"Alone! And much too far away." Grandmother turns toward you. "Tell me, where is he? Where's my Pero?"

You tell her that Grandfather died a long time ago. Turn to page 345

You say that you're not sure, but that you don't know anyone who spends a long time with the dragons by choice. Turn to page 323

GAVRILO ARRIVES SHORTLY BEFORE DAWN. Sretoje and a man you don't know are with him. Their clothes are spattered black, as though from lamp-blacking. You are sitting with your sleeping grandmother. Marija has left.

Gavrilo nods when he sees you and Grandmother. Sretoje gives you an affectionate hard smack in the head. You hug and kiss each other. The stranger holds his left arm tight against his body, and there are little streams of dried blood on the back of his hand.

Gavrilo sits down next to Grandmother and asks what's up. His eyes are shining as he looks at her face. "We can help," he says, as though answering a question from her.

You say you're looking for Grandfather. She thinks he's still alive. Grandmother believes she's in a time when he took a trip around here.

"To the fire cliffs," Gavrilo says.

"How'd you know?"

"I guessed."

"When she wakes up, if not sooner, she'll have forgotten all this and I'll take her back. Oh, and to explain why Grandfather's not here and to make the trip seem more exciting, I told her that his disappearance had something to do with dragons."

When they hear the word "dragons," all three men turn to face you. Do they want you to say more? What else is there to say? That of course you don't believe in dragons. There are just as few dragons as there are Grandfathers. Or just as many.

The men stand up. Their boots crunch, their blood roars, their bass and baritone voices quiver as they all bellow at the same time: "Who says there're no dragons?"

Gavrilo adds: "Your plan's pretty idiotic, if you ask me."

At which point Grandmother, with her eyes still closed, cries, "Speaking of plans, when do we leave?"

We leave on page 337

DRAGONS HAVE INHABITED THE EARTH FOR FIVE THOUSAND YEARS. Where today's dragons come from is famed in song and story: the legendary realm of the Caucasus and Mesopotamia. Without the migration patterns of the past few millennia, there would be no dragons in the Oskoruša region. As it is, when you stop the rental car and get out with Grandmother, you hear in the clouds overhead a mighty beating of wings.

"What was that?" Grandmother asks.

"Just the forest rustling in the mountains," you say.

Grandmother yawns. And you shudder in the depths of your soul.

You drape your jacket over Grandmother's shoulders. The light inside the car goes out and the world with it.

Cellphone flashlight on, and off you go through the woods on page 315

GRANDMOTHER LEAVES THE ROOM AND STARTS TALKING. "Pero and I were in a hotel like this recently. Only it was much nicer. And by the sea. In Kotor. With Asim and Hanifa. Swimming, walks, hikes. Things like that." She decides to take the stairs; you hold her arm. "When you see Hanifa and Asim, tell them I'd be happy to get a visit from them."

Grandmother starts telling the story of a theft in the hotel. Then the lights go out. And right away come back on again. In one of the dark seconds, Grandmother stops talking.

You ask what was stolen and who stole it. Grandmother looks at you, annoyed, and keeps walking.

Hanifa and Asim fled Višegrad in the war and never came back. They've been dead for a couple of years. There's no need to mention that.

"A trip every summer," Grandmother says in the hall with the pictures. "Not always to a nice place, no. A lot of the time it was really boring. But we're together. That's all that matters." She stops in front of the field of clover. She says she knows where that is. "I want," she says, "to get out of here, do you hear me? With Pero. Not right away. I'm not being unrealistic. When I'm better."

The sound of the garden shears clacking in the rose hedge outside is much too piercing. Will the hunchback even let you leave with Grandmother?

You decide to see what happens, and you walk Grandmother out of the building through the main entrance. Turn to page 322

Do you try to find another exit? Turn to page 308

THE LIGHT IS ON IN GAVRILO'S HOUSE. You and Grandmother peer through the window. She whispers the name of the woman who's setting the table inside: "Marija." The fact that she recognizes Gavrilo's wife makes it easier for you to decide to knock.

The woman of the house opens the door without asking who's there. She smiles and kisses first Grandmother then you. "Come in, come in." Like it was nothing. Not the late hour, not the nearly a decade since the last time you saw each other.

Are you two hungry or thirsty? Since you say yes to both, she gets water, beer, and bread and invites you to sit down. "I thought the men would be back from the fire cliffs by now," she says, cutting the bread into thick slices.

You and Grandmother eat.

The photographs of the war criminals have disappeared.

Grandmother dunks the bread in her water.

You ask what the men are doing on the fire cliffs.

"Bickering with the vilas." Marija looks you up and down; you laugh, embarrassed. "They're burning the garbage," she says then. "It's safer up there. There's only cliff, the forest is far away. And it doesn't stink up our lungs." She turns toward Saint George and the dragon. Or the dragon and Saint George. They both stare back, unmoved.

Grandmother puts down her fork and yawns.

Marija asks how she's doing. She doesn't ask what brought you to Oskoruša. Grandmother admits she's tired. Wouldn't mind lying down for a bit.

Of course.

She lies down on the sofa, her hand covering her eyes. Marija puts a blanket over her.

You wish your grandmother good night.

Turn to page 302

YOU LEAD HER INTO THE COMMON ROOM by the entrance. There are tables here and there, a few chairs, two armchairs with creased leather, and in every corner a rubber plant in a bad mood. A game of Parcheesi has just been played. Red won, the other colors didn't play.

Grandmother spins the dice between her fingers. "We made our toys ourselves. Father liked that: carving and whittling. My little sister used to play with me a lot."

You look for the back door, but all the doors lead to bedrooms except for the one to the cafeteria. The rubber plants eye you. The TV set eyes you. The cafeteria menu and the calendar eye you.

An empty birdcage is hanging on a column. You don't know if it's supposed to be art or if the bird's coming back.

"Is there any way out of here, Grandma?"

She hands you the dice. There are two doors left.

You roll.

The dice come up odd: You open the door on the north side of the room. Turn to page 313

The dice come up even: You open the door on the east side of the room. Turn to page 317

YOU WAIT.

The gardener grins.

Grandmother says: "When I was a child I used to cry in the night a lot. When a child cries a lot in the night, people say that witches are eating up its insides. My Zagorka drove off the darkness and comforted me. I called her Little Sister. Even though she was older. She died in my bed. In the beginning she took care of me, in the end I took care of her. That's how it has to be.

"My little sister taught me a lot," Grandmother says, raising her arm, and suddenly the air around you is glittering and bright.

Turn to page 312

THAT WAS EASIER THAN YOU'D THOUGHT. The two of
you stroll down the street. You help Grandmother into the car.

She asks if you can play some music.

You can.

"Then please don't," Grandmother says, shutting her eyes.
After a few moments she falls asleep.

You let out your breath.

You are lying to your grandmother. You're lying to her by
confirming her belief that her husband's alive. You're uphold-
ing an illusion to spare her, a dementia sufferer, the unalterable
truth of the fact that he's dead. On the other hand, with the
truth, which she'd have to be told anew every day, he would die
again every day.

When she wakes up, she presumably won't remember
where you were going. So what now?

*You wait until Grandmother wakes up and take her back inside the home.
Turn to page 318*

The light is green. Off to Oskoruša. You start driving and turn to page 304

IN RESPONSE TO YOUR WORDS, THE DEMON RAISES THE LAMP TO YOUR FACE. His fingernails are thorns, the pupil of his eye a red rose. Something is crawling under his eye patch. He grins and takes a deep bow like an actor at a Christmas market. The hedge too—as the wind picks up—bows. Both freeze like that. The two of you duck past him and through the hedge. The creature smells extremely sweet, like he's gone overboard somehow with aftershave or chocolate.

Escape from here to page 310

THE BLINDING LIGHT turns into a piercing pain behind your eyes. Red, trembling spots. Only gradually does the world regain its contours. Grandmother, back straight, stiff as a soldier, is standing in front of the rental car. The two of you are on the street.

There's a shout from behind you.

"Let's get out of here!" cries a voice, maybe your own. You see a movement out of the corner of your eye, jump into the car, and open the door for Grandmother. She gets in, which takes a while, there's the sound of metal on metal, shears on enamel, doesn't matter, you got full insurance, and you're off.

Turn to page 304

BEHIND THE DOOR THERE'S ANOTHER BEDROOM.
A night-light gives off a little light. Three bodies on three beds.
You can open the window. It's about five feet to the ground. To
get to the street from there you wouldn't have to go past the
gardener, or through the thorny hedge.

You put a chair under the window so Grandmother can
climb up more easily. You're already getting a little nervous at
the thought that she'll have to jump out.

Grandmother bends over a sleeping woman: "Is that me?"

"Grandma?"

"You've ended up all over. Fine. I understand. I understand
your reasons. You call and ask how I'm doing. You drop by, have
a coffee with me, feed me. You tell me my toothbrush is old. You
say I have an apartment. This isn't my apartment. This isn't my
wall. How am I supposed to be doing between some strange
walls? You tell me. This isn't a hotel, or a spa. Because they don't
leave me alone here. They try to make me comfortable. That's all
anyone does with me: feed me, lie to me, make me comfortable."

Grandmother puts her hand on the sleeping woman's forehead. Strokes her hair.

The nurses say that she sometimes wanders around like a child
and tickles the other residents. Some of them like it, some don't.

You don't know how to reply. You'd prefer to simply say that
now you're here for her. But that isn't exactly true either. And
so: onward. Something else, maybe say something true: This
isn't a hotel.

---

*You try to convince Grandmother to flee out the window—"Then let's get
out of here!" Turn to page 310*

*It's much too risky. You decide to try the other door from the common room.
Turn to page 317*

YOU GET GRANDMOTHER DRESSED. She has goose bumps. You roll the socks over her feet and up to her knees. Her skin is rough and saggy. A blouse. A sweater. Wool pants. You try to force her foot into a boot, but the boot is much too small.

"Those aren't my shoes."

There are more shoes in the wardrobe: a pair of flats and a pair of turquoise-blue glow-in-the-dark sneakers. You pick the sneakers.

While you're kneeling in front of her, she asks what people need. Against dragons.

"Weapons. Preferably magic ones."

The sneakers fit.

"Hopefully we won't need to fight at all. We'll just find Pero and bring him back."

Grandmother's possessions are in the wardrobe: Some items of clothing. Her hairbrush. A comb. Nail clippers. An empty plastic bottle. Her watch. The diapers. A half-eaten bar of chocolate, badly hidden under the family photo album. This is her life. You should have labeled the photos with names and dates.

You leave on page 305

THE FOREST PATH IS A CHALLENGE, MUDDY AND UNEVEN. You make slow progress. Even so, Grandmother asks you to go slower. The two of you rest on a fallen tree trunk. Your phone is at 33%. The reception goes in and out.

You reach the first house after an hour. Grandmother stops and looks at it. A blue door to a ruin. The pole for the power line is on a roof full of holes; the house is hanging from the power cables like a marionette.

"Look how dark it is when the lights are out," Grandmother says. "Inside, the darkness is all clammy between the stone walls. But you've got your family around you. You can hear them breathing. Father. Mother, blinded at a young age. Little Sister, my Zagorka. She let me sleep in her bed. Sweet-smelling breath, sour-smelling breath."

Grandmother seems to think she's in Staniševac, her childhood village. "Should we wake Little Sister up?" she asks.

"This is your house?"

"Yes." Grandmother thinks it over. "Wait. No. Ours . . . ours has two stories. And the roof is whole. We eat and relax downstairs. Sleep upstairs. Nine children and six grown-ups, two brothers' families.

"Strange. I don't know what I have to do tomorrow. By nighttime everyone knows their task for the next day. You go here and you go there. This one watches the cows. That one the sheep. We have a hundred and seven sheep. Two of us have to bake the bread and prepare the meals. One stays home and looks after the chickens and takes out the garbage. This and that. Now, in the summer, there are things to do in the fields. No one asks or is asked what they'd like to do. You just need to be able to do it. Lately I've been darning socks all day."

Grandmother turns to face the blue door. "This isn't Staniševac, is it?"

You avoid her gaze. "No."

"I know where we are." Grandmother pinches your cheek. "It'd be better if we had horses." Grandmother starts walking.

"What, now?"

"Horses see better than you, you donkey. Anyway, I know the path." She points to the mountains behind you. Vijarac's peak towers up into the cloudy sky, and somewhere up there fires are burning. Lots and lots of fires. Flickering and dying out. Flaring up again. Licking, waving ribbons. Going out. Flashing on in several places at once. It's like someone is painting with fire on the canvas of the night. Someone, or something.

"Dragons." You're whispering.

Grandmother laughs and puts her arm in yours. "Well it's not butterflies, you donkey."

Today is October 29, 2018. I just wrote: "Well it's not butter-flies, you donkey." My phone rang. My grandmother has died at the age of eighty-seven in Rogatica.

Sretoje's farm is on the hill to the east, on page 321

You'd rather go in and see Gavrilo. It looks like the lights are still on at his house. Turn to page 306

THE NURSE BOLTS UP OUT OF HER OFFICE CHAIR.
She asks what's happening, smoothing her white coat, her
cheeks reddened from sleep. Before you can answer, Grandmother has shouted: "We want to hunt dragons in Oskoruša,
Ana, my dear."

You shake your head and act like Grandmother's not in her
right mind, muttering something about a little outing.

The nurse has heard enough. Residents aren't permitted
to leave without being signed out, and never in the middle of
the night. While she's talking, she slips her arm into Grandmother's and guides her to the stairs. Just joking with her,
Grandmother titters.

In the room the nurse helps her get undressed. You hope
Grandmother will defend herself. She yawns. The nurse leaves
the two of you alone, not without giving you a last accusatory
look. She even turns off the light in the room.

"Grandma? Everything okay?"

you say into the half darkness on page 345

IT IS EARLY MORNING IN ROGATICA when you wake up. Grandmother's gone. She fell asleep in the passenger seat, you didn't want to wake her up, and you must have nodded off yourself in the parked car. You can't find her anywhere outside the old-age home either. The hedge looks like hedges do. Pretty roses, if you like that sort of thing.

The old people are hunched over their steaming plastic cups on the porch. A nurse comes toward you in the hall. Yes, Kristina, she's here watching TV.

Grandmother is sitting on a stained leather sofa combing her hair with her fingers. The TV above her is screeching a morning show. The hostess asks a little dog a question. The little dog doesn't answer. The hostess now tries asking the little man. He runs a school for nervous dogs.

You sit down across from Grandmother. She smiles.

Have you seen her brush.

You have.

Would you brush her hair.

You get the brush from the wardrobe in her room and brush your grandmother's hair.

She says, "Good morning, Saša."

"Good morning, Grandma."

"What do we have planned for today?" Grandmother turns off the TV and looks at you.

"What would you like to do today, Grandma?"

"Maybe we can go visit Zagorka? Last time you made it all the way up on foot. I didn't have to carry you at all. From the valley to the house."

"I'd like that," you say. Zagorka's house is in ruins, you think.

"The plum harvest is soon," Grandmother says.

You help her up. The two of you take a stroll around the home. Then it's game time. Dominoes are handed out. Your grandmother's fingers are too quick for the other old people, she wins every time. Your grandmother's still got it. For lunch, there's turkey with potatoes and vegetables.

THE END

"AND WHO ARE YOU?"

You say you're her grandson.

"So?" The hunchback leans on his shears and peers past you at Grandmother. "Kristina. You never told me you had grand-children." Grandmother sniffs a rose. "Is that your grandson, Kristina?"

She shakes her head.

You go over to her and say you are. You say your name.

Grandmother waves you away with a laugh. "My Saša goes to school. He's a good boy, always gets the best grades."

You mention Grandfather, and you tell the gardener that you can get your ID from the car if he wants, the same last name, etc.

Grandmother asks if she can pluck a rose. The gardener plucks one for her. As he does, his face flinches as though he'd pulled out one of his own hairs. He gives Grandmother the rose and walks her into the building, to the nurses' break room.

You follow them onto page 317

THE HOUSE IS DARK AND SILENT. Sretoje's dog, Cigo—that's not this dog. This dog's crazy barking says to keep away as you and Grandmother get closer to the property. This dog is blacker than night. It pushes against the fence and screams at the mountains. You talk to it. But its fear is more important to it than you are.

If Sretoje were here, he would no doubt have woken up a long time ago. Still, you pound on the door a few times. Nothing. You try the handle. Locked.

Today is October 30, 2018. Memorial candles are burning in the window of our apartment in Hamburg. I'm looking at photographs of my grandmother. In one of them I'm sitting on her lap. I am six years old and forty years old. It's hard for me to remember her as a healthy woman. It's hard for me to keep my grandmother here, *alive.*

The horses whinny. Grandmother goes into the stall. You follow her. She is already dragging a saddle along the ground.

Come on, help her already, on page 329, what are you doing standing around like that?

THE GARDENER IS WAITING FOR YOU. He has shouldered his shears and is standing guard in front of the hedge. Legs apart. Back hunched. The shears seem even bigger than they did when you got here—they clang like swords. The hedge seems even more disheveled, with branches shooting out and waving like tentacles in the wind.

"Where are you going, my dears?" His voice is scratchy. He sticks his pinky under his eye patch, as though to wipe his eye.

You position yourself in front of Grandmother and wait, without a word, to see what will happen on page 309

You say, "We're having a little outing, we'll be back tomorrow evening at the latest." Turn to page 320

You have read enough Southern Slavic folklore to know that you're dealing with a demon whose life is eternally linked to the life of the plant. He lives with the rosebush, he will die with the rosebush. So you shout: "Out of my way, spawn of Hell, or I'll slice your jugular open!" Turn bravely to page 311

"DRAGONS? ON VIJARAC?" Grandmother squeezes your hand.

"Tree dragons. Cave dragons. Shape-shifters. Many-headed monsters. Serpents that write poetry. Saint George wasn't too thorough, it seems."

"What's this nonsense you're talking?"

"Nonsense? Okay. Then we'll just wait here for Pero to come back."

She jumps up. "No more waiting," she shouts, so loud that you're worried she'll wake up the other woman in the room. Then she has to laugh, at the top of her voice, in the stale air of the room, in this world furnished with lavender to keep the moths away. "Dragons," she shouts through the laughter. But she turns serious again when she asks: "Tree dragons?"

"Tree dragons collect shiny things."

"Then we better not dress in gold, if we think we might meet one," Grandmother says, opening the wardrobe. "Now help me get dressed."

"Where are we going?"

"To hunt dragons like you said, you donkey! To hunt dragons."

The hunt begins on page 314

IT'S LIGHT OUT. Grandmother has disappeared and so have the dogs. You get out of the car and call for her. Like before: *Throw the ball down, Grandma. I'm hungry, Grandma.* Her head would appear in the window and she'd do what you wanted, or else wouldn't.

Your grandmother's head appears in the window.

You shout, "I was worried."

Grandmother shouts, "So?"

Mother is making coffee when you come in. She gives you a kiss. Father, Uncle, and cookies are waiting for the mourners in the living room. A woman and her son are already there. He knows you; the two of you used to play soccer in the stairwell as children, he says. You can't remember this and you say you remember it.

Grandmother sits on her sofa listening. The praise for the dead. They've thrown out the pink blanket. Today is November 1, 2018. Grandmother has been dead for three days. On the little table, the one with the glass surface and the crocheted doily, there are four cellphones. Mother serves the coffee.

Zorica, the neighbor from the third floor, hugs you, takes a cookie, and says that when she was at the market she ran into the priest who's going to be doing the ceremony at the cemetery.

You're surprised.

"She wanted that," your uncle says.

"By the way, the youngest male relative carries the cross to the grave," your father adds. "That's you."

This must be a joke, you say. If you picked up a cross then either the cross or your hand would burst into flames. Probably both.

Grandmother says, "Don't be egotistical."

"If Grandpa ever finds out that an Orthodox priest is dancing around his grave," you say, "he'll dig his way out and punch him in the face personally."

"In that case," Zorica says, "he probably would have done it when the priest blessed his own grave."

"The priest did what?"

"Afterwards. Kristina asked him to a few years ago."

"That can't be true."

"I took him there myself, I swear by my mother. Kristina was in the hospital. And he couldn't help making a comment about the star on the gravestone. He told me to tell Kristina to get rid of it. That sure made her mad."

Two older women and a thick cloud of perfume come into the room. Grandmother rolls her eyes and disappears into the bedroom. You follow her.

"I think that's strange, about the priest," you say. "Since when are you religious?"

"It's just a precaution. In case any of it's true. If not, well, you've spent a little money and had to listen to some singsong. Actually you have to listen to it, I don't." Grandmother grins.

In the next room, Father is telling the story about trying to help Aunt Zagorka cut down some trees. He tried and tried, couldn't do it, and then Zagorka came up, took the ax out of his hand, and bam, chopped down half a forest. Grandmother waves her hand to brush away the stories and they fall silent.

She opens drawers. Standing by the wardrobe, she presses her nose into her blouses. Her Complete Crochet Works are in the glass-fronted cabinet—tablecloths, coasters, wall hangings, cushion covers. How many hours did she spend on them?

She runs her fingers over the patterns, takes some pieces out and presents them to you. These are clearly the especially good ones but you can't tell the difference.

"I'm sorry we didn't find Grandpa."

"Doesn't matter." She sits down on the couch. The green fold-out couch, older than you are. She strokes the surface. You know the Bosnian word for the fabric but not the German word. You know exactly what it feels like. Hairy, soft, but a little rough at the same time.

"I should have been there for you more," you say. "We all should."

"It's all right, sunshine. We had our time together. Let's just talk a little more."

"About what, Grandma?" You sit down next to her.

Grandmother takes your chin in her hand and kisses your forehead. "Oh, you know, maybe we won't say anything after all. And then I'll go. They're calling again outside. Let them wait a bit longer."

They're calling again outside.

Grandfather's calling, you hope.

The girl, and the soldier too.

Asim and Hanifa.

The siblings. Loudest of all: Little Sister, Zagorka.

Grandmother shuts her eyes.

Grandmother listens.

Grandmother asks: "Is that me?"

THE END

No, not the end. Someone you love dies. Has died. "Is that me?" were Grandmother's last words in the old-age home in Rogatica, spoken to no one. Just what I've been asking myself in this book: Is that me? Son of these parents, grandson of these grandparents, great-grandson of these great-grandparents, child of Yugoslavia, refugee from a war, ending up by chance in Germany. Father, writer, character. Is all that me?

I remember the sound of my nickname, when Grandmother used to say: "Everything's just a game to you, Sašice." It was a gentle childhood without much strictness.

Am I still that?

All the short visits to see her after the war. Every time we were a bit more foreign to each other—the familiarity was the past. I was always rushing around, she was always there.

With my girlfriend and our child to go see her, nine months after the child's birth. Grandmother pushed him through town in the baby carriage. She wasn't used to steering and let the carriage go faster and faster, ran behind it, talking sweetly to her great-grandson while she ran.

I put my hand on her cheek. I wish my grandmother a good night. I wait until she falls asleep. I sit down in the common room.

There's a canary in the birdcage. I open the file WHERE_ YOU_COME_FROM.doc. I write:

I put my hand on her cheek. I wish my grandmother a good night. I wait until she falls asleep. I sit down in the common

room. There's a canary in the birdcage. I open the file WHERE_
YOU_COME_FROM.doc.

THE END

And I close it again.

I write: Grandmother saw a girl on the street. Don't be scared, she shouted from the balcony to the girl, I'll come get you. Don't move!

Grandmother goes down the three flights of stairs in her stocking feet, and it takes time, it takes time, her knee, her lungs, her hip, and when she gets to where the girl had been standing the girl is gone.

THE END

YOU'VE NEVER SADDLED A HORSE IN YOUR LIFE. Grandmother has, but she's forgotten how it's done. She helps by saying sentences that start: "I think you need to . . ." But that's not how it's done. Or: That is how it's done but you can't do it. The horse's patience comes to an end relatively quickly; it is no longer calm.

You pull out your cellphone. No reception. When you're standing in the gate to the stable, something appears on the phone: "2G." You search for *saddle horse* on YouTube. There are countless videos. You are standing under a sorb-apple tree in Oskoruša and waiting for a video to show you how Mia from Schleswig-Holstein, Germany, saddles her horse.

Grandmother grabs for your phone. You let her take it away from you, because that is right. She touches the screen until it goes black.

"When Father says before bed, 'Kristina, you'll do the horses,' I'm happy," Grandmother says, and she strokes the horse's flank. "We have two. One for riding, the other for work. Zekan. That's the riding horse's name. The other—I don't remember. I can ride fast, but I always ride slow, to take as much time as I can. The riding horse is named Zekan, the Germans took him and . . ." Grandmother pauses. "Did the soldiers? . . ." She doesn't expect an answer. Grandmother gives the horse a little slap and goes out into the yard.

"Should we keep going on foot?" you ask.

"No. Let's sleep and keep going tomorrow," Grandmother says.

"Good. We can see if Marija and Gavrilo are at home and spend the night with them. Or we can drive straight to Višegrad."

"I'm cold," Grandmother says, and she starts running. You catch up to her and lead her

. . . *to Gavrilo's house: Turn to page 306*

. . . *to the car and drive back to Višegrad: Turn to page 336*

THE LEAVES OF THE BEECH TREE FLUTTER RED AND
ORANGE IN THE WIND. Bushes and underbrush snatch at
the horse's fetlocks. You have to dismount and lead the horse by
the reins. Grandmother is the only one who stays in the saddle;
Gavrilo leads her horse and his own through the woods.

"How are you doing, Grandma?"

She takes a deep breath. "I used to love riding, but didn't
do it often enough," Grandmother says. "I don't recognize this
forest. This isn't the road home, is it?"

"Where do you live?"

"My sunshine," Grandmother says. "My joy. My little donkey. Try to finally understand. It doesn't matter where something is. Or where someone's from. What matters is where
you're going. And in the end even that doesn't matter. Look
at me: I don't know where I'm from or where I'm going either.
And I can tell you—sometimes that's not such a bad thing."

*I can't think of how I might answer. I've been in Grandmother's
apartment in Višegrad for hours. People have been dropping by all
day, giving us condolences and staying for a coffee or a quick drink
or whatever. I didn't know this was the custom. The family needs to
be there between the death and the burial, to receive guests.*

"I'm dead?"

"I didn't know this was the custom. The door stays open
all day."

"How did I die?"

"Your sons and their wives are here, your grandchildren too."

"How did I die?"

"In your sleep."

"As they say."

"A neighbor's brought pita."

"Potato pita? That must be Nada."

"She's crying."

"What is she saying?"

"That she's thankful. To you. She says the pita's for the children. That their mother and grandmother was a good person. That she helped her . . ."

"When she needed help most."

"Exactly. And the policeman's here too."

"Andrej?"

"Yes."

"Is he sad?"

"Everyone's sad, Grandma."

"Andrej looks so good when he's sad. And where are you?"

"In your bedroom."

"Are you writing your stories?"

"Yes."

"How does this one continue?"

Do you know? Turn to page 340

Do you not know? Turn to page 340

BECAUSE OF THE RAIN, YOU MAKE SLOW PROGRESS ON THE SOPPING WET CLIFF. Every step's dangerous. Pebbles clatter down into the abyss from under your feet. You cross a stream that plunges down into the valley as a steaming waterfall. The water's warm.

Grandmother dismounts and wipes her face. She wants to keep going on foot. You take turns at her side—sometimes it's Gavrilo holding her under her arm, sometimes Sretoje takes her hand, sometimes you. Grandmother is pale and indefatigable.

More and more loose stones and boulders are on the slope. Rocks shimmering red cover the crest like scales. The fire cliffs. Here is where Father, decades ago, woke the snakes and woke in you a fear that you've carried with you your whole life in a word.

The peak looms directly overhead, a steep cliff wall, chalk-white. Gavrilo takes a narrow path parallel to the ridge. Columns of smoke shoot out of the cliff. The taste of sulfur in your throat. A hawk on the ledge screams, and Sretoje says: "They're waiting."

You would have missed the cave entrance if Gavrilo hadn't stopped. A fissure in the rock, just wide enough for a person to slip through if they're not too big. Gavrilo walks up ahead with the lantern. Marija hands you a torch and walks into the tunnel behind Grandmother and you. Sretoje stays outside the entrance.

The tunnel passes through the cliff, sloping down slightly. A bright beating sound is coming from inside the mountain, accompanying your steps—a massive, steel heart! At the first fork in the tunnel, you pause, and the beating stops. You drink. When Grandmother starts up again, the hammering comes back.

You pass a second crossing, then a third. Gavrilo leaves chalk markings on the wall. At every additional branching off, he hesitates longer. Talks it over with Marija. She takes the lead but soon she too stops at an intersection of several paths. She and Gavrilo turn toward you.

"The cave is alive," Gavrilo says.

"Be careful," Marija says.

"The paths through the cliff are never the same for anyone."

"There's not a way in for everyone. In other words," Gavrilo says, and Marija completes the sentence: "We're going in circles." She points to the chalk marking. "Whichever way Gavrilo or I choose, we always come back here. There's no path forwards for us."

"It's not your trip, is what Vijarac is saying. Vijarac would let us wander around for a thousand years."

"Only going back," Marija says. "Out. That's the only possibility."

It's warm. Soft, clattering drips on the stone.

"No way we're going back." Grandmother speaks. "It's not *your* trip." She hugs them both. "A good story," she says, "is like our Drina used to be: never a silent trickle, always wild and wide. Tributaries make it bigger, it roils and seethes, overflows the banks. There is one thing that neither the Drina nor a story can do: go back." Grandmother looks at you. "I want us to finally get there."

"And from you, Marija," she says, holding out her hand, "I want the rapier."

Silence. In the cave. In the old-age home in Rogatica. At my grandmother's grave in Višegrad on the morning of November 2, 2018.

"What's waiting for us if we keep going?" you ask.

"Only you know that," Grandmother says. "I'm in Rogatica. I'm in Višegrad. I'm the character."

It's time to leave the cave. Take Grandmother back to the old-age home on page 318

Today is October 31, 2018. For me it's time to leave this fiction behind. My grandmother is no longer alive. Today the mourning guests are coming to pay her their last respects. Your grandmother is still alive. You bring her home on the next page.

Never stop telling stories. You descend deeper into the mountain on page 341

A LITTLE BEFORE VIŠEGRAD, GRANDMOTHER FALLS ASLEEP IN THE PASSENGER SEAT. You drive on through empty streets. The streetlamps whitewash the façades a warm gray. A pack of dogs trots behind your car.

The bridge over the Rzav and the eternally spawning fish. No fishing today. A gap in the architectural row of teeth where the pharmacy used to be. The china shop. A neighbor once told a story about a Chinese baby, full of amazement, like she was talking about a circus act. Conclusion: "Even though it was Chinese it was unbelievably sweet." The second mosque wasn't rebuilt. In the building over there was the arcade, with the tempting tinkling of video games and pinball machines. Today it's a betting office. A woman in her midthirties has her shift there from ten to ten; between three and six, her two black-haired children (three and six) are with her.

The inventories need to stop sometime.

You park in the lot. The dogs consider their next move. You won't get out of the car until they leave. They spread out around the car and lie down on the pavement. Grandmother snores softly.

You close your eyes for a minute too. On page 324, you wake up

GRANDMOTHER KNOWS EXACTLY WHERE SHE IS and knows why she's here.

She insists: "We should go."

Gavrilo doesn't try to talk her out of it. "Where we're going," he says, "we need to be at full strength. Are you at full strength, Kristina?" He wants to help her up and she shows him her strength: she gets up on her own.

The men wash up at the faucet. The injured man talks to Gavrilo and leaves the house. Something's in the air. The table was set for six, and there are six of you.

Marija walks into the room. And how—hair in a braid, a golden circlet adorning her brow. Gavrilo stands up and hugs her. The pommel of a weapon is sticking up over her shoulder. No one asks any questions, so you don't either. It's that kind of night. The weapon: a rapier.

Everyone sits down at the table. The room is warm, your eyelids heavy. Gavrilo and Grandmother are whispering at the head of the table. You can barely follow the conversations.

The wounded man comes back. There is no more blood on his hand. He nods at Gavrilo, and you understand too: time to head out.

"Can you ride?"

The horses are waiting in the yard. Not having been in the saddle for many, many years—that's one thing. Ending up with the most stubborn, refractory horse—that's another. Before long the path gets very steep, and you can catch up to the others.

It starts to get darker, but the sun is still there behind the clouds. A first hint of thunder rumbles above Vijarac's peak.

At the edge of a beech wood, whose leaves are autumnal red despite the time of year, you take a break. The turning of the pages smells like the storm in a final chapter.

You ride deeper into the forest on page 331

YOU LEAVE THE FOREST. Whipping wind and rain spur you on. There's no shelter up here—Vijarac's other face is practically bare rock. Moss and lichen, crippled bushes.

You check your phone again for the time, and it would have surprised you if it still had any charge, this close to the finale.

"Peroooooo!" Grandmother suddenly screams. An echo comes back. After a few moments it's raining on your grandmother's name too. The mountains call for Kristina in a man's voice, a voice that makes your grandmother smile.

Up to the peak, on page 333

AT THE EDGE OF A CLEARING, a meadow gripped by a cloud of fog. Women singing. The vocabulary almost familiar, but still somehow foreign—an old-fashioned dialect, maybe?—and so lovely that Gavrilo warns you to be careful and gives you a sign to detour around the place.

The clouds dance.

A steep drop-off to the right; lines of song growing ever more urgent from the clearing to the left.

The horses shy.

You follow Gavrilo and Grandmother, with Marija and Sretoje behind you and the stranger bringing up the rear. You don't even know his name yet. He's probably the guy who has to die at some point, like the anonymous member of the *Star Trek* crew on missions outside the ship.

And you slip—a misstep on the dewy grass. You slide down the slope and clutch the meadow to stop yourself.

The grass is warm. The blades writhe like they're trying to free themselves from under your hand. A choir is singing at the back of your neck, *crescendo*. The wisps of fog float toward you.

You're thirsty. A sudden, uncontrollable thirst.

Conveniently enough, there's a clear spring in the middle of the clearing.

It's also convenient that you suddenly understand the words being sung. They're an invitation:

If a man only knew what it meant
to drink from the spring with us,
he'd never drink with anyone else

Obviously a trap. You return to the safety of the woods on page 344

Water and mythical female creatures who want to drink with you on page 300!

"THEY SAY THAT WHEN A VILLAGE DIES, SO DOES ITS WATER." Grandmother plays with a little rivulet seeping out through the rocks. She drinks from it. Lets it flow over the blade of the rapier. "Our water source in Staniševac wasn't very convenient. The village was up on the cliff but the water was at the foot of the mountain, below the lowest house. Not too well thought out, you'd have to say. Hauling water up the mountain your whole life. But since we were people who'd rather move a mountain than a house, that's how it stayed."

Grandmother starts walking again, then stops right away, puts her hand on her breast, and gasps for breath. Sheer willpower drives her onward. She sets the rhythm of the beating from the depths.

You've marked every crossing you pass, and you're not going in a circle. At the next crossing, you decide to take the wider of the two tunnels, and a roar shakes the mountain—so loud that it sounds like it's coming from around the next bend. A wave of hot air hits your faces.

Grandmother's knees buckle. The hammering gets slower until it stops entirely.

You hurry over and she waves you away. Rubs her eyes. It smells like burning grass now. Your eyes itch too. Grandmother spits. Onward. She wants to keep going.

The tunnel ends at a narrow ledge. The cliff opens up into a huge round crater. A burned-out landscape spreads out below you, its foundation a fire-blackened layer of rock dotted with green islands: fields, even a little village, shielded by bright columns from the charred or still blazing remains. A river of flame borders it all in a ring of fire. There is simply fire everywhere, sparks and smoke everywhere. And dragons everywhere.

An incomprehensible, teeming, dazzling, scaly scene. Dragons small and large, most of them winged, resting and eating and breathing fire, crawling alongside the village on clawy paws. Serpents with paws, cave dragons, long-necked basilisks with horned skulls soaring up out of the fiery river.

There is a footbridge of light wood crossing the river; despite all the fire nearby, it seems untouched. At the place where the bridge reaches the other shore, the cliff has opened its maw. A mighty breach in the stone yawns with darkness that can't stay put: shadows reach out from it into the world.

A three-headed monster is guarding the bridge. Each of its wrinkly heads is bickering with the other two, judging by its violent movements. It's not clear whether the dragon is guarding the bridge so that nothing crosses over to the other side that doesn't belong there, or so that nothing that mustn't enter our world escapes.

The walls of the gigantic cavern are lined with openings, honeycomb-style. You and Grandmother are standing in one of them. Dragons come out of them, or fly in—like this one, a reddish specimen with a long tail ending in a flipper and huge, see-through wings with which it effortlessly takes off and sets its course . . . straight at you.

Grandmother raises the rapier on page 348

YOU FEEL THE COLD WATER IN YOUR THROAT and a cold grip on your neck. Something pulls you down into the depths. Something dances with you. How does it look? Decide for yourself. The Devil is different for everyone. Anyway, it certainly seems that your trip has reached

THE END

"That is so stupid!" Grandmother cries. "We've come this far and you let the Devil trick you?"

"I made a deal with him."

"Tell me."

"Tomorrow. It's late now." Grandmother grumbles but goes and lies down. I take off her slippers. My grandmother was the good vila of my earliest years.

"Sašice?" She's whispering. The echo of my nickname from the past. "Everything's a game to you, Sašice."

I pull the blanket over her and stay sitting with her for a while longer.

THE END

YOU CLAMBER BACK UP THE SLOPE as fast as the muddy soil lets you. Sretoje holds out his hand and pulls you up. The song is still tempting. But the forest is growling. Marija has pulled out her rapier, and Gavrilo talks to her, trying to calm her down. Everyone needs to keep calm.

The rear guard is too quiet. The stranger doesn't seem to be there anymore. You shout for him, go back a bit on the path, look for him. Nothing. The women's singing comes to a joyful conclusion. That's a good sign.

"Vilas." Grandmother spits three times.

Gavrilo, Sretoje, and Marija confer. They keep looking up at the sky. The first raindrops fall.

"Onward!" Gavrilo cries. "We'll worry about it later. Maybe this time they only want to dance. Let's keep going."

He quickens his pace to page 339

YOU'RE TALKING TOO LOUD. The roommate stirs in her bed. Smacks her lips.

Grandmother lies down. "Tuck me in? I'm so tired."

You tuck her in. She tucked you in hundreds of times when you were little. You wish your grandmother a good night.

"It's good we're here," she whispers, feeling for your hand.

You don't know what she means by "we." Nor do you know where her "here" is. Whoever, wherever—anyway, something's good.

THE END

THE FIRST SWEET SIP SLAKES YOUR THIRST AT ONCE. You can't do anything but drink everything in the vila's hands . . .

. . . and the next thing you see is the clearing from overhead. You're floating in the air, the vilas are dancing with you, it's really nice, somehow, to be so light, and you know all the dance steps, but you're going to get tired at some point. You want to keep going . . .

. . . now it's autumn. You hadn't thought vilas would be such cleanliness fanatics. You have to sweep their tree houses every day, and wash their dishes in the mountain streams, with no dish soap of course . . .

. . . and winter is here. You don't have any clothes except what you had on when you came to the clearing. The vilas laugh at you. Sometimes they keep you warm . . .

. . . and spring comes. You never get any rest anymore, it's all playing and dancing and cleaning, and the vilas don't have a Netflix subscription but at least they can add new songs to their repertoire. You sing along, feed yourself on ecologically correct lines, wear a shirt made of leaves. You're not one of them but you're integrated, in their sense, with neither equal rights nor freedom.

You start trying to work out an escape plan.

THE END

"What do you mean, THE END?" Grandmother shouts. I am sitting on her bed, next to her outrage. The roommate woke up at some point and listened to the story. She, too, cries: "No, no, no!"

"Why didn't you just ask me? If you drink with them, they've got you!"

"You're a bit late with the advice, you know."

"Late nothing. You don't drink the water, all right? You don't do a thing but get out of there. So, that's how it continues. Out of the woods. I want to make it to the peak."

Well all right then. Turn to page 339

"STOP."

"Grandma?"

"People are connected to each other for very different reasons. I'm not going to list them for you."

"Grandma."

"Telling stories won't keep me alive, Saša! You're getting sparks mixed up with embers. You're exaggerating! Where you come from is a giant cavern full of dragons? And one is guarding the bridge over the river to the other world?"

"It's your bridge, Grandma."

"What?"

"I have to cross it with you."

"That's gruesome."

"This is a conversation with myself."

"That's even worse." Grandmother lies down.

We are in Višegrad. I am her grandson and four years old or fourteen or twenty-four or thirty-four. Grandmother is saying I shouldn't go outside with wet hair.

We are in America. On a warm night, Grandmother asks me about my time in Heidelberg. I tell her how Wojtek army-crawled all the way up to Emmertsgrund. I tell her how we grilled a lamb on a spit in the forest and a woman with a dachshund strolling by asked if that was a dog we were roasting.

We are in Belgrade, at a bus station. It's late. We're waiting for the bus to Višegrad. We're tired. There are letters on the wall. I ask what it says. I'm maybe four, five at most. Grandmother says, impatiently, that I should read it myself. I say: "Exit." Grandmother smiles, grabs my chin, and kisses my hair.

We are in Rogatica. Stacking dominoes into a tower until there are no pieces left. Counting them down together: "Three, two, one—" My grandmother's laugh.

We are discovered. After three or four beats of its see-through wings the dragon is hovering in the air right in front of us. It sniffs the air. The yellow fire of centuries is in the pupils of its eyes.

"*Salve, draco*," Grandmother says. The dragon blinks. Grandmother lays down her rapier. The dragon blinks again, and then it's like it's bowing, its skull right in front of the ledge we're standing on.

Grandmother takes the first step, then another. She climbs onto its neck. I follow her—of course I follow her, you don't let your own grandmother go off alone with a dragon—and it turns around and hurtles into the teeming mass.

We fly over an island village, then a stone house on a lake of the clearest blue. There are fruit trees too, and flowerbeds, and a dozen dancing figures in front of the house.

"The maidens," Grandmother cries. "Looks like they're having fun."

We land, not exactly gently, in front of the three-headed guard of the bridge. The heads stop their squabbling and the right-hand one says apologetically: "I'm from a Russian dragon legend, I shouldn't be here at all." It closes its eyes.

"I take it my husband is in there?" Grandmother says, turning to the other two.

"First and last name please?" the middle head says.

"Petar Stanišić."

It takes out a gigantic notepad and starts turning several pages at a time to run through the list of names. The left head asks if we'd like anything to drink while we're waiting. There's blood, water, sorb-apple compote, and every foreign language. I take Spanish. Grandmother takes water. The glass I drink from has a little crack in it.

The middle head spits a little fire, turned politely to one side, and says: "Found him."

"Can he come out?" Grandmother asks.

"Never seen that before," the dragon says.

"So, he can?" I say.

Already my grandfather is strolling out of the darkness and over the bridge. He has a mustache. He is wearing a shirt and a sports jacket. He looks dazzling. Grandmother thinks so and says so, anyway. Grandfather is too stunned for compliments.

"Kristina, what are you doing here?" he asks, his eyes open wide. In a few steps he is with her, holding her tight in his arms and she him. At some point they turn toward me.

"Look who brought me here."

"Is that . . ."

I hold out my hand to my grandfather. I think about how hard it's appropriate to grip, and before I know it the hand-shake's over.

"Are you coming with us?" Grandmother asks her husband.

"I really can?"

The middle head says yes, he's allowed to. "Isn't that strange, for thousands of years no one's ever thought to just ask if they can have someone back. Except the Greeks, but that didn't go too well."

The dragon has a cute little lisp, but I keep that to myself, you don't want to stir up trouble with dragons.

"Sign here, please," it tells Grandfather. "And you sign here, please," it says to Grandmother. As we're leaving, it adds: "The comrade is to be brought back within forty-eight hours maximum."

Gavrilo, Marija, and Sretoje act like they don't notice the dragon that brings us to the mouth of the cave. They seem happy and relieved to see us. They hug Grandfather as if he's come back from the dead, I almost wrote.

There's only one more thing to tell about the descent of Vijarac: on our way we run into a horned viper, but I wouldn't venture to say that it's Ajhendorf.

I have read most faithfully
The words, simple and true,
And as they poured through all my soul
They turned inexpressibly clear.

We want to go straight back to Višegrad—forty-eight hours isn't much time. We apologize for losing the rapier and say goodbye to the Oskorušans.

I get into the driver's seat. Grandmother and Grandfather are talking in the back seat. This and that. And what did you do then? And then? Tell me! Grandmother remembers flawlessly. Tells him everything. About the war, too—just when we drive past the aggressive Serbian graffiti. I expect political commentary from Grandfather, but he just slides a little closer to Grandmother.

At home we have coffee. "Our first coffee together," Grandfather says.

"He's already tasted coffee," Grandmother says. "Tried it before he was four years old."

It's nice. We have no more questions. I close my eyes.

When I close my eyes, on November 2, 2018, here behind my lids are a number of things I have:

Grandmother Kristina and Grandfather Pero.

My granny Mejrema, who read my future in kidney beans. One time she prophesied that I would have many lives. Like a cat? I asked.

That thing about cats is just a superstition, she whined.

My grandfather Muhamed, who braked trains. One time he got stuck in a raging snowstorm with a wood transport train. He pulled his coat tighter around him and went all the way back to Višegrad, almost twenty miles, on foot through the snow and the bitter cold. The story had only one point: survival. (Mother remembers her father's icy eyebrows, and that he didn't shave that day or the next.)

A ceramic bird from my last vacation with my parents, the kind you fill with water and when you blow up its ass birdsong comes out the front. I liked it because I liked that vacation.

Bburago model cars, 1:43 scale. I owned around forty. Brumm, brumm. Had to leave them behind. My son collects cars, although he doesn't yet understand the concept of "collecting": he *has* a lot of cars. The models from back then cost between eight and twenty-five euros today on eBay. I ordered the white Porsche 924 (original packaging).

I open my eyes. Grandmother and Grandfather are sitting there, looking at each other.

Now I don't know how it continues.

I say: "See you later." And run out, to play.

THE END

Or would you prefer another ending, *how it really happened?* The burial? The family gathered at the cemetery on November 2. A nephew carried the cross. The priest sang the liturgy. He sang for a very long time, to the point where it got on the mourners' nerves. Everyone cried only when the coffin was lowered.

And then the coffin was too long. The gravediggers had been afraid of that, and had already taken off the handles. Still, the coffin stuck up just above ground level in the grave. A little slanted, in fact.

The men pulled on the ropes, one of them stepped on the coffin, maybe to try to make it lie level, but nothing happened. They decided to leave it like that. It was deep enough, and not that crooked.

THE END

ACKNOWLEDGMENTS

I would like to thank my parents for the happiness they made possible. My grandparents for their kindness and their stories.

The ARAL gas station in Emmertsgrund. Rahim, Fredie, Werner Gebhard, Joseph von Eichendorff, ICSH, and the two clerks at the foreign registration offices of Heidelberg and Leipzig responsible for the letter *S*, for asking me what I planned to do later.

Maria Motter for facts and certainties.

Katharina Adler, Christof Bultmann, David Hugendick, Martin Mittelmeier, and Katja Sämann for their gracious support.

SAŠA STANIŠIĆ was born in Višegrad (Yugoslavia) in 1978 and has lived in Germany since 1992. His debut novel, *How the Soldier Repairs the Gramophone*, was translated into thirty-one languages; *Before the Feast* was a bestseller and won the renowned Leipzig Book Fair Prize.

DAMION SEARLS is an award-winning translator from German, Norwegian, French, and Dutch, and the author of *The Inkblots*, a history of the Rorschach test and biography of its creator.